WAR TORN

BOOK 3

THE AFTERMATH

JAN LLOYD

Disclaimer

War Torn Book 3 is a work of fiction. Names, characters, places, and incidents in this book are either the products of the author's imagination or used in a fictitious manner.

Copyright © 2025 by Jan Lloyd

All rights reserved. No part of this book may be reproduced or used in any manner without written permission of the copyright owner except for the use of quotations in a book review. For more information, address: oghanlloyd@ msn.com

First paperback edition March 2025

Book cover design by Nabin Karna
Interior design by Damian Jackson

Chapter 1

PARIS, SPRING 1946

"Come on, Sleepy Head, wake up."

Frances turned over and looked towards the door of her bedroom. Through sleepy eyes, she focused on Mueller standing in his underpants, holding a tray with two mugs of coffee and a plate full of toast. She yawned and sighed, returning his smile.

"I must have done all right then, from that smile on your face," he said, giving her a suggestive grin.

"I don't know what you mean. I'm smiling because you've brought me breakfast in bed. I didn't realise that you were so well trained."

"Well, you can thank Anna for that when you see her. I'm brilliant at toast-making just as long as there's bread. Which is all I could find in your food store, by the way."

She sat up, pulling a couple of pillows behind her back for support. Mueller passed her a mug of coffee and a slice of toast and seated himself on the side of the bed.

"Here's the plan, then. I will go and clean up." He rubbed his hand across his stubbled face. "And shave. Pack and check out of my hotel and return here as soon as possible. I think I can walk it inside an hour if I get a move on, and I'll drive back. Then lunch, and you can take me sightseeing for the day, followed by dinner and—" he gave another suggestive smile. "Then back here. It's a good plan?" he asked. Frances moaned.

"Please don't be angry with me," she said, "I meant to tell you last night, but I didn't want to spoil things."

Mueller exhaled. "What? What haven't you told me?"

"I have a concert tomorrow."

"That's all?" he said with relief. "That won't interfere with our plans." She screwed her face up.

"It will. It's in Brussels. I have tickets for a train at 4 p.m." Mueller scowled at her whilst sitting on the edge of the bed, munching at his toast. "Kristian, I'm sorry I—"

"Shush." He sat, thoughtfully formulating a new plan. "Right, first off, forget your train."

"I can't. I can't just not turn up."

"Shush and listen. Forget your train. We'll drive to Brussels, you see. It's on the way home. Almost, anyway. What time do you have to be there?"

"I have a rehearsal at 2.00 p.m. tomorrow."

"So, we carry on as planned, but you must pack. Pack everything you will need. We can fill the car if we must. As you can imagine, there is little to be had of anything back home. We'll eat early tonight, come back, and sleep."

"Sleep?"

"Sleep. We must, for some time at least if I'm going to drive. Then we leave at 5 a.m. That will give us plenty of time to get you there for rehearsal. Have you got a hotel booked?"

She nodded.

"So, a night in Brussels and back to Schonen Felder, or a second night in Brussels?" She sat up and wrapped her arms around him. He was anxious to return home and take her there with him, and she wondered how his family would react.

Betrayed, she'd left his home when he returned from the war

and told them all there was someone else. They'd had a last encounter that had ended with them making love. Only it hadn't been love. Anger or some such thing had driven them to it. And then that night he'd turned up at the Christmas Ball for the British Officers, where she had been part of the entertainment. He'd gone there to meet Adenauer and later had asked her for a last dance 'in remembrance, for old times' sake,' he said. And he'd held her in his arms, and she could scarcely bear the pain of longing she felt. She'd run away because she didn't want to hear the words she was convinced he would say, that it was over. But it wasn't over now, and he asked her back to Schonen Felder. To his home where she'd seen out the war with people who should have been her enemy. People she had learned to love. She missed them all dreadfully. It had been six months since she had seen them, six months since she had run away from Kristian .

"Let's go home, shall we?" she said.

"Hmm." He nodded in agreement. "Now, are you sure there is nothing else you have forgotten to tell me?"

"No, no, that's it."

"Good."

"Apart from I have six concerts in America."

"Bloody hell, Froggy. When? How?"

"The end of this month…

"What!"

She laughed at his response. "That's when it was to have been. I've put it back for a year due to, well, circumstances." She patted her bump.

Mueller leaned over her, kissed her cheek and then her abdomen, giving it a rub as he said, "You've always wanted to go to America, haven't you?"

She nodded.

"How the hell did you sort it all out?" he asked.

"I still have friends, you know. Charles Munch knows me from the Conservatoire. He conducted my first performance at the theatre where I played last night. Do you remember me telling you I had no idea how everything was organised for our escape from Paris to Fecamp?" Mueller gave a nod. "It seems quite a few resistance members were working at the Conservatoire. I always suspected Jacques was involved too, you know. Anyway, that's how. Charles has many friends in America. He sorted everything. I think he may even move there in the future."

"Excellent cover, using the Conservatoire," said Mueller thoughtfully. "So, Frau Mueller, how long will you be leaving me and our children for when you take your trip to America?"

"Maybe a month or six weeks. I can go, can't I?"

"And if I said no, would that stop you?"

"No, but I'd rather go with your blessing."

"Then it's just as well that you have it. I suppose I will have to get used to playing second fiddle to the little bastard in the black box, won't I?"

"Are you jealous of my violin, Kristian?" she asked.

"Pfff," he huffed, then reconsidered. "You do pull a dreamy face, though, when you hold it."

"I pull a dreamy face when I hold you too, don't I?"

He cast her a look as he carried on with his toast thoughtfully before saying, "You know, you pull some extraordinary faces when you play. I'm not always sure you're enjoying it. Anyway, I'd better make a move, or we will miss lunch and breakfast."

She grabbed him, preventing him from standing.

"Just a minute, Herr Mueller," she said through slit eyes, "I most certainly do not pull faces when I play."

"Ha! Frau Mueller, you most certainly do, and I love every one of them." He pulled himself free of her and threw on his clothes from the night before, then gave her a brief kiss. "I'll be back as soon as possible," he said, leaving.

"Phone for a taxi. There's a number by the phone downstairs.

They are just up the road and will be here in no time, and you can return even quicker."

Mueller nodded and went downstairs to make the phone call. The thought crossed her mind that she might never see him again. He could just leave. She was relieved when he quickly reappeared.

"It'll be five minutes," he said.

She jumped out of bed, throwing her arms around his neck, kissing him, and getting her desired response. They were both lost in time until the sound of a motor-horn outside brought them back to the present.

"Right, I will try to return within the hour, so you need to get moving." He was almost out of the door.

"Kristian, say it," she called.

"What?"

"You know what? Say it. Tell me again." Mueller sniffed.

"It's taken me thirty-two years to say those three damn words. I'll say it again to you when I'm sixty-four." And with that, he was gone, down the stairs. She stood, watching him leave the house from the window upstairs. Watching as he climbed into the taxi. He jumped back out instead of pulling away, and she heard his footsteps running back up the stairs to her. She looked around to see what on earth he'd forgotten. Throwing the bedroom door open, he crossed the room and kissed her again. He took her chin in his hand and smiled into her eyes. "I love you, Froggy," he said, and then he was gone, leaving her spellbound.

* * *

She had wasted time and knew he'd be cross if she wasn't ready. Instead of bathing and packing, she had spent a good half hour playing her violin and looking in the mirror to see if she pulled the faces he accused her of pulling. She had found it rather challenging to come to a proper conclusion, as she quickly realised she also spent much time playing with her eyes closed.

Deciding that maybe it wasn't the right time to spend time on such a matter, she hurriedly bathed and threw on her robe. She gathered the few cases she had and began packing her clothes. She started by separating summer and winter dresses, folding each item carefully to cut down on the creasing. Then, panicking that time was of a premium, she changed her approach and rammed everything into the nearest suitcase. By the time an hour had passed, she had most of her clothing inside suitcases and, by sitting on top of them, did up the latches and, for extra measure, put straps around them.

Next, she went to one of the spare bedrooms to sort through her coats. Mueller hadn't mentioned returning to Paris anytime soon, which meant the house would have to be locked up. She would have to make time to call in on the neighbours or contact her lawyer to keep an eye on things.

Delving into one of the enormous wardrobes, she removed some coats that were quite old and certainly not fashionable anymore. Oddly, she thought, Otto had left even her clothing in place, and she shuddered at the thought of him running his hands over her belongings. She made a pile of clothes she no longer wanted on the spare bed, and as she cleared most of the coats from the wardrobe, she found an old biscuit tin on the floor, amongst some shoes, and knew immediately what it contained. That is how Mueller found her, kneeling on the floor and getting on for a hundred old and not-so-old photographs laid out before her.

She didn't hear him arrive. She didn't hear him at all until he touched her and spoke. "Froggy, you're not ready."

She turned to him. "Look, look, Kristian, see what I've found. They're all here—all of them. Look. There's Papa and Mummy, and that's me," she said, pointing to a professional photograph of her parents holding a baby. Mueller knelt beside her, picking up one photograph.

"I know who that is. That's your Aunt Edie, isn't it?"

She nodded, and he saw her swallow. "That's Jacques, see, and these I've put over here are all Steven. That's the day we married." She picked up a photograph. Mueller took it from her and strangely felt no jealousy. He'd always wondered about the man, and in his head, he'd turned him into a spectre, afraid to mention him even. The photograph showed him a dark-haired man with a neatly trimmed beard who had clearly made an effort for his wedding day. He was wearing a dark suit, somewhat uncomfortably, thought Mueller. The man looked out from the photograph with bright eyes set in an intelligent face, and even though the face had no features that could set him aside and classify him as handsome, Mueller thought it was an honest, kind face.

"So, this is the man, then?" he said, smiling at Frances. She nodded, and he nodded back. "I'm glad I've seen him. Thank you for showing me." He paused, not wanting to rush her. "I think we could both do with some food and fresh air now, couldn't we? Come on, Froggy, we'll take them back home with us, and we can look through them together if you like, eh?"

She nodded again. "I would like that. I'm glad I found them. There are such memories here. Yes, let's put them with things to be packed."

"I'll take this lot down to the car while you finish getting dressed. Come on, we need to go shopping." Her face lit up.

"Shopping, are we going back into the city?"

"Do we need to?" asked Mueller.

"Don't know. What do we need?"

"Plenty of that perfume you've been wearing for a start. I noticed the bottle on your dressing table is nearly empty."

"Balenciaga, you have good taste. I think we'll manage that in Neuilly. Give me five minutes, and I'll give you the tour."

<h1 style="text-align:center">CHAPTER 2</h1>

Lunch, followed by the tour, went well, and Mueller admitted he could see why people found Neuilly such an attractive place to live. He thought it would be a perfect location if you had to live near a city. You can take in all the sights of Paris and then retreat to the quiet at the end of the day.

There was an excellent choice of restaurants, and they found most of what they thought they might need, though, as everywhere else in Europe, choices were limited. Frances stocked up on even more baby clothes, and Mueller decided it would be a clever idea to buy several sizes until she pointed out he had to make colour choices. Having no idea whether he was buying for two boys, two girls, or one of each, he passed.

By five thirty, Frances was worn out, and even though rain threatened, they found a place to sit quietly by the river for a while. Relaxed in each other's company and enjoying the physical closeness of one another, they found they didn't need to make small talk.

By six, they were both hungry and went searching for dinner.

After that, they made their way back home. Once there, Frances insisted she had to practice for the next day's concert. Luckily, the piece chosen had been Sibelius's violin concerto in D minor, which she knew well. As an encore, she would play the good old Paganini Caprice, which she hated but the audiences seemed to love.

"They just want to see if you can play it," she complained to Mueller. He had taken himself off for a walk to give her space and, since returning, had amused himself by mimicking her facial expressions as she played the Paganini piece.

"You're not funny, you know," she huffed. "Kristian, I really do need to practice, and you're not helping." He grabbed her around the waist from behind.

"Do you think you could play that while I've got my arms around you?" he asked.

"Yes," she said, wriggling free, "but I'd probably take your eye out with my bow."

"I bet you can't," he teased, "If you can, I'll leave you alone to practice some more."

"I bet I can," she said, rising to the challenge. "Come on, let's see."

He moved behind her again, placing his hands on her hips and bending his neck so that his cheek lay gently against the right side of her head. As she raised her bow and played, he felt her take a deep breath. He swayed gently to the music, taking her with him. He let her play the first twenty or so bars until he felt her relax into the music and then slid his hand between her thighs. There was a screech from her and the violin together. He jumped back quickly from her, laughing as she turned and struck out at his shin with her foot.

"That was a filthy bloody trick," she snapped.

"Come on, Froggy, that's enough. Wrap the little bastard up and put him to bed for the night. We've got an early start tomorrow morning, and I've plenty more filthy tricks to share with you before then." Despite trying not to, she began to chuckle, finally joining in with his laughter.

"All right, you win. Make yourself useful while I sort a few things out. Grab two glasses and a bottle of wine and give me five minutes."

"Just five, promise?"

She put down her violin, reached her arms around his neck, and kissed his mouth. "Promise," she said, "But if I make any mistakes tomorrow, it's your fault."

* * *

The alarm was set for four thirty a.m., and Mueller wanted to be on the road by five, making sure they could traverse the city and be on their way before Paris woke to the wet morning. With a brief stop off for breakfast on the way, they made Brussels by eleven thirty a.m. and checked into their hotel on Avenue Louise. Their suite was spacious and comfortable and in the middle of the busy city centre, which brimmed with restaurants, one of which they took advantage of for lunch. Afterwards, they returned to the hotel and ordered a taxi to take Frances to rehearsal at the Henry Le Boeuf Hall, which was too far away for her to walk, especially in her condition.

"What time will your rehearsal finish?" Mueller asked.

"Hopefully by 4.30. Why don't you meet me there?"

"Where?"

"The Centre of Fine Arts. You might find it interesting. They say the hall is acoustically brilliant. I've seen photographs, and the inside is amazing. Ask at the desk for directions. I think it's about a half-hour walk away. It will give you a chance to see some of Brussels. Rue Ravensteinstraat, I think. Check downstairs anyhow." She gave him a brief kiss. "See you in a couple of hours, yes?"

He grunted. "Playing second fiddle again, you see. A beautiful day, a beautiful city, and I've been dumped."

"Kristian, you will come, won't you?"

"Of course, I'll come. Go on, you'll be late. Don't keep me waiting though. 4.30, you said."

As it was, the rehearsal didn't finish until later, and she found Mueller outside the Centre of Fine Arts waiting for her. She invited him into the hall, and he was tempted but refused, knowing time was short. He hailed a taxi to take them back to the hotel. Even though Frances was not due to perform until the second half of the program, the conductor insisted she was to be in the building before the concert began. Time ran away, scarcely giving her any chance to rest and just enough to bathe, tie back her hair, and change into the loose black evening gown she'd worn two nights previously. Mueller was concerned that she hadn't eaten since lunchtime and ordered a pot of coffee and eggs on toast to be delivered to their suite, for which she was very thankful.

* * *

By the time they got back to the hotel, it was late. The evening had gone extraordinarily well, with the Henry Le Boeuf Hall filled with over two thousand people in the audience. Mueller stayed in her dressing room with her during the concert's first half and was surprised by her nervousness.

"I'm always nervous just before," she said. "When you stop being nervous, you stop giving your best, you know."

She sent him to his seat at the start of the interval to give herself time to prepare mentally for the performance. It was her largest audience for a long time. As it was, she need not have worried. The performance of the Sibelius piece went very well, and the Paganini, as always, received a standing ovation from the audience and orchestra alike. After signing programs and shaking hands with well-wishers, she was tired out, and Mueller thought it best to go straight back to the hotel for a late dinner rather than eat out in the city.

"I thought that was an excellent choice of pieces tonight. I was proud of you, Froggy," he said as he opened the door to their suite. "All in all, Frau Mueller, a rather good day. Tomorrow, back home. How are you feeling?"

"Good, but tired. I'm going to get out of this dress and flake. Shall we have a brandy before we turn in?" she asked, and he nodded.

"I'll get us one sent up."

She returned to the lounge in one of the hotel robes, her hair brushed down as he liked it, and she joined him at the window where he was looking down onto the busy Brussels Street. He'd removed his jacket as soon as they got back to the room, and now he'd removed his bow tie and opened the neck of his shirt. She smiled to herself, knowing how much he hated anything formal. As she joined him, he placed one arm around her shoulders and toyed with her hair with the other hand.

"It's almost like it was when we met. I love it loose like this. Don't ever have it cut, will you?"

She shook her head and, taking his hand, laid it on her bump. "They're at it again. Can you feel?"

Mueller chuckled as he felt the movement against his hand.

"It's all right for you, Kristian," she continued. "They seem to wake up when I want to sleep. Where's that brandy? Perhaps that will knock the little devils out for a few hours."

"They're taking their time with it. I'll call the desk again," he said, making his way to the phone. As he crossed the room, there was a knock on the door, and a boy arrived with two large brandies on a tray. Mueller paid him a tip and, taking the drinks, passed one to Frances, who had stretched out on a sofa. He returned to the window with the other and looked out onto the street below.

"I wish you'd sort things out when we get back home," she said.

"Eh? What things? I didn't know there was anything to sort," he replied, still looking down onto the city.

"You know what things, Kristian."

"Do I?"

She saw him shrug and the back of his body tense. She wondered whether she should stop now and change the subject, but she decided she had gone too far.

"Isn't it time you forgave her?" she asked. She noted his shoulders rise and fall as he inhaled deeply and exhaled with a sigh.

"If you mean my mother, Frances, keep out of it. It's nothing to do with you."

"Nothing to do with me? I'm your wife, aren't I? And Mutti, well, I care about her. Kristian, I find it hurtful that you don't think your family affairs have anything to do with me."

He turned and faced her, jaw tensed and mouth taut, set in the hard line, which she knew from experience was a warning.

"As I said before, keep out of it. You know nothing about it. It's family business. And well done, by the way. You've ruined what was a good evening by bringing this up."

Worn out and nerves stretched to the breaking point, she exploded. "Then damn you if you don't recognise me as a member of your family. Damn you! I'm going to bed."

"Good!" he shouted after her as she slammed the door to the bedroom.

* * *

She tried to sleep; she wanted to so that when he came into the room, he would see that she didn't care, but after more than an hour of tossing and turning, she gave in and pushed open the door, going back into the lounge. She found him in the same position: back to her, staring out of the window, standing too straight to be relaxed. He knew she was there, but he refused to turn and acknowledge her. Padding across the room, she touched him gently on the shoulder and braced herself for another verbal onslaught. It didn't come, and he didn't move.

"Come to bed. I'm so sorry. I shouldn't have brought it up now. It was the wrong time. Come to bed, Kristian, please," she pleaded, and he sighed.

"I adored her. You know, Mutti. We did everything together; she was always there for me. She taught me everything. How to walk, read, my numbers, play chess even. Then it all suddenly changed."

"Were you jealous when Karin came along then?"

He turned to her and gave the question some thought. Then smiled in recollection. "For a day or so, maybe," he said, "and then I was captivated. I couldn't take my eyes off her and would guard her like a dog. That's not when it changed. It changed when Karin died. I needed Mutti, you see, and she wasn't there. She just removed herself from my life because she blamed me for Karin's death."

"No, you're wrong. Your mother didn't ever blame you," she argued. Mueller chewed on his lip.

"How would you know you weren't there?" he snapped.

"I know because I've often spoken to Mutti about it. You're all we ever talked about."

"Of course, I was forgetting; you're best friends now," he said, with more than a hint of sarcasm. Then he turned from her again and continued his vigil at the window. "I've done without her for over twenty years. I learned to do without her."

"Kristian, you must stop this. Can't you see that you are viewing what happened through the eyes of an eight-year-old?

Mutti was suffering from depression. That's why she locked herself away from you. She didn't want you to see her like that." He gave a snort, which Frances ignored. "She loves you more than anything. You need to move on and see what happened through an adult's eye now. She told me you were her saviour. That if you hadn't been there, she would have given up. No one has ever blamed you for Karin's death. Yes, your father was cross with you, and that's why you got a beating, which, from what I was told, you deserved. But blame you for Karin's death? No. The only person who ever blamed you for that is yourself, the boy of eight who needed his mother. Well, let me tell you, she is getting older, and now she needs you." She watched him as his shoulders rose as he took each deep breath. He refused to face her, continuing to stare through the window, but he spoke gently.

"Go to bed, Frances; you need your sleep. I'll come soon; I promise."

* * *

She woke again when dawn was breaking. He was lying on his side, turned away from her. She touched him very gently, not wanting to wake him if he had found repose.

"Are you awake?" she asked in a whisper.

"What do you think?" came the tired reply.

"Can I say something?"

"Can I stop you? Haven't you said enough already?"

"Yes, I know. I've said too much, I suppose. But I was thinking, there must be millions of people out there tonight who wish they could talk to their parents, children, or loved ones. And they can't, Kristian, because this war has taken them away from them. I think I was lucky. I know I lost everyone, but at least we all knew we loved each other. It must be dreadful losing someone you love, not having told them how you feel. Please talk to Mutti. We don't know what's around the corner, do we?"

He rolled onto his back and, turning his head to her, stared into her eyes. Then he lifted her arm and moved into her warmth. Laying his head upon her breast, he sank into a much-needed deep sleep.

CHAPTER 3

Someone was shaking her awake, and for a while, Frances hadn't a clue where she was. Remembering the night before and her dogged persistence, she tried to put off opening her eyes so she wouldn't have to face him.

"What time is it?" she eventually groaned.

"Almost nine," came his reply. She quickly came around.

"But we must be out of here for ten, and I'm starving."

"Which is why I have had breakfast sent up to our room. Here, coffee," he said, offering her the cup. She opened her eyes and was met with a smile from Mueller, which she hadn't expected. He'd bathed and was dressed already in a white shirt he'd opened at the neck and a pair of casual dark trousers.

"How do you do it? Hardly any sleep, and you're up and at 'Em. I'm going to have to wear the same clothes as yesterday. Everything clean is somewhere in a suitcase in the damn car."

"I won't tell, Froggy. Come on, get some breakfast down you, then a quick bath, and we're off on the last leg of our journey to the rest of our lives."

She climbed out of bed, grabbed a robe, helped herself to some food off the trolley, and joined him at the table. He appeared to have shaken off his moroseness from the night before, which relieved her. A long journey in the car or a U-boat with a peevish Mueller was not something anyone would want to undertake. She thought back briefly to the crew of UBA. As it was, he seemed to be full of smiles, probably because of the thought of home. Despite all he'd said the night before, he loved Schonen Felder.

He sat for some time, watching her eat as he sipped away his coffee. Then he gave a sniff, which she knew usually preceded some derogatory remark. This time, however, he surprised her. "I always thought I was the intelligent, philosophical one out of the two of us, you know," he said.

"You are," she replied through a mouthful of food. "You always have all the answers."

"Yes, I do," he began, "but you, my girl, seem to have all the questions." She raised her eyes at him, wondering if he was starting an argument based on her behaviour from the night before. He nodded at her, and there was a smile just tugging at the corners of his mouth. She decided to be magnanimous and accepted it as his attempt at an apology.

* * *

It took almost four and a half hours to get to Bonn, and they still had nearly a further hour to drive home. Frances was filled with excitement and nervousness and couldn't wait to get the initial homecoming over. She was surprised and a little miffed when Mueller wanted to call in at the Party Office before making for home. He took her inside, introduced her to Maggie, and asked if Konrad was there. It was mid-afternoon on a Friday, and everyone was shutting down for the weekend.

"He is, as a matter of fact," Maggie said. "I'll let him know you're here."

"No need," came the voice from the office as Konrad

Adenauer opened the door. "Looks like you had a successful trip then," he said, giving them a wide smile. He crossed to Frances and kissed her on both cheeks. "I'm glad for you both." His eyes fell on Frances. "You, my dear, are looking bonny."

"If you mean I've put on weight," Frances said with a laugh, "I'm pregnant."

"And there's two of them," added Kristian.

"Two at a time, impressive. You'll soon catch me up. I have eight. When did I tell you to come back in, my boy?" he asked.

"Tuesday, Sir. Is that still all right?"

"I have meetings all day on Tuesday, don't I, Maggie?"

"Yes, you do, Herr Adenauer," Maggie replied, flicking through the diary.

"Then spend an extra day together and come in bright and early on Wednesday, Kristian."

Frances squealed with delight and thanked Adenauer by returning his kiss.

"You may not thank me for long, my dear. Things are getting busier and busier by the day. Believe me, I'll take my pound of flesh from Kristian."

* * *

She had wondered why he had taken her to Bonn and not straight home to Schonen Felder. It hadn't been just the office. After calling to see Konrad, he'd taken her to a block of apartments about a ten-minute walk away. She'd shrieked with laughter when he swept her into his arms. As he climbed the stairs to the second floor with her still in his arms, a door opened just above them, and a professional-looking, middle-aged, somewhat overweight man stuck his head out of the door.

"Ah, Kristian, it's you," the man said with a grin.

Kristian stopped. "Meet my wife, Manfred. Shake hands with Manfred, Frances; he's my neighbour."

The man stretched out his hand, which she took with a giggle and a blush.

"Well, I won't keep you," said Manfred with a knowing smile. "I think you are probably in a hurry. Pleased to meet you, Frau Mueller." And with that, he closed his door and was gone, leaving Mueller ferreting in his jacket pocket for the keys to a neighbouring apartment. He struggled to hold on to her while he searched.

"Why don't you just put me down?" she suggested.

"Not the way it's done?" He chuckled. She worried he would drop her and was relieved when he said, "Ah, got them."

He struggled even more to get the key in the lock and open the door with her still in his arms but eventually managed it. They both fell through the door into the apartment, laughing. Only then did he agree to put her down.

"Well, what do you think?" he asked.

The first thing she noticed was how tidy it was. Nothing was out of place. It reminded her of his cabin space on UBA. The second thing she saw was the size of the apartment, which was small. Another reminder of his cabin space. It was little more than a bedsit, but there was a reasonable kitchen and a bathroom.

"I don't understand. Who does this place belong to?" she asked.

"Me. I've lived there for the past five or six months. I've been renting it, you see. Easier than commuting every day from home, Froggy, and I haven't had to worry about fuel either. So, I live here Monday to Friday and then go home and help on the farm over the weekend. And——"

"And what?"

"And everyone was so damn miserable without you. I guess I needed time out on my own to reassess my life."

He had moved out of Schonen Felder and lived a bachelor's existence in Bonn for the last few months. She asked him if he had seen any other girls, and he told her he hadn't, and she wanted to believe him.

Their lovemaking had become less desperate but no less passionate, as they now accepted that they were each with the other because that was how they both wanted it to be. Frances looked at the man sleeping beside her and, not for the first time, was overwhelmed by the love she felt for him. He was shattered, having had no sleep the night before and having driven them to Brussels the previous day. Then he drove them from Brussels to Bonn and still made love to her. She looked down at him again, surprised to find him awake. He'd been watching her and smiled at her as she noticed.

"Pfennig for them, Froggy. Did you sleep at all?"

"A little," she lied.

"We'd better get moving. I usually get home at about six, but we'll be much later. I'll have a quick bath and shave first."

She put out her hand and caressed the stubble on his chin. "It reminds me of when I first saw you. Why don't you leave it?"

"They'll know something is going on if I turn up like this. I want to surprise them. Do you want the first bath?"

"Kristian, I need my clothes brought in. I can't wear the same ones again."

He puffed his cheeks at her. "Which suitcase then? You have a bath, and I'll grab it from the car. It will take me just a few minutes. I'll be back before you're finished."

"I don't know which suitcase. I just shoved everything in, anywhere, and kept back my evening gown for last night's concert, plus a change of underclothes. I need them all."

"That's a bit of a waste of time. Just wait until you get home. Then you can unpack the lot."

"I need my clothes here, surely."

"Here?"

"I am staying with you, aren't I?"

"Not here. You'll stay at the farm, and I'll come home at weekends."

She stiffened. This was not what she had expected. "But I don't want to stay at the farm and see you at weekends. I want to stay here in the week and then go home with you at weekends."

He turned away from her, not wanting to argue, and opened his wardrobe, looking for a change of clothes for himself. "When will you become a good haus frau and do as your husband says?" he muttered. Crossing the room, she struck him hard on the back.

"Know this now," she said. "I will never be told what to do again by anyone." He turned around, giving her one of his boyish smiles.

"Hey, it was a joke, Froggy. You haven't forgotten what a joke is, have you?"

She scowled at him; the thought of him being in the flat all week had rattled her. "Well, it wasn't very funny, was it? And if it isn't funny, it's not a joke!"

He turned back round to his wardrobe once again. "It made me laugh," he said under his breath. She was tired and pregnant, and she cracked.

"Do you know what? I wish I hadn't come back with you. If we are not going to be together, I wish I'd stayed in Paris."

Turning back round to her, Mueller shook his head, crossed the room, and took her in his arms. Her leaving Paris was something that he hadn't given much thought to. He had made it clear that he wanted to be with her, that he loved her, and had assumed that they would return to Germany and that she would be all right with that. But why would she? Germany, with the memories it held for her, was the last place she would want to be. He hadn't given the matter a second thought until then. He stroked his hand through her hair and lifted her chin so that he could look straight into her eyes.

"I'll never make you do anything you don't want to do. I never want to. I'm sorry, I didn't think things through. I didn't even consider that you might not want to return to Germany. It has unpleasant memories for you. Would you be happier if we stayed in Paris?"

His apology and suggestion moved her. She reached up and touched the side of his face. "You'd move to Paris for me?" she asked.

"I'd do anything for you. Don't you know that Froggy?" he said gently. She reached up her arms, clasped her hands behind his neck and, pulling his head down to her height, kissed him.

"You'd do anything for me?" she asked. He pushed his fingers into her hair, cradling the back of her head, returning the kiss.

"Anything," he replied.

"Then I can stay here with you during the week, and we'll go to the farm at the weekend," she said, giving him a triumphant smile. He looked at her and nodded slowly.

"I think I've just been stitched up, haven't I?" He kissed her forehead. "And I'm glad I have. I want you here, you know, but I just thought that having people around you would give you more time to rest," he said. "You're going to need support. I don't want anything to go wrong. With the pregnancy, I mean."

* * *

It was later than Mueller liked when they got to the farm. Frances had insisted that he bring all her suitcases and boxes into his apartment while she bathed, and then while he bathed, she searched through her luggage, trying to sort it all out into what would fit her still, what she would need at the farm for the weekend, and what she wouldn't need until the cooler weather. They'd come to a compromise that she would stay in Bonn until the babies were born, and then afterwards, she would spend some weeks at the farm. That way, she could get support and help from Freya and Anna. She had to admit that looking after

23

two babies on her own would be too much. During that time, while she was at the farm, he would look for a larger apartment in Bonn to start a family life together.

* * *

As the car crackled up the drive, Mueller told Frances, "Stay low." He was going to drive the car to the front of the house, and once he was inside, she could go to the kitchen and hide. He wanted her return to Schonen Felder to surprise them all.

"But how long will I have to stay in the kitchen?" she asked.

"Not too long. I want a little time with Mutti first, you see. I've bridges to build, haven't I?"

It was the first time she had heard of his intention to make things right with his mother, and she gave him a squeal of glee. "And Anna, what should I tell Anna?" she asked.

"Anything you like, but if I were you, I'd tell the truth, or you will be in trouble. Come on, duck down and wait until I'm in the house before you leave the car. Mutti and Pa will meet me in the hall as always, so they won't see you."

And so, as Mueller entered the house at the front, Frances went to the back and entered the kitchen. Sneaking up on Anna, she touched her shoulder and said, "Hello," giving her one of the biggest shocks she'd ever had. She screamed and jumped away, standing momentarily, staring, trying to decide whether Frances was real.

"My God, child, where on earth have you appeared from?" she cried out. "I need to sit down to recover myself. You are lucky I hadn't got a rolling pin nearby to use as a weapon." Then, she was across the kitchen, taking hold of Frances in a tight embrace, almost stifling her. "Sit, sit, and tell me everything. Does Kristian know you're here? He's been driving us all mad. He's been so miserable, and Peter has been trying to get hold of him on the telephone all this week."

24

Frances told Anna all that had happened over the previous few days: how Mueller had turned up at her concert in Paris, declared his feelings for her, and brought her home.

"Are you sure there is nothing you have left out?" Anna asked after Frances had finished her tale. She shook her head and struggled to conceal a smile.

"No, that's it. I've told you everything."

"You're a terrible liar, young lady. I know you are hiding something."

"Anna, there's nothing else," she said as the kitchen door opened and Mueller entered. He grabbed Anna and swung her around in his usual manner.

"Ah! And why do you look so happy?" she asked, referring to the broad smile on his face as he put her down. "This girl says she has told me everything, but I don't believe her. What do you know?"

Mueller shrugged. "What has she told you?" he asked.

"It's what she hasn't told me I'm interested in. I would say you're about five months pregnant. Am I correct?"

Mueller and Frances looked at each other and burst into laughter.

"How on earth did you know, you old witch?" asked Mueller.

"Look at you both. This girl is blooming, and then you come in with a silly look; plus, you've spent several days together, and there hasn't been a murder. You're both still in one piece, so something must have prevented you from killing each other. Have you told your parents yet?"

"No! I want Frances to be the first surprise; then we'll tell them together. Right, woman. A pot of coffee, the good stuff if you have any, and five cups, Anna."

"Five cups?"

"You want to join us, don't you? Come on, I'll return to the sitting room, and Froggy, you come in with Anna in a couple of minutes."

Mueller returned to his parents, leaving Anna and Frances to put together a tray of coffee.

"It happened the morning you returned for your clothes to say goodbye before you left us, didn't it? Before that, in Bonn? Kristian came back from that in one hell of a mood. What on earth did you say to him?" asked Anna. Frances shrugged. "I knew something had happened. Why on earth did you run away from us?"

"I didn't think he wanted me," said Frances. "I thought there was someone else. You heard what he said the day he came home." She bit on her lip.

"There's something still bothering you, isn't there?" Anna hung on to Frances's gaze until she nodded.

"What is it? What's bothering you still? Come, child, you can tell me."

Frances wiped her hand across her forehead and sighed. "Anna, you don't think it's just because I'm pregnant that he's brought me home, do you?"

Anna gave a harsh laugh. "Listen, my girl. That boy has been climbing the wall and driving us all up there with him. He did not know about your pregnancy, did he, when he found you?"

"No."

"Well then, you foolish thing. He came to look for you without knowing that, didn't he?" She shook her head at Frances. "Right, now that's sorted, come on, into the lion's den."

* * *

They made their way to the sitting room, devising a plan for Anna to go in first, put the tray on the table, and then for Frances to follow her. Kristian had left the door wide open, and as they both approached, Frances could see that mother and son were deep in conversation on a couch and that Freya was holding her son's hand. Peter Mueller was seated in an armchair with a newspaper obscuring his view of the door. Totally changing the plan, Frances took the tray from Anna and crossed the room, placing the tray on a low table near the couch.

"Thank you, Anna," said Freya, not taking her eyes off her son's face.

"It's not Anna, it's me."

There was an audible intake of breath from both. Freya turned towards the sound of the voice, and Peter let the newspaper drop into his lap. Then, they were both up and full of questions.

"I told you I had a surprise for you both, didn't I?" said Mueller, crossing the room and placing an arm around his wife. He drew her into his body and kissed her forehead.

"This is the best surprise ever," screeched Freya Mueller with more excitement than she'd felt in years. "How?" she asked, jumping up and embracing Frances.

Once the initial surprise, kisses, and excitement had abated, and they all sat down with a coffee, Mueller recounted the story of his trip to Paris one more time to the delight of both of his parents. Anna just sat with a knowing smile on her face.

"It's wonderful, just wonderful, the best thing ever," said Peter. "I'm so happy for you both. I'm happy for us, too. We always hoped that you would work things out eventually."

"We've another surprise for you, haven't we, Froggy?" said Mueller. "Do you want to tell them, or shall I?" Frances beamed back at him. She was feeling relaxed. The worst part was over, and she had been accepted back into the Mueller fold.

"I will. I'm pregnant," she announced. "You're going to be grandparents."

There was a brief silence while Peter and Freya digested the information. Then they all dissolved into laughter as Peter Mueller asked, "How?"

"Have you forgotten how it's done then, Pa?" said Mueller,

grinning at his father. "Froggy is five months through her pregnancy, and…"

"There are two," said Frances, cutting in, "and I believe I can thank you for that, Peter." She threw a smile in Peter's direction and turned to Anna. "And that's something you didn't know, Anna, isn't it?"

"Anna knew?" questioned Freya crossly.

"I guessed, Freya. There is nothing to get worked up about. I'll see if I can save the dinner, shall I?" She left the room, mumbling on her way back to the kitchen. "Fifty minutes late. If it's ruined, it's not my fault."

* * *

The dinner was wholly edible but not one of Anna's best. They all agreed that it should be a secret just between themselves. Mueller had seated himself next to his mother for the meal and glanced over to her from time to time, finding it much easier to smile at her than he had ever thought possible, and Freya relaxed more than she had in years as she drank in every one of those smiles.

Following the meal, Frances told of her up-and-coming visit to the States, and Mueller excused himself.

She found him sometime later in the garden, looking towards the distant lights of Cologne and Bonn. He didn't hear her approach and only knew she was there when she stood behind him and wrapped her arms around his chest, laying her head on his back.

"Hello," he murmured. Then he took her hand and pulled her to his side, wrapping his arm around her shoulders and hugging her close. "Hunter's moon, Froggy," he said, referring to the full moon's brightness in the nearly cloudless sky.

"You miss it, don't you?" she said.

"Huh," he said, rubbing his hand across his chin. "I don't

miss people trying to blow my head off." He glanced down at her.

"I don't mean that," said Frances.

"I know you don't mean that, and yes, I miss them, all of them. The men. Paul." He blew out his cheeks and exhaled.

"Have you visited Inga Werner, Kristian?" Frances asked, and she watched him shift uncomfortably.

"No, though I have written a couple of times. I know I need to go to see her. I've been putting it off. I don't know what to say, you see. I can hardly say Paul died for a noble cause, right?"

She turned to him, wrapped her arms around him, and gazed at his face. "You'll think of something to say when you see her. Should I come with you?"

"I'd like that," he said. "We'll put it on the list of things to do. I've been thinking about something else, too."

"About what?"

"Pa told me there was a baby at Auschwitz, after all."

Frances was immediately filled with emotion, feeling an overwhelming love for the two she was carrying.

"He also told me that Mengele chap told you he'd buried him. Do you believe him?"

She shrugged. "I don't know, though there was no reason for him to say he had if he hadn't. Under the apple tree in his garden is where he said," she murmured.

"I'd like to find out. I want to bring him home if he's there. He shouldn't be left in a place like that." Mueller watched her eyes fill with tears.

She took a deep breath before replying, "There are many people left in places like that who shouldn't be there, Kristian."

"I know, but he's ours," he said, and she took his hand.

"I'll come with you then," she said.

"You most certainly will not! Who knows what horrors it could unleash? Just look at you now. I need to do this on my own, Froggy. Let me. I need to see if our child is there, and I need to see the place for myself. Don't make things any more difficult."

In the distance, they heard the nightly alarm carried on the wind from the towns and cities, which signified the beginning of curfew.

"Ah, there we go. Looks like we lost the war again then," said Mueller. "I wonder when they will get fed up with those bloody sirens. I mean, it's not like we need a bloody daily reminder, right?"

Frances smiled at him. It hurt his Germanic pride to be on the losing side, even though he knew now and accepted that the cause he had been fighting for was rotten to the core. Still, the way the Brits rubbed their noses into Germany's defeat every night irked him.

"Childish bastards!" he spat. Then he turned to her and, with a smile, and inquired, "Well, are we going in?"

"I don't mind. It's a beautiful night."

"We could go for a walk," he suggested.

"I think that's a lovely idea."

"Come on, I'll grab a torchlight from the boot room. Do you need a coat?"

She shook her head. "Don't think so. It's quite a warm night."

They made their way to the kitchen door, which also housed the door to the boot room. Although the hour was now getting late, Anna was still at the sink clearing up. As Mueller closed the outside door armed with a torch, she wrapped the window and opened it.

"If you're off to the stables, make sure you get the hay off each other's backs before you come into this house!" she ordered.

"What hay, what are you on about, woman?" said Mueller with a wink at Frances, who was trying to suppress a fit of the giggles.

Anna wagged a finger at them both. "You know what I'm talking about."

"Haven't got a clue," returned Mueller, taking Frances by the hand and heading towards the stables.

"Liar!" came the shout. Mueller stopped and turned back to the window, giving Anna one of his best boyish grins and a shrug.

"I'll leave the kitchen door off the lock for you, then," she yelled. "Goodness, there'll be five, six, seven babies here before we know it," she grumbled in the background behind them as they walked on.

"If we end up in the barn, which I'm thinking is highly likely, no biting, Froggy, promise?" said Mueller.

"Promise," she agreed, with an impish smile.

Chapter 4

I t was their second weekend at Schonen Felder. Frances rolled onto her back as she heard the latch pull back on the bedroom door. She threw a sleepy smile towards Mueller as he entered, fresh from a bath and clothed in a white towelling robe. He returned her smile and sat on the side of the bed.

"How are you all today?" he asked, leaning over and kissing her stomach.

"Good," she replied with a yawn. "I could have done with another half hour, but the phone ringing woke me up."

"It was Sara. Mutti told me she was on her way over. It seems she has news for us," Kristian informed her. "Knowing Sar, she'll be here soon, so up you get, Frau Mueller."

"Not until I get a good morning kiss." Frances pouted.

Mueller threw himself onto the bed and took his wife into his arms."

"I don't think I can get close enough to kiss you," he teased, pursing his lips.

"Well, you'd better try a bit harder," she instructed and rolled on top of him. He groaned.

"My God, you've turned into a whale." He gasped.

"It's your Mueller offspring responsible for that," she reminded him, bending her head forward and kissing his lips. He was about to return the kiss when there was a hard knock on the door.

"Kristian, Frances." Freya Mueller sounded on edge. "You are both up, aren't you?"

"I am," Mueller replied. "I've been trying to get Frances up for ages, Mutts, but she's refusing to move," he continued, receiving a knee in the thigh from Frances.

"We'll be down in a minute," shouted Frances. "Sara isn't here yet, is she?"

"No," came the reply, "but you know Sara. She likes an early start to her day. Come on, you two, please. Anna got breakfast half an hour ago, and it's almost nine o'clock."

"We'll be down in five minutes, Mutti, promise," Frances answered.

They both listened to the staccato sound of Freya Mueller's heels tapping across the landing and down the stairs.

"We're going to be in trouble," Mueller said through a grin. "You're teaching me bad habits."

"Doesn't hurt now and again. I rarely get to see you before mid-morning at the weekends. You're always off doing something or other first thing. And anyway, it's Sunday. Surely a lie-in is permissible on a Sunday, isn't it?"

"Not when Sara is on her way here. Come on. Up, otherwise I will call Anna."

"No, I'm up, really I am." She laughed, pulling herself to sit and swinging her legs over the side of the bed. "You get dressed, and I'll be five minutes. A quick bath," she said, opening the bedroom door and crossing the landing to the bathroom. "And save me some breakfast; we're all starving."

They were finishing their breakfast when the dining room door burst open, framing Sara, wearing her usual riding attire. She crossed the room and joined them at the dining table, giving each a peck on the cheek before pouring herself a coffee and seating herself next to Kristian.

"You're looking pleased with yourself, Sar. What's going on?" he asked.

"I've got some news," said Sara, "Guess what?"

Mueller shook his head and shrugged. "Haven't got a clue."

A huge smile split Sara's face. "We're getting married," she announced.

Frances shrieked and jumped to her feet, quickly followed by Kristian, who wrapped his arms around Sara in a brotherly embrace and kissed her on the forehead.

"When?" he asked.

"They're letting you marry?" asked Frances.

"God, yes. Where have you been?" asked Sara.

"But I didn't think it was allowed."

"Might not be in our wonderful British zone," Sara said, "but the Yanks have allowed their men to marry their sweethearts since last December."

"I suppose I'm a bit out of date with things having been away. That's wonderful, Sar." Frances gave Sara a warm hug. "I'm so happy for you both. So come on, fill us in on the particulars."

"Well, Jack and I are off to America."

Frances couldn't contain herself. "What? You can't." she screeched.

"Frances, calm down," said Mueller, who looked far from happy. "It was always on the cards that if Sara and Jack married, she would go to America."

"Ah, but I haven't told you everything, so shut up, Kristian," Sara admonished. "The best bit is, we're coming back, both of us."

Frances screeched again. "That's brilliant. Is Jack staying in the forces for the time being?" she asked.

"No. It's even better than that. You know, Kristian, that pop has always worried about what would happen to our farm when he was too old to run it. He couldn't possibly let me, of course, being a mere female."

Mueller nodded. "Quite right." He gave a lift of his brows and a chuckle. Sara looked at him through slit eyes.

"Shut it!" she said, continuing, "So, you see, now there is Jack. I can stay home, where I want to be, and raise a family like you two."

Kristian stood and embraced Sara again as the door opened, and Freya walked in, casting a look at the other three.

"What have I missed?" she asked.

"Just the best news ever," Frances said, and Sara repeated it all for Freya's sake.

"So, when do you leave for America, Sara?" Freya asked.

"A couple of weeks. We'll probably stay a few months, have a simple ceremony for Jack's people, and then come home and do it all again here."

"Two weddings, lucky girl," said Frances.

"And you're doing it all again for your family and friends, which is more than can be said for these two." Freya cast a disparaging look at Frances and Kristian who blew out his cheeks and huffed.

"If I have a second wedding, it will be with a different woman, Mutti. Are you up for that? I could do with one less bossy, for starters."

"Huh!" Frances looked across the table, casting him a filthy look. He held her glance, a smile tugging at his lips.

"Maybe a few years younger, too," he added, throwing Frances one of his lopsided grins.

"Hah, hah, very funny, Kristian Mueller. You wait," Frances threatened.

* * *

Back in the small apartment in Bonn, Frances sighed with satisfaction and lay back on the bed, nestling herself into Mueller's arm.

"Should we still be doing this?" he questioned.

"Doing what?" she asked sleepily.

"You know, making love. It feels odd knowing they're in there."

"I'm sure they're fine, Kristian. Besides, I can't think of a better way for them to get to know that their father is a dick." Mueller turned his head towards her grinning face and blinked, unable to think of a suitable comeback. "And that," said Frances with a chuckle, "is A: for telling me I was starting to resemble a whale and B: for considering swopping me for a new model."

Mueller sniffed and pushed himself up onto his elbow, finding her gaze. "I'll hang onto you for now, Froggy. But if Mutti keeps pushing for this second wedding— well—"

"Down to me to hit that on the head then, isn't it?" she said. "Great news about Sara and Jack, though."

"'Tis," said Mueller. "I've been thinking the last few days—"

"Well done," Frances interrupted and threw him a cheeky grin. Mueller merely raised his eyebrows and continued.

"About a few things. You are sleeping better now, aren't you? You're in a better place?"

"I'm with you. If you'd seen me in Paris—" she shook her head.

"Bad?"

She nodded. "There were nights when I scarcely slept. The bed was too hard, too soft. I'd dream I was taking part in a selection. Sometimes I was selected…At one point, I thought I was going mad. I swear I could feel others in bed with me. It was the concerts that saved my sanity. I had to think about something other than…." She trailed off and he took her hand.

"How are you feeling now you're home?"

"Home. That's a word I've yearned to hear. I'm here with you now. And Mutti and Anna and your father."

"You said you would come with me to Berlin. I've been putting it off, waiting to see if Konrad would need me there, you see." He sighed. "You know that's an excuse, Froggy. I can get time off to go anytime."

"To see Inga?"

He nodded.

"Well, when then?" she asked.

"Are you up to it?"

"I'm not ill, Kristian. I'm pregnant. I'm definitely up to it, are you?"

"I'm dreading it," he confessed.

Chapter 5

As it was, they waited until the following weekend to make the car journey to Berlin. Mueller decided it would be wise to stay the night at Schonen Felder and make for Hannover which would cut a considerable amount of time off the long journey.

It was coming up a year since the war had ended, and Frances was still upset and surprised by the number of displaced persons they came across, particularly in and around the larger villages and towns.

"It's all far from over," Mueller stated. "If we have another poor harvest this year, and by all accounts, it's looking that way, then there are going to be many more deaths from starvation."

"I don't understand why you are relying on wheat and grain crops when you and your father have complained that the seeds are poor. And you can't rely on the weather where we are either."

"It's what we do, Froggy. We've always managed to produce enough, but now, with all these extra mouths to feed…You can't blame these people for turning to crime, can you? They're fighting for their very existence and that of their loved ones. At least I only had myself to worry about on my journey back from France." Mueller went quiet for a while, reliving some of the horrors he had encountered. After a few minutes, Frances drew him from his reverie.

"You know, when I visited England…"

"Ah, when you ran out on me, you mean," Mueller said, briefly casting his eyes on her.

"Yes, which you deserved," she returned. "Anyway, listen. Many of the Brits were growing their own food. They were encouraged to do it during the war and continued. If they have too much, they take it to the market and sell it to others. Market Gardening, they call it. They grow salad and potatoes. Can't we do that rather than rely on poor seeds and poor crops?"

"The weather isn't right, Froggy."

"But we could build greenhouses, and then you are removing one of the unknowns."

"Greenhouses?"

"Huge greenhouses, Kristian, which will keep the wind and frost off the plants. Just think, fresh salad, tomatoes, new potatoes, carrots even."

"Can't see Pa going with that."

"But you could sow the seed, so to speak." Mueller took his eyes off the road and glanced at her, giving her a nod.

"I'll sow the seed," he said.

* * *

The closer they drove towards Berlin, the more depressing the journey became, and the quieter Mueller became too., Frances decided to try to take his mind off the carnage they were driving through.

"Tell me about your time at university. Tell me about what you and Paul got up to."

"Froggy, I'm not sure I should tell you."

She watched with relief as a smile of recollection creased his face.

"Come on, Kristian Mueller. I want to hear the lot."

"I bet you do." He was quiet for a while and then gave a sudden chuckle. "It was wild, suffice to say. You know the authorities kept an eye on the universities, particularly when Adolf seized control. So many great lecturers left the country, sadly. I suppose we were the lucky ones. We crept through before it got too bad and still had some brilliant minds lecturing us. We also had a whole load of Nazi ideology forced down us, though."

"As part of your course?"

"I suppose you could say it was extracurricular. But we were expected to attend lectures and speeches, you see."

"Tell me how you and Paul met."

"Our rooms were next door, and we were both reading law. It didn't take us long to get talking." He took his eyes briefly off the road and turned to her. "It didn't take us long to recognise like minds and become close." He was thoughtful for a moment and then said, "We had mental times with girls and alcohol until Paul met Inga." He laughed before continuing. "I spotted her first. At the end of our second year, Inga was starting her first. She was reading classics. My God, she was beautiful." Frances felt a touch of irritation as he continued. "Paul, the cheeky sod stole her from under my nose."

"She'd have definitely chosen you, of course, if you'd moved faster."

Mueller flashed her a smile. "Of course, and you'd have missed out. Aren't you lucky?" She sniffed derision. "They were right together from the start, you see. She was gentle, like Paul."

They passed a sign that said Berlin, 1 kilometre, and Mueller pulled to the side of the road and stopped the car. As they looked towards the city, all they saw was utter devastation. Both were horrified.

"My God." Mueller gasped.

They drove forward into what was once Germany's capital and was now kilometre upon kilometre of bombed-out buildings. Women and men, though mostly women, were sorting through the rubble in groups, looking for stone and bricks that could be reused in the hope that Berlin could rise again from the ashes like a phoenix. Many stood in the debris, passing heavy buckets of what was considered useful to the end of the line.

"It's worse than I thought," said Frances. Mueller nodded.

"This isn't right." He sighed. "Bombing civilians isn't right, Froggy. Someone should be held responsible for this. But it won't ever happen. And do you know why?"

She shook her head.

"Because we lost. I need to stop and try and get my bearings. Every damn street looks like every other, you see. There are so few landmarks left."

"Why not go and ask where we are, Kristian? There are plenty of civilians and troops about." Mueller nodded and drew up on the side of the road.

"Stay here then. I'll go and find someone to ask."

He walked away and approached a group of women sorting through a pile of rubble. Their children stood in a group watching him, and even at a distance, it was clear to Frances that they were near starvation, their eyes huge in their emaciated faces. She had the ridiculous thought that they could have bought eggs from the chickens back home. But a few eggs could cause a riot, she thought. You'd need enough to feed the city or, at the very least, enough to feed an entire street, and even they had nowhere near that amount of food to give away. She watched as Mueller walked back towards the car.

"I've got my bearings now. I wasn't far out. It's up the road a little more and then a left turn," Mueller said as he clambered back into the driving seat.

"I can't wait to meet Inga, and I'm so excited about meeting the children too," Frances replied as they drew away and made for the home of Paul and Inga Werner, having no idea if any of it was left standing.

* * *

Mueller was inflamed. "What the fuck has she done?"

"I don't know, Kristian; what has she done?" Frances pointed to the women and elderly men across the street, whom Mueller had approached briefly before. "Calm down and tell me what they said. Inga is okay, isn't she?"

Mueller shook his head. "God knows. She's left the remains of her home and moved into the Russian zone. They called her whore and all kinds of names, but at least they gave me an address. I can't think why she would move away from her old neighbourhood. She's left old friends behind there. Or that's what I thought. I need to sort this out. Come on, we have to make for the Pariser Platz."

"I remember. That's the square leading to the Brandenburg Gate. When Steven and I came here, it was about all we got to see of Berlin before we were thrown out. Though, we did visit the Tier Garten, of course. Oh, and we saw the Reichstag. That's not far away, is it?"

"No, just a block," Mueller replied, seemingly paying little or no attention to her comments on her visit to Berlin with her first husband.

"It was quite badly damaged when we saw it."

"What?"

Frances bulked at Mueller's sharp answer. She realised that he hadn't been listening to her at all. "The Reichstag," she repeated. "It was quite damaged when Steven and I visited."

"Not as damaged as it is now, by all accounts."

They drove until they reached the Pariser Platz, the far end of which was the Brandenburg Gate.

"Ah," said Mueller. "It's certainly changed a bit since I last saw it. The horses had heads for a start. It will take some fixing," he said with a frown.

He drew up on the side of the road and parked the car. Frances was aware it was one of very few. Most of the other vehicles were military. Bicycles had become the main means of transport for many Berliners, and she had a flashback to her attempts at cycling around Paris during the occupation. The darkest of times, she thought, and yet here she was, sitting next to her German husband, six months pregnant with his children. Mueller dragged her from her reverie.

"Froggy, I just want to sit and watch for a while. This is all quite extraordinary, isn't it?"

"What is?" she asked.

"All of this," he said, indicating with his hand the goings on outside on the street.

"You mean how people are going about their business as though nothing has happened?" Frances asked him.

"Hmm," said Mueller, rubbing his jaw thoughtfully. "I don't know whether it's a good thing or a bad thing."

She touched his arm. "Life goes on, hey?"

He turned to her and nodded.

"Suppose so."

They both sat in the car for some minutes, lost in their own memories and looked at the lives of the bustling Berliners as they crossed from the Russian zone into the British and vice versa. Businessmen carrying briefcases. Women, some dressed to the nines and sporting up-to-date fashion, on the arm of men equally well dressed. Mothers chastising their children for misbehaving. War-weary, worn-out women, so obviously peddling their wears in public, hoping for a man to show interest. Someone who could give them enough money to buy a meal or, at the very least, a crust of bread. And then there were the really desperate. Children with no mothers, who were left on the street to beg. And folk who had lost everything other than the sad remnants of their past. They pushed them around in carts towards the Brandenburg gate and the black market, hoping someone might buy one or more of the sorry items they had left over from better times.

Frances drew Mueller's attention back. "Should we go?" she asked.

He sighed. "We should. Shall I drive us into the Russian zone, or are you up for a walk?"

"Let's walk. It will do us both good to get out of the car for a while."

"We may not have one when we return, but I agree. I need to stretch my legs." He opened his car door and walked to the passenger side to help Frances out. She took his hand deep in thought.

"Why was it built, Kristian?" she asked. He gave her a questioning look. "The Brandenburg Gate, who built it?" she asked.

"One of the Prussian Kings. Frederick William the Second. He wanted a grand entrance towards one of his palaces. Only royalty was allowed to use the central arch. Now by the looks of things, anyone can use it. It was built originally as a testament to peace, and now, it divides this city into East and West. What the hell is Inga thinking of, huh? Come on, Froggy, let's see if we can find out." Frances took his arm, and they walked towards the Russian zone.

* * *

"Here we are. This is it. The white house, across the road. Hardly salubrious," Mueller said, turning to her and raising his eyebrows. "But I guess once upon a time it was."

"I should think there are very few salubrious homes left in Berlin, Kristian."

He grunted.

"At least four walls are standing, and it has an entire roof. It's odd, isn't it? This side of the gate is no different to the British side."

"Except for the enormous poster of Stalin, of course. There are as many British uniforms this side of the gate as the British side," he remarked. "All very friendly. I wonder how long it will last, Froggy. Eh?"

"Come on," she said, taking his arm. He blew out his cheeks, exhaled, and stopped walking.

"What the hell do I say to Inga regarding Paul? I haven't got a clue."

"You'll know when you see her. It'll be fine." She took his arm again, and they crossed the road, passing a group of children given sweets by a couple of Russian soldiers. Once they reached the house's front door, Mueller rapped hard on it with his knuckles. Seconds later, the door was opened by a fair-haired young boy of about seven who stared at them wide-eyed. Frances saw the likeness immediately.

"Uncle Kristian?" the boy muttered under his breath. Then the door was flung open wide, and Frances and Mueller watched as he raced to the back of the house yelling. "Mutti, Mutti, It's Kristian. Kristian is here. He's come. I knew he would."

Frances and Kristian stepped into the wide hallway of what once upon a time had been a well-to-do house. Now stripped of most of its furnishings, it stood sad and empty.

"Kristian?" A woman's voice echoed through the hallway towards them, and Frances watched as a beautiful but careworn, too-slender young woman appeared at the far end of the hall and stood beaming at them. "Kristian," she repeated before dashing into Mueller's arms, followed by the child, who grabbed him around the legs.

Some seconds and many tears later, the woman pushed herself out of Mueller's embrace and turned her pale blue eyes onto Frances. "You must be Frances," she said. "Paul wrote of you. You're as lovely as he said."

Frances stepped forward and wrapped her arms around the tearful woman. "And so are you. Paul showed me photographs, and this must be Johanne."

"And where is my godson? Where is little Kristian? He must be what? Coming up five. Where's he hiding?" Mueller asked, casting a gaze around the building.

Inga Werner choked on her tears as she lifted her gaze to Mueller's and replied, "He's gone, Kristian. My little boy is dead."

There was absolute silence in the hall of that house until Mueller muttered through a clenched jaw, "How?"

Inga Werner lifted her hand to her head, drawing it through her hair. She raised her eyes and met their gaze.

"There was no food, no milk," she said, choking back the memory. "I tried so hard to find something for him. I went looking. But you have seen how it is still. Almost a year on, Kristian, and there is still so little food." She shook her head with worry. "There will be people dropping like flies this coming winter. It will mostly be the elderly, babies, and young children. Which is why you find me here." Inga straightened up and looked Mueller in the eye. "I know you, Kristian. You'll think I have cheapened Paul's memory by moving in here with a Russian." She sighed with relief, it was said.

Mueller exploded, causing Johanne to burst into tears as he vented his anger. "You are living here with a fucking Russian? Huh, too right I think you have cheapened Paul's memory, and you've cheapened yourself, too, Inga."

Inga grabbed the lapels of Mueller's jacket, searching his face for a little understanding. "Do you think there was a choice? You don't know what it was like, Kristian. How could you? No one could imagine hell on earth."

Having experienced hell on earth, Frances identified with the woman's trauma. "You need to hear this, Kristian. Let her tell you how it was," she said.

Mueller turned on her. "What I need to do is to leave this damn place!" he spat. Frances grabbed him by the arm and drew him back towards the front door.

"Stop it. You owe it to Paul to listen to what Inga has to say. She has lost a child, for God's sake."

"She's sold herself. The Russians are animals."

"And your countrymen, people like Otto, and those who ran the camps were not?" Mueller pulled his hands through his hair in consternation as Frances continued. "She's young. She wants to live and yearns to see her child grow to manhood. Paul would want that too." She took Mueller's hand, laid it on her belly, and turned her flaming gaze on him. "Would you want me to let these two children of yours die if I had a way of saving them, no matter what?"

Mueller looked into the amber of her eyes. Eventually, he nodded, took a deep breath, and exhaled. He then walked back up the hallway towards Inga. "Tell me how it was. I need to understand."

"Come," she said. She took Mueller's arm and led him up the hall to a large kitchen at the back of the house, and Frances followed. Inga prepared a pot of coffee, found four cups and poured a little milk into three of them, topping up the fourth for Johanne. She gave the boy a loving smile and ruffled his hair. "Why don't you go and play Johanne or read for a while," she said. "I don't want him to listen to it all again. He's been through enough." She turned her eyes to Frances. "Could you?"

Frances tried hard not to feel like she was being dismissed, but she failed. She had no alternative but to go with the child.

"Show me around your house, Johanne, why don't you?" she encouraged. What else could she do? "And then, if we have time, maybe we can walk around your neighbourhood." Mueller gave her a brief nod as she passed Johanne his milk, picked up her coffee cup and, taking Johanne's arm, led him from the kitchen. She looked back as she reached the doorway and saw Mueller pull his chair close to Inga and take her hand. She felt her stomach knot.

* * *

Mueller took a deep breath and exhaled. "I miss him, Inga, every fucking day, you see. You must blame me for his death."

She shook her head and searched his face with her eyes. "Why would I?" she questioned.

"It was me who recommended that he take over the running of the old tub when I left. Did you know that?" The suspicion of a smile flitted across her lips.

"Of course I know that. Paul was beside himself when he took over from you. Kapitan Leutnant Paul Werner. He was honoured, Kristian. You know as well as I that the odds were stacked against him coming home, and he knew that, too. You were one of the lucky ones, and I'm glad of it. If I had lost you both, I don't know what I would have done."

He gave her a weak smile. "So, tell me about you. I don't need to ask you if it was bad. To bomb civilians the way they did." He shook his head. "I just said to Frances that someone should be held accountable." She stretched out her hand and touched Mueller's cheek.

"But it won't happen, Kristian." She gave a deep sigh. "It was terrifying. Of course, it was. Night after night of it. Skulking below ground, hoping there would not be a direct hit. Did you go to the old home?" Mueller nodded. "The fact is there is very little left of it. Very little left of the entire street. But you saw that for yourself."

"I'm so sorry, Inga," he said, and she smiled briefly, then her brow knotted as she continued.

"The bombing was just the start. There was a shortage of food, and my boys were getting weaker and weaker. And then, one day, I lost my Kristian. Some falling masonry hit him. I warned both the boys to keep away from the buildings. I was with them and turned my back for just a moment to speak to a neighbour. For some reason, he tottered back towards the house; he was weak and —" Inga gave a little cry as she re-lived that day all over again. "They said he'd have known nothing about it. Knowing that didn't help. If it hadn't been for Johanne, I wouldn't be here—We knew the Russians were approaching the city. We slept in the cellar at night: no water, no gas, no light. Johanne was so scared and so very hungry. Then, this one night, we heard artillery and knew they had reached Kaiser Platz. Then that was it. Our building was hit by artillery fire over and over again. I was scared, Kristian; I was scared to leave the cellar to cook. Then they arrived."

She stopped speaking, and a sob caught in her throat. Mueller squeezed her hand and looked deep into her eyes, holding her steady. Inga took a deep breath and continued, "A group of them found us in the cellar. And then it started." She clenched her jaw before continuing. "Five times. My old neighbour held Johanne close so he couldn't see what was happening. Thank God they left my neighbour alone. She is in her sixties. I believe it would have killed her. I bit my lip for my boy and stayed silent throughout the ordeal."

Another sob wracked through the body of Inga Werner, and Mueller held her closer.

"You don't need to say anymore," he said.

"Yes, Kristian, I do. You need to know to understand. I want you to understand. I should be telling Paul all of this. You're the closest thing I have to him."

She continued her story. She told Mueller that she and Johanne moved out of the cellar of their old home and searched for what they thought would be a safer place. They found what was left of a bombed-out apartment not far from the Potsdamer Platz.

"We liked it. There were still a few trees left standing and some greenery about," she said. "Then, a couple of days after the fighting stopped, a horse-drawn baggage train arrived just outside. It belonged to a Russian tank regiment. They hobbled the horses and let them graze. We were afraid, but we couldn't stay inside forever. Besides, we saw female soldiers and men. We went outside; other Berliners were there, too, and the Russians gave the children food. The one that gave Johanne food —" She met Mueller's eyes. "Well, he smiled at me. And that's how I met Alexei."

"Alexei," Mueller repeated. "So that's his name then. Did he hurt you? If he did, I'll kill the bastard. You don't have to stay with him, Inga. You can—"

Inga Werner laid a hand on Mueller's arm. "He seemed nice. So, when he walked off, I followed him." She looked away, took a deep breath, and continued with her head down. "I offered myself to him. I said I would be just his. He could do whatever he liked to me if he gave Johanne food."

"Christ, Inga! What the hell were you thinking, to offer yourself like that?" Mueller snapped.

She shrugged. "I was thinking of my child Kristian. I want you to know that Alexei has never hurt me, and I believe he never would."

They both jumped when the front door banged. "Can we come in?" Frances's voice echoed down the corridor to the kitchen. Inga stood and made her way out.

"Come, Frances, of course," she said, taking Johanne into a maternal embrace. "More coffee?"

"I'd love some," Frances replied.

The two women and Johanne made their way back to the kitchen. Mueller was standing, and Frances immediately saw that he wasn't happy. She gave him a questioning look, which he ignored.

"We should leave, Frances," he muttered. Inga stretched her arms and placed them around Mueller's neck.

"I'd like you both to stay and meet Alexei, Kristian."

He shook his head. "How can you ask——"

Frances cut in, "We'd love to."

"I'm so glad," came a voice from behind.

Frances and Mueller turned as Inga smiled at a lanky, well-decorated Soviet officer standing in the doorway to the kitchen. The officer had just spoken.

"This is Alexei. Alexei, this is mine and Paul's greatest friend, Kristian Mueller, and his wife, Frances."

The two men eyeballed each other as they grasped one another's hands. Mueller spoke first, his jaw clenched.

"Kapitan Kristian Mueller, Kriegsmarine."

"Kapitan Alexandr Kuznetsov. Soviet Tank Division."

The two women looked at each other, eyebrows raised, looking from one man to the other, as neither man wanted to be the first to let go of the other man's hand. They broke the stalemate by interceding, taking their partner's hand, and leading him to the kitchen table.

"We were just about to leave," Mueller said awkwardly.

"I insist you stay the night," said Kuznetsov. You don't want to be out and about with your wife. There is still a great deal of crime, and the hotels, to be honest, are …" He threw his hands wide and shrugged his shoulders. "We can share notes, Mueller, hey? Both spent our war years inside a fucking tin can, didn't we?"

"But mine was bigger than yours," Mueller returned, holding the other man's gaze, and it was with relief that both women watched the corners of their men's mouths twitch before they both burst into laughter. Grabbing each other's hands a second time, they gave a friendlier shake.

"Inga, what have we in the larder?" asked Kuznetsov. "We have friends staying, huh?"

"A little cold meat, today's bread, and some cheese," she replied.

"And I have plenty of vodka, and today, I managed to get hold of a few bottles of wine. So, Mueller, let's talk tactics and drink," said Kuznetsov, "while these women sort some food and prepare a room for you and Frances. Where is Johanne, Inga?"

"He is reading in the front room, Alexei." Kuznetsov sniffed. "Good. Reading is good for him. He must read Tolstoy."

"I agree," said Mueller and received a warm smile from his host.

We will take the dining room then. Tactics, Tolstoy, and drink." And with that, he ushered Mueller out of the kitchen towards the dining room.

Chapter 6

Mueller woke up with a groan. He could scarcely remember getting into bed and hadn't a clue how he got up the stairs. Frances turned towards him with a sigh.

"Serves you right. What time did you get to bed, anyway?" she asked.

"Haven't a clue. Feels like about an hour ago."

She looked at her watch, pulled herself to sitting, swung her legs over the side of the bed, and made for the window for some light.

"It's 8:30," she said, pulling back the curtains.

"Ah. It probably was about an hour ago," groaned Mueller. "Close the damn curtains, Froggy, please. I've one hell of a hangover, you see."

"Yes, I do see, Kristian, and you'll get no sympathy from me at all. You should know your limits."

"Couldn't let Kuznetsov drink me under the table, now, could I?" He gave her a lopsided grin.

"How childish," snapped Frances. "Come on, we can't stay

up here any longer. It's downright rude." She jumped as someone wrapped the door and spoke.

"Mueller, are you awake?"

"Kuznetsov," Mueller muttered under his breath. "The bastard sounds too bloody perky," he whispered.

"Mueller," Kuznetsov repeated. "Are you awake? I thought you might like the grand tour of what's left of Berlin, hey?"

Mueller groaned and gave Frances a wide-eyed look. "Okay… Give me five, Kuznetsov. I'll meet you in the kitchen."

He quickly dressed and tipped some water from the jug on the washstand into a bowl. Splashing some on his face, he hoped it would help with his hangover. It didn't.

"Are you okay if I leave you with Inga?" he asked, making for the bedroom door.

"Of course I am," she replied.

"Then I'll see you later." He turned to close the door.

"Kristian, no more vodka, promise?" she said.

He raised his eyebrows and left with a boyish grin on his face.

* * *

Mueller went to the kitchen and found Inga, Johanne, and Alexei Kuznetsov having breakfast. Alexei stood when Mueller entered. "How are you feeling?" he asked. Mueller straightened up and tried to ignore the banging in his head.

"Fine," he replied.

"Really?" answered Kuznetsov, "I feel shit, I can tell you."

With relief, Mueller flopped down onto a chair. "Thank Christ for that," he said, drawing laughter from Inga and Kuznetsov.

"I'll cut you some fresh bread," said Inga. "Johanne has been out already to pick up today's ration, and Alexei has a stash of

54

coffee. You look like you could do with some." Mueller smiled his thanks.

"Is Frances all right?" Inga asked.

Mueller nodded. "She'll be down in a minute. Your vodka got me in trouble, Kuznetsov."

Alexei Kuznetsov wrapped his arms around Inga's shoulders and kissed the top of her head. She looked up at him and smiled, and he chucked her under the chin.

"Me too," he said. "So come on, Mueller, let's sample the delights of Berlin or what's left. We'll stick to our zone. Anywhere particular you would like to go?"

"How far to the Cecilienhof Palace?" Mueller asked.

"Under an hour. You want to see where your country was carved up, eh?"

"Yes, I think I would; after all, history was made there. I should move my car first, though."

"Where did you leave it?" asked Kuznetsov.

"The other side of the square from the Gate. I didn't think we would be long."

"Wasn't expecting to be made welcome by a Russian, eh?"

Mueller couldn't think of an answer.

The two men walked to the Brandenburg Gate and across the Pariser Platz, which took them back into the British zone. Mueller remarked that Russian, British, German, and Yank were going about their business as though they were the greatest of pals.

"It won't stay like this, of course," Kuznetsov remarked sadly. "We all have different ideas about what's best for you Germans. At some point, it will become East against West. I can see the future; a united Europe will not benefit us Russians."

"My work with Adenauer is about bringing that to fruition, but I don't think it will happen overnight."

"The French?" asked Kuznetsov.

"The French. I know how awkward they can be, being

married to one." Mueller pointed across the road to his car, which had survived the night, and he was thankful for it.

"We'll drive it back to the house. I've got an idea, Mueller. Let's take the girls and Johanne with us to Potsdam. We can go to the lake after. What do you say?"

"You can just make up your mind about what you do?" Mueller asked with surprise as he climbed into the car.

"To be honest, it's pretty lax," Kuznetsov commented, climbing into the passenger seat. "As long as I put in an appearance, make sure somebody sees me round and about. I'll give a few orders before we leave my district. What do you say?"

"If Inga and Frances agree," said Mueller.

"I'm sure Johanne would like some time with his Uncle Kristian, hey? He talks about you all the time."

"I'd like some time with him, too," replied Mueller as he started the car.

"He's a fine boy," Kuznetsov said and then asked, "What was he like, Mueller?"

Mueller glanced at him as he pulled away and headed towards the Brandenburg Gate and the Soviet zone. "Paul?" he asked and got an answering nod. Chewing on his lip for a few moments, he exhaled. "He was the most decent man I have ever met. He was fair and just. He was my conscience. I loved him like a brother and miss him daily."

"And Inga?" asked Kuznetsov, leaving Mueller unsure what the question was.

"They were the perfect couple. Beautiful inside and out, you see."

"So, do I stand any chance at all, do you think?" They had reached Kuznetsov's neighbourhood. "Park over there," he instructed, pointing to a space in the road near the house.

As Mueller parked the car and reached for the door handle,

Kuznetsov put a restraining hand on his shoulder. "You haven't answered my question," he said. "I'm in love with Inga, Kristian. I won't be here much longer. I'm a lecturer back home, and I want to go back. I want Inga to come with me. Will you stand in my way?"

"Are you free? Will you wed her, or will she be the other woman you might tire of someday?"

"I'm mostly free," Kuznetsov said with a nod and continued. "I have a son a little older than Johanne."

"And his mother?" asked Mueller.

"Is dead. I didn't think I could love again but Inga. Well, Inga has stolen my heart. So, will you get in my way, Mueller?"

"I think what happens, well, it's down to Inga."

"But you will have an enormous influence on her decision. She sees you as being so close to Paul that you are almost the same person."

"Kuznetsov, I assure you one hundred percent that I am not. In comparison, Paul was a saint."

"Ah, there you are." Caught in having a conversation, both men opened their doors and got out of the car. "We wondered where you had got to. What with the jeep not gone." Inga remarked. "I thought you were going off somewhere."

"Kristian left his car parked over the Brits' side."

"First name terms, well done." Inga gave them both a smile. "Frances is in the kitchen with Johanne, and there is coffee on the stove." Inga threaded her arm through Mueller's and led him up the hall to the kitchen as Alexei followed.

"Inga," called Kuznetsov, "Kristian wants to visit Potsdam, the Cecilienhof. We thought perhaps we could all go and carry on to Sacrower See and then go to the Waldfrieden for some food, maybe? And Kristian and Frances must stay another night with us, eh?"

That sounds like a plan, Frances thought with relief. Another day before travelling would benefit her in her condition." What do you think, Inga?" Frances said, sticking her head out of the kitchen door. "There are a couple of handsome men here. Should we walk out with them?"

* * *

"So, this is where it happened," said Mueller, placing his hand on Johanne's shoulder. "This is where the fatherland had the soul ripped out of him." He cast his eyes over the exterior of the Cecilienhof Palace.

"And he bloody well deserved to, didn't he?" Frances remarked, voicing what she was thinking. She noticed the look between Inga and Kuznetsov and quickly recovered herself, remarking on the building. "It looks very British. Tudor in design."

"It didn't look so good before the conference," said Kuznetsov. We had to bring trees and bushes in to make it look the part. It's taken a bit of a beating, but I'm afraid we use it as a club now. I can get you in for a look around if you like. There are one hundred and seventy-six rooms, I believe. Vodka is now consumed in most of them."

"Do you want to go inside, Kristian?" Frances asked.

"If it's now a club, should we give it a miss, particularly with you girls here? Who knows what we could walk into."

"Let me go and see who is about," said Kuznetsov. "I could get you into the conference room at least and show you where some of the photographs were taken in the gardens. Give me a couple of minutes."

A few minutes later, inside the conference room, Frances remarked, "It's quite something, isn't it? To think that the President of the United States, the Prime Minister of Great

Britain, and the leader of the Soviet Union, were all seated together in this room. And just the smell of all the wood. The panelling is superb here."

"I was there when they all arrived. Truman, Churchill, and Stalin. They all came with an entourage," said Kuznetsov. "That room was packed to bursting during the conference."

"I didn't think Churchill was there. I thought he was booted out of office," Mueller said.

"Attlee replaced Churchill, and the government changed," Frances added.

"Only the Brits would sack the chap that had just won them the war. Pricks!" Mueller scoffed. "So, shall we make our way to the lake?"

Inga took Mueller by the arm. "It will bring back sad memories, Kristian. Do you remember we came here when I was pregnant with your namesake?"

"Didn't stop you from joining in with the swimming." Frances watched as he gave her a broad smile. "It was a special day, Ing."

"Are we going swimming today?" Johanne asked.

"Well, you can if you like. No one will mind you being in your underpants, I'm sure," said Inga.

"Back to the jeep then. Sacrower See, here we come, hey?" shouted Kuznetsov. "Come on, the rest of you." He loped back to the car on his long legs with Johanne at his side as the others followed at a more sedate pace.

The weather was good, and Sacrower See was not busy. Frances removed her shoes and enjoyed the feeling of the sand between her toes.

"Should we take the circular walk around the lake?" Kuznetsov asked.

"That's about a 10-kilometre walk, isn't it? I'm up for that. It's a good day for it," said Mueller.

"Too much for me," Frances said. I'll walk up to the forest and sit for a while."

"And I'll join you on the forest walk," said Inga. "We've so much to talk about, Kristian."

Frances felt emotional as Inga took Mueller's arm and walked off, deep in conversation. She was unsure which emotion she was feeling. How could she be angry when Inga had welcomed her into her home? What she wanted to do was run after them, shouting 'wait for me', but in the heat and with the additional weight of carrying two babies, she had had more than enough walking after a couple of kilometres.

"I'm going to sit down here and wait for you all," she told Kuznetsov. He threw himself down in the sand beside her.

"Johanne and I will wait with you," he said. It will probably take them maybe two hours to get back to us here. Are you up to walking to the restaurant? It's back where we parked." He leant towards her. "The lemonade is homemade. Yes?"

"Please don't ruin your day for me, Alexei," she replied.

"How can it be ruined if I am taking a beautiful woman for a drink?" He called over to Johanne, who had his shoes off and was paddling in the lake. Johanne, would you like a lemonade?"

The boy was back in no time. "And a cake, Alexei?" he asked.

"And cake all around," Kuznetsov announced.

They found a place to sit outside with views down to the lake. After lemonade and cake, Frances insisted that she would be fine for a while if Johanne and Kuznetsov wanted to return to the waterfront. Men were fishing, and the two thought they would see what fish had been caught.

It was getting on for an hour later that Frances spotted Mueller and Inga walking towards Alexei and Johanne, who were still down on the water's edge. She watched as Kuznetsov pointed towards the restaurant, and seeing her, Inga waved madly and ran towards her, smiling.

"Frances," she said when she reached her. "I've had such a lovely time with Kristian, reminiscing. It's been wonderful having someone to share my memories with. Thank you for letting me borrow him. It's done me the power of good."

"Well, I'm glad you have had such a nice day," Frances replied as the men arrived.

Mueller immediately picked up on Frances' tone. "Are you all right, Froggy?" he asked as Kuznetsov, Inga, and Johanne went searching for more cake and lemonade.

She looked him in the eye. "Of course, shouldn't I be?" she asked.

* * *

They stayed a while longer at the restaurant at Sacrower See, and once back at Kuznetsov's house, they all sat in the kitchen, chatting. Once Johanne had gone to bed, Kuznetsov produced a few bottles of wine and spoke of his son, Ivan.

"How long has it been since you have seen him?" Frances asked.

"Too long. It's been two years since I managed to visit. I will see a big difference in him. It will be good to get home and get back to lecturing."

Frances shot her eyes to Inga to see how she was taking the news that Kuznetsov couldn't wait to get home. Inga appeared utterly unfazed by it, which made Frances think that maybe the relationship between Inga and Kuznetsov wasn't as close as she had thought, and it rattled her.

"What do you lecture in?" Mueller asked.

"Languages. I am fluent in German and French and have a good knowledge of Polish and English. They have come in useful lately, I can tell you." He turned to Inga with a smile and took her hand. "Very useful indeed," he said.

"I hope it won't be too long until you're reunited with your son, Alexei," Frances said. Again, there was no comment or reaction from Inga.

"Where in Russia is he?" Mueller asked.

"Near St Petersburg. He spent the war with my mother-in-law. I hope she hasn't spoiled him too much. So, what's it to be for you, Mueller? Two boys, two girls or one of each, huh?"

"The devil knows?" Mueller replied.

"It doesn't matter what as long as they are healthy, Kristian," Inga said. "And what of Schonen Felder? I was always meant to visit there with Paul, but now that won't happen."

"You can visit Schonen Felder whenever you like, Ing. You'll always be welcome," Mueller reassured her.

"Paul told me all about it. He had a secret admiration for your cook," she said through laughter.

"Anna," said Mueller and started to chuckle too. "Suffice to say she is a force, isn't she, Froggy?"

"She is," Frances agreed. "But a good one."

The conversation continued into the early hours. They mostly talked about home and losing loved ones, places, and people they missed. By the time they went to bed, they were each full of memories, not all of which were good.

Frances found she couldn't clear her mind of the way Mueller had held Inga close at what seemed to her to be every opportunity. They had walked arm in arm along the beach at Sacrower See, and disappeared from view for more than two hours.

She had looked on with Alexei as they whispered heads together for most of the day.

When Mueller strode into the room from the bathroom, she couldn't contain herself any longer.

"Are you in love with Inga?" she asked. Mueller was taken aback; he momentarily looked at her with surprise before replying.

"I've always been a little in love with Inga," he said as he undid the buttons on his shirt and turned to place it on a hanger. Frances felt her heart lurch. She was pregnant with his two babies, and he admitted he was in love with another woman.

"Do you want to be with her, Kristian? Because it very much looked that way to me." Mueller exhaled noisily.

"What? What do you think you saw? You have been in a strange mood all day. What on earth is wrong with you, woman?" he snapped.

"You are what's wrong with me. All the whispering together and walking arm in arm. I'm surprised Alexei hasn't said something."

"Alexei has said something, Frances, as a matter of fact," Mueller said, holding onto the look she gave him.

"I'm not surprised," she spat and then, dreading his answer, asked, "What? What did he say?"

"He asked me to talk to Inga about going to live in Russia with him. He asked me to find out how she would feel about doing that."

"Oh." Frances deflated and flopped down onto the bed, letting go of her pent-up anxiety. All she felt now was her exhaustion. She repeated, "Oh."

As the tears began to fall, Mueller sat down beside her.

"Hey, why the tears?"

She turned to him, her face screwed up with emotion. "I'm so tired, Kristian. I feel fat and ugly, and Inga is here looking so damn pretty. God, I'm so bloody fed up with being pregnant."

He pulled her to him, and she laid her head on his chest. "You're seven months through, Froggy. You've done brilliantly. I can't imagine what it must be like to carry all that extra weight around. You've got a few more days, and it will be over."

Frances sniffed, and Mueller delved into his pocket for a handkerchief to dry her tears. "You haven't told me what Inga has decided. Has she decided?" she asked, giving another sniff.

Mueller nodded. "She has. She's decided to go to Russia

when Alexei goes back. She said there is little in Germany for her now and too many unhappy memories. I think I could have changed her mind. I wonder if I should have done it. They are quite different to us, the Russians. I think her life will change quite a bit."

"But she'll be with a man who loves her, won't she? She'll have someone to take care of her. I like Alexei," Frances argued.

"And so do I, and I told her that." Mueller took her hand and looked into her eyes. "I'm unsure whether I should tell you this, but we agreed no secrets, didn't we?"

"Yes, what?" she asked. He saw the worry on her face.

"Alexei was part of the Russian army that freed Auschwitz."

"What?" she gasped. "When did he tell you?"

"The first night. When we drank too much."

"Did you tell him I was there?"

"No, Froggy, I didn't. I wasn't sure how you would feel. Whether you would want to visit there again."

"I visit there every day, Kristian. I thought you knew that." He took her hands and found her gaze.

"Hey, I know that. I didn't want to stir anything up, that's all," he explained. "It looks like I have just by mentioning it."

She drew her hands away from his, and he watched as, for a moment, she was back there. She wrapped her arms around herself protectively. "Tell me what he said anyway."

"They drove tanks through the electric wire. That's how they got in. He said he has never got over the hell he saw there."

Her eyes widened as she saw it, too. "I wonder if he came across any of the orchestra girls," she said. "Should I ask him?"

He shook his head. "Sweetheart, I think it's highly unlikely he would have seen anyone you know."

"But I found Miriam, didn't I?"

"Yes, you did, and how unlikely was that?" He tucked some stray hair back from her face, behind her ear. "Try and let it rest,

Froggy. When we get back to Schonen Felder, I will arrange my visit to Auschwitz. We need to bring our son home if he's there."

"I want to come with you." She searched his eyes.

"No, this is something I want to do alone. Please, don't make it difficult."

CHAPTER 7

JUNE 1946

What is it that Mueller felt? Anger, frustration, guilt, horror, pain, anguish? He felt all of this. Seating himself on a random block of concrete, he was mentally and emotionally drained and surprisingly physically drained, too. And yet all that he had done that day was take a tour around Auschwitz, or what was left of it.

He'd journeyed from Cologne to Krakow the day before and had found a half-decent hotel to put him up for the night. That morning, he had taken a taxi and arrived outside the foreboding gates of Auschwitz, which declared that "Work makes you Free." It had been a mean lesson that he'd learnt that morning. The only freedom the inmates of Auschwitz achieved was through dying, and he realised Frances's escape from death was one in a million.

They'd tried to turn him away when he had arrived at those gates, stating that the museum was not yet open and that he should return in a week or so. He'd argued that he had come a long way. All the way from Cologne, which made little difference. It wasn't until he mentioned that he believed the body of his son was buried in Doctor Mengele's Garden under an apple tree that someone did take notice of him. A man stepped forward and introduced himself as Isaac Lensky.

"I work with Tadeusz Wasowicz; he is in charge here. You're German. Why would your son be in Mengele's Garden? Were you one of the guards here?" he asked.

"Christ, no!" Mueller replied. "My wife was sent here from Paris; she was pregnant with our child. She told me Mengele had told her after she miscarried that he had buried the child in his garden."

"It all sounds very far-fetched. Why would Mengele put himself out for a dead child? After all, he spent most of his time killing them." Isaac Lensky regarded Mueller through slit eyes. "What are you really up to, I wonder?"

"I'm telling the truth. Look, I agree it sounds far-fetched, but for some reason, Mengele formed an attachment to my wife. She was a musician and played in the orchestra and, sometimes, for Mengele at his house."

The man nodded. "I've heard such stories. "What is your wife's name?"

"Frances, Frances Meyer," said Mueller

"Violin? I believe I heard her play at one of the sham concerts. I'll go and speak with Wasowicz. Run you past him. Stay put."

Mueller did stay put and was exceedingly uncomfortable as several people eyed him up until Lensky returned. Another man came with him who introduced himself as Tadeusz Wasowicz.

"You're a few days too early, Herr Mueller," the man said in passable German, "but perhaps we can make use of you. We have been putting together an exhibition here for some months. I wonder if we could use you as a guinea pig, so to speak. Would you allow our director Kazimierz here to give you a tour? You can tell us what you think." Mueller nodded his agreement. He wanted to see the site anyway, though he didn't expect it to have such a visceral effect on him.

"Were you here? Before… you know?" Mueller asked the man as they set off.

"Was I a prisoner?" Kazimierz asked. Mueller nodded, and the man continued. "Yes, I was here for some months. I am told your wife was here too."

"Yes, in 43."

"She's lucky to have survived."

"I tell her that, but she is filled with guilt, Kazimierz."

"Ah yes, guilt. I think all of us who have survived here know guilt intimately. Please call me Kazi."

"I had to come. I needed to see for myself, you see."

"Too fantastical to believe?" Mueller nodded. "She was a lucky one, being in the orchestra."

"She wasn't in the orchestra at first," Mueller explained. "She told me they shaved her head and sent her on work details."

Kazi nodded his understanding. "All done to dehumanize us, Mueller. Some fell for it. Most did. They gave up, just as they wanted us to. And if it hadn't been for the Red Army, so might I have done. So, how did Mengele get his paws on her?"

Mueller pulled a hand through his hair as he tried to remember the term that Frances had used. "It was through something called a…a selection?" Mueller said.

Kazi nodded a second time. "She met Mengele during a selection, and she survived him. Remarkable. But your child did not, Mueller?"

"No," Mueller replied, surprised by the emotion bubbling inside him.

"Is your wife a Jew?" Kazi asked.

"It's a long story, but no," Mueller replied.

"Well, Mueller," said Kazi, laying his hand on Mueller's shoulder, "It's a long walk around this camp, so let's hear it while I take you on a journey like no other, eh?"

Mueller gave Kazimierz as much of Frances's story as he

knew, starting with how they had met and how the SS had arrested her.

"I always felt there were huge gaps in what she told me," he told Kazi, who gave him a sad smile.

"And maybe there are many things left in the minds of those that have experienced such a place as this that are better unsaid," he replied."

As he toured the camp, Mueller gleaned a greater understanding of the horrors which were Auschwitz. The Death Wall, where so many were executed, between huts 10 and 11. The remains of the crematoria in Birkenau and the burning pit where thousands were buried. The reconstructed crematoria in the main camp that the SS had tried to destroy to hide their crimes. The shower houses where hundreds were gassed at a time, and the cruel interiors of the brick and wooden barracks where prisoners were held until they were selected for block 11 or saved their captors the trouble of selection and died of malnutrition or disease.

Kazi showed him the warehouses, which were stuffed with the belongings of the unfortunate who had ended up in Auschwitz. Piles of suitcases, still with the names of the owners on them. Vast heaps of men's, women's, and children's clothing, Thousands of pairs of spectacles and shoes, and worst of all, the tons of hair, which took Mueller back to the hotel room where Frances had told him that her incredible mane of hair had been shaved off to be used for the soles of pumps for U boat crews.

His mind flew back to the hotel room in Munich. On the night following her release from Dachau, He had accused her of madness when she told him of the persecution and torture of the poor souls who had found themselves in Auschwitz and Dachau. It had been so much easier than accepting the truth. Now, as he stood side by side with Kazi, total acceptance was his only option.

"I'm surprised you haven't had break-ins. There's so much stuff here, and so many people now have nothing."

"Oh, we've had break-ins, all right. There are quite a few things that go missing. We have turned a blind eye to some poor folk who have turned up here with only rags on their backs. The ones I hate, though, are those who sneak in to scratch around in the firepits looking for gold teeth or jewellery. They sicken me, Mueller. They disturb the sleep of those thousands of souls whose remains are there."

* * *

Once he had told Frances's story and the tour was complete, Mueller felt as though he had been cut into tiny pieces and littered across the Auschwitz site like parts of a jigsaw. He doubted that he could ever be put back together again entirely. A few pieces would always remain at Auschwitz, left behind here, where he forced himself to bear witness to the crimes of his countrymen. Being made to bear witness was becoming a habit. Frances was the first when he rescued her from Dachau. Then Adenauer had sent him to the trials of the war criminals at Nuremberg as a looker on, to see fair play. He had come away from there disgusted with those so-called leaders of his country, the masterminds. And now, he bore witness for a third time as he understood the horrors their evil minds had set into motion. He'd had enough now. He wanted to leave the place to try and get on with his life, but he worried that every time he looked at Frances, guilt would take a bite out of him.

Lost in his dark thoughts, he jumped when he felt a gentle touch on his shoulder. It was Lensky, returned.

"Mueller, I can take you to Mengele's Garden if you are ready," he said.

Kristian Mueller lifted his eyes and, finding the man's gentle gaze on him, was overwhelmed with emotion.

"How can you bear to even speak to me? I'm one of them, Lensky?" he said.

Lensky sat beside Mueller on the concrete block and held him with his steady brown gaze.

"You know," he said, "God gave us the great gift of forgiveness, Mueller. What a dreadful thing it would be if we didn't use it." Witnessing Mueller's pent-up emotion, he leaned forward and wrapped his arms around his shoulders in an embrace. Overcome, Mueller collapsed into him and clung to him like a child. A few moments later, he pushed himself out of the embrace and looked Lensky in the face.

"Lensky," he said, "I've always considered myself a good German. I'm unsure now that there is such a thing. Can you be good and German, do you think?"

"I'll answer that with another question," Lensky replied. "Do you think there is such a thing as a bad Jew?" Mueller was silent, unsure how he could answer. He feared giving some kind of offence, so he sat mute. "I'll try and answer that question with yet another question, shall I?" Lensky continued. "A Jewish father was talked into working as an informant for the Nazis in Warsaw. It might have saved his family, but in so doing, he sacrificed his friends. Was that Jewish father a bad man? What do you think, Mueller?"

Mueller sat, thoughtfully contemplating his answer. "My wife is carrying our two unborn children. I would do anything to save them had the tables been turned."

Lensky gave a harsh laugh. "This is what I thought, and I ended up here anyway. Oh, for a while, we were safe. Now, I have lost my entire family and was responsible for the deaths of I don't know how many of my friends and associates. And yet here, in this place, I have found acceptance, forgiveness, and friendship from most anyhow, though not from myself. But, Mueller, I am working on that. You should do so, too."

* * *

Mueller looked at the little wooden coffin on the table in his hotel room in Krakow. It was the strangest feeling to know that Josef Mengele had been true to his word and that the dried-out remains of his tiny son were inside that box. Within twenty-four hours, he would be back at Schonen Felder, and they would be able to arrange to lay this child to rest finally and, hopefully, some of Frances's demons with it.

He gave a little thought to Mengele, the doctor of death. Frances had told him a little of his vile experiments. The man seemed to have a sordid fascination with twins and the colour of people's eyes. Frances was lucky not to have had hers end up in one of his collections. He'd never seen anyone else have eyes quite as beautiful as hers. And with that thought, he was able to put Mengele and Auschwitz to the back of his mind, at least for a moment, and find repose. Tomorrow, he would make the journey home. He would try to leave all his negative thoughts behind him in the hotel room in Krakow.

* * *

Mueller was scarcely out of his car before Frances threw herself into his arms. "Have you got him?" she asked. She'd stayed at Schonen Felder in case she went into labour while he was away. Close on her heels were Peter and Freya.

"Good God, woman, you weigh more than you did three days ago," Mueller remarked, kissing her on the cheek.

"My good home cooking," Anna shouted over. She had heard the car draw up, had left the kitchen, and joined the others at the front of the house. "This girl is going to eat us out of house and home if these babies are not born soon."

Frances was madly pulling on his sleeve. "Kristian, was he there? Did you find him?"

72

He nodded and took her arm, leading her into the house. "Stay here, and I will get him. He's in the car. Go inside with the others, and I'll bring him in." He took her by the shoulders and looked into her eyes. "He's home now, sweetheart. We will arrange a funeral if that's what you want. Go on, get yourself into the house, and make me a coffee. I'm gasping."

He turned back to the car to fetch the remains of their child from the back seat, with Frances still at his side. Bending into the car, he removed the little wooden box, holding it as you would a precious gift. Treating it with love and respect as he carried it past his parents and Anna and laid it on a table in the study.

"He can stay here until we can organise a funeral and lay him to rest. Is that all right?" he asked Frances. She nodded, and he put an arm around her shoulder to remove her from the room, but she shook him off and found his gaze, holding onto it tight.

"What was it like there? What did you see?" she asked. "Tell me. Is there anything of it left?"

"Yes. A good deal of it is left," Mueller told her.

"Well, there bloody well shouldn't be," she spat. "It should be ripped down and bulldozed."

Mueller took her by the shoulders. "I disagree," he said.

She shook him off. "How can you disagree? The place is evil. Didn't you feel it?" What he felt was her tension. He spoke calmly.

"Do you want me to tell you?" he asked.

"Of course I want you to tell me."

"Then calm down a little, hey?" She took some deep breaths and turned her head towards him.

"Go on then," she said.

He took her hand. "So, the railway line is still there, just as you said. And the gates."

Mueller told her of all that he'd seen. He told her everything. He didn't bother shielding her from the horrors; she had lived in the place for several months, and they were ingrained in her still and probably always would be.

"I don't understand why they've left it standing," she said as he finished.

"It's a memorial. Can't you see that?"

She shook her head.

"Many people returned there, Froggy; they had nowhere else to go. Lensky told me they came back in their hundreds at the start. Seeking family and friends. Many of them stayed on to share in the work."

"But it's ugly and cruel—"

"And it's the resting place of thousands of people. It can't just be bulldozed. There were so many survivors working on preserving it. I spoke at some length with a man called Kazimierz, another survivor. He said he and others spoke of it having to be a memorial, even before they knew they would survive themselves. They are proud of the work they've done, and they should be."

Frances screwed up her face. "I just don't get it," she said.

"Sweetheart, it's not just a memorial to the dead; it's a reminder to the living, you see. It's proof of the crime, my crime if you like. It's a warning that we must never tread that road again." He kissed her on the forehead. "Come on, let's get a coffee. We have a funeral to plan."

* * *

Mueller woke in the night. He turned over in bed and stretched out his arm towards Frances. She wasn't there. He was still tired from the journey and the stressful visit to Auschwitz, and it took him a few moments to come around and a few more before he realised where his wife would be. He let loose a couple of expletives as he searched for his slippers and gown and then ran downstairs to the study, where they had left the little coffin that housed the remains of their first child.

He saw the light creeping through the underneath of the study door and pushed it open. There was no sign of Frances or the little coffin either. He turned around in the hall, wondering which way to go, and saw the light coming from the open kitchen door near the stairwell. And then he heard it. The tap of metal against wood, and then quiet. He silently made his way to the kitchen and was met by Frances's back. She was looking down at something cradled in her arms.

Mueller walked softly towards her and gently wrapped his arms around her. She leaned back into his body. Bending, he lay his cheek on her head and spoke softly. "You didn't believe me, did you? You didn't think he was in there." She muttered a little questioning mewling noise, and he repeated. "You thought I was lying. That the box was empty."

Then, after taking a deep breath, she answered, "No. I knew you wouldn't lie to me about bringing him back. I had to open it, not to see if you were lying, just so I could hold him, Kristian. Just for a while. I wasn't sure you would understand."

"If it helps you, Froggy, I'm all in favour. But let's put the child to rest now, hey?"

She nodded. "I've wrapped a lace shawl around him, see? One of the ones we bought in Paris. I can replace it next time we go there. Do you think we might visit before the babies are born?"

"Are you up to it?"

"For a weekend, yes, I think so."

"Then let's see what we can do, eh?" He tried to steer her from the kitchen. "Come on," he said, "you need your sleep, and so do I."

"I'm coming, Kristian; go if you like. I want to wrap him up. To keep him warm. You don't have to stay."

"I want to stay Froggy. He's my son too, you see."

* * *

The funeral was a small affair and took place at the church in the town at 2 p.m. a few days later. The last time Frances had been there was Christmas Eve, 1944 and the church had been brimming with people and Nazi propaganda. Now there was just her, Kristian, Peter, Freya, Anna, and Sara's parents, Eva and Gunter Kohl. They all fitted onto the front pew.

"There are so few people to witness that our baby ever existed," she said to Kristian on the way out to the churchyard. The child was finally laid to rest in a plot of ground close to Mueller's grandmother. He put his arm around her shoulder and pulled her in close.

"Not many people, Froggy, but a whole load of love, and that's what counts, I'd say."

* * *

After the burial, they returned to Schonen Felder and ate together. Peter had wanted to take them all to a restaurant "to give Anna a rest," he said. But there was still an enormous food shortage, and what they had at the farm was much better than anything they would find in a local restaurant. And so, the day before, the women had pulled together and produced a wholesome meal of chicken and vegetable stew with freshly made bread. And to follow, plum pie and cream, made from last year's glut of plums, which Anna had thankfully and thoughtfully bottled.

During the meal, the Kohls informed them that Sara and Jack would be back in a few months for good and that a wedding celebration was the next thing on the cards. After leaving, there were still a few hours of light, and Mueller and Frances decided to walk back home across the fields. They ended up at the coppice where two years previously they had sat down together for a picnic. It was to have been a special day. The day before, Mueller returned to U-boat duty at Kiel. The day all their arguments were to have been set aside and their love for one another consummated.

"I'd forgotten how lovely it was here," Frances muttered. "There's a good view of the Kohl's farm, isn't there?"

Mueller wrapped his arms around her and looked over her shoulder towards their neighbour's property. "I hate myself for how I behaved that day, Froggy."

"I hated you for how you behaved that day," she said.

"We could make up for it now, you know. Put it all behind us."

She felt his breath hot behind her ear as he kissed her neck and nuzzled her. Her breathing quickened along with her heart rate, as it always did when he touched her. "We can't, Kristian. What if someone should see?"

"No one comes here. This is my place, I told you." She turned into him, and he lifted her chin and kissed her gently at first and then with mounting passion. She wriggled out of his embrace.

"Kristian, I'm seven months pregnant." He pulled her back into his arms.

"And?" he questioned.

She looked into his eyes, unsure whether he was teasing her, noticing the twitch of his lips as he fought back a smile. "Are you joking?" she asked.

He shrugged. "Don't think so," he said.

"But look at me. I'm enormous. Hardly attractive."

"There's just more of you to love." He chuckled.

"You are joking, aren't you?" He pulled her close, and it was obvious to her that he wasn't.

"It's not possible, not here. Not now. We should wait until we're home. Tonight."

He was grinning at her, showing the gap in his teeth, and she felt her entire body respond.

"How?" she asked.

He threw himself onto the grass, and the dark blue of his eyes held her amber gaze.

"You'll have to come on top," he instructed. She fought to control her laughter.

"I'll crush you," she said.

"It's one hell of a way to go, Froggy." He gave an ecstatic groan as she lowered herself onto him.

CHAPTER 8

MID-JULY 1946 EVENING

Frances reckoned she had at most another month to go until she gave birth. Doctor Neumann had been keeping a close eye on her and had a midwife at the ready to call in to assist him when she went into labour. She had spoken to them both about her worries regarding not being able to carry to full term or not being able to give birth to a living child, and they had both done their best to reassure her.

She had been thoroughly miserable for a few days, as the temperature had risen to an uncomfortable level, forcing her to spend the hottest part of the day inside with her feet up, either reading or resting. She had to force herself to practice the violin for several hours. Thankfully, the weather had cooled a little and was hovering now at a couple of degrees above 20C.

She had taken herself outside and was sitting on the seat in the garden against the wall. Kristian was at the office, and Peter had gone to Bonn on business early that morning. Freya was visiting Eva, leaving herself, Anna, and the dogs around the house. She reached over for her book, which had fallen on the floor, and received a hefty reminder from the babies she was carrying of their presence. As she sat back up, she caressed them, rubbing her hand lovingly over her swollen abdomen. These children would be born into a loving home. They would want for nothing and would be safe. Things had certainly changed in a little over four years.

The thought shot through her that giving birth to two healthy babies was by no means a certainty. She had cruelly lost a child already, and it wasn't a certainty that she would give birth to two healthy children at all.

Four years ago, she had thought she was safe. Yes, she had been living in an occupied country, but her life was still comfortable. Food was on the table, and restaurants managed to carry on trading, albeit the clientele was mainly German. She sat for a while, reminiscing about those years she had spent in Paris and remembering the people she loved—those who had gone now.

If the war hadn't happened, would the children she was carrying now be Kristian's children? Could they ever have been Steven's? She dwelt on that for a while, seeing the image of Steven's slight, bearded form standing before her. Would he be angry that she had married a German, she wondered. More than that, would he be angry that she had fallen in love with Mueller to such a degree that she barely thought of him?

Steven had been rounded up and thrown into Drancy, and though his time there had been brief, it had been enough, she was sure, to cause his illness. They said the French police were behind the appalling treatment of the Jews in Paris, but everyone knew who was behind the French police.

Would Steven ever forgive her for sitting in this beautiful garden at Schonen Felder? She thought about that for a while and eventually concluded that Steven would not judge her. He had been more of a father and a teacher to her than a husband, and thinking back now, she knew it was improbable that they would ever have had children together.

She was certain he would have denied her the chance of

motherhood, but she believed he would be happy for her. He would not judge an entire race for the treatment of his people. He was too intelligent for that. A rose petal blew over from a climbing rose growing nearby and landed in her lap. There was something significant about it landing just at that moment, and she felt the fleeting presence of Steven Meyer and thanked God for him.

And what of Edie, her dearest Aunt Edie, her father's sister who had taken her in with such joy when her father had passed away, leaving her alone in England? Warm, large, and loving, she had loved Edie back with a vengeance. Would her Papa have agreed with the freedom Edie gave her in their life together in Paris? Probably not, she thought, though he did not need to worry because she was so thoroughly into her music that she had given little thought or time to the flagrant excesses of Paris. She probably was a bit of a bore for the years she was studying, unlike Otto.

She sat bolt upright. What right had Otto to invade her musing? He was nothing to her anymore. He had committed the ultimate crime against her womanhood, the bastard. And yet? And yet, there had been a time when they were close. She had enjoyed his company and helped him with his amours. Had she led him on? She didn't believe so. If she had, then was she responsible for what had happened that night in Munich? And if so, then she was ultimately responsible for his death at the hands of Kristian.

She had never asked Kristian how it had happened. It had always been enough that it had, and she was glad of it. But now it was niggling at her; she wanted to know. It was because of Otto that they had to rush to flee from Paris. Because Otto, Edie, Steven, and Jacques were dead.

Jacques, ah Jacques, and now the tears fell as they always did when she thought of the brilliant Jacques Cuvier, her teacher and friend. Many saw him as a doddering old fool, but that's what he wanted them to think. She got to know that it was all a front. Everyone knew he was a brilliant musician and teacher, but how many knew he, along with others, was using the Conservatoire as a safe place for Jewish students? How many knew that he was involved with the French underground? She only found out that when it was too late. When he stood on the deck of the small fishing vessel, the Etoile, after ordering her to the hold and then opened fire on a German E boat with the cry of 'Vive La France.'

She fought to hold on to the image of Jaques in her head. Grey-haired, Dickensian Jaques, bumbling and warm, who could put her in her place when he had to. But there was another image fighting its way into her thoughts. The last time she had seen him, his brains had been smattered over the deck of the Etoile.

"Pfennig for them?"

Frances physically jumped. The voice of Peter Mueller encroached upon her memories. She exclaimed, "Shit!" and he laughed at her reaction.

"Sorry, my dear. You were well away. Where on earth were you?"

"In the past, Peter," she replied.

"Not always a good place to be. Look to the future; that's my advice."

"When did you get back from Bonn?"

"Half an hour ago. I've just had a chat with a couple of our men. It seems there are a few displaced people around and about. We need to keep an eye. Can I join you? I need a rest." Frances nodded and shuffled along the bench to give him more space.

"Are you okay, Peter?" Frances asked, "You look tired."

Peter Mueller laid his hand on her arm. "To be honest, Frances, I feel a little worn out. Things that used to be easy are— well, they are not so easy anymore. I believe it's called old age."

"Rubbish! You're not old." She laid her head on his shoulder. "I won't allow it."

"Then I will do my best to pretend it's not happening. So, what are you up to for the rest of the day?"

Frances gave a tut. "What can I do apart from sit here and vegetate? You have all forbidden me to ride." She turned to him. "It wouldn't hurt, you know. I could sit on Majesty and go for a walk and—"

"Risk having a fall? Frances, these children you're carrying are precious to us all."

"But I'd be careful. I'd be fine, and I'm so bloody bored, Peter, and I miss the horses so much."

"I'm not saying you shouldn't spend time with them. Just don't put yourself in danger."

"But Majesty would never hurt me. She wouldn't hurt anyone," argued Frances.

"No, not purposefully. Why don't you give her a good groom in her stall? You'd be safe enough there."

"I do that already. I wait until it's quiet and spend a couple of hours with them."

Peter Mueller tried to look angry. He was, in fact, worried, though not enough to prevent him from fighting the smile tugging at the corners of his mouth. "Of course you do," he said. "Now, while it's just you and me, suppose you tell me about this great idea the Brits have."

Frances gave him a confused look, and he continued. "The gardening thing? Kristian said you had some idea involving giant greenhouses."

She straightened up. "I have. It's a brilliant idea."

Peter Mueller couldn't suppress a smile; she was so enthusiastic.

* * *

Frances waited for the night to draw in and for everyone to settle. Peter was reading that day's newspapers, and Freya was resting on the couch, eyes closed, digesting her meal. Kristian had returned from the office late and was still eating dinner in the kitchen, where Anna was washing up. So, she knew everyone would be tied up for a while and made her way down to the stables to spend time with her beloved Majesty and her beautiful son, Kapitan, who was grazing the paddock just outside the stable block.

As she entered the barn, Majesty picked up on the sound of her footsteps and her scent and gave a low wicker. Frances entered the stall and was met with a friendly nuzzle from the mare, who then pushed her nose into her pocket to check for carrots, which she found in abundance.

"I just want to sit on you for a while," Frances cooed to the mare. "We won't be able to go far, and it will be just a walkabout. What do you say, Majesty? You'll take care of me, won't you? I know you will."

She walked over to the tack room and grabbed Majesty's headcollar, having decided to rider her bitless and bareback. No one was about; she would be safe as houses on Majesty, as she always had been right from the start when she was a novice. Now, she was a practised horsewoman. Once the head collar was on, she attached the end of the lead rein to the other side, making crude reins. She then walked the mare over to a bale of hay, which she stood on to help her onto the mare's back. Majesty stood relaxed and still as Frances threw her right leg across her and settled into her.

"Good girl," she said. "I don't know what all the bother is about. We're fine, aren't we?"

She gently pulled on the right rein to turn her and made for the barn door. She and Majesty walked out into the failing evening light, making for the open fields. Frances loved the feeling of being on Majesty's back again. It had been too long. They had all kept an eye on her, forbidding her to ride in her state. Yes, she was pregnant but wasn't ill. She had told them time and time again that she would be careful and only ride at a walk. Frances took a deep breath, rejoicing in the cooling evening air as it blew gently, ruffling through Majesty's mane and blowing across her face. It was the most comfortable she had been in days; she'd enjoy it, and they wouldn't even need to know.

She had no idea how long or how far she had ridden. The time had stood still, and Frances was lost in the enjoyment of the peace and stillness, the only sound being the gentle, continuous rhythm of Majesty's feet. They turned for home. The mare hadn't put a foot wrong, and Frances was convinced she understood her condition and knew she had to take care of her rider. They were less than half a kilometre from the stables when they both heard it. There was no mistaking the frightened squeal of a horse, which carried towards them through the night air.

Majesty increased her pace with scarcely any action from Frances. They both knew something was wrong when a horse squealed at Schonen Felder. As they approached buildings, Frances saw the movement of a beam of light from inside the barn. Someone had a torch, and from the frightened screams of the horses, she didn't think it was Kristian, Peter, or any of the men who worked for them. There were strangers in the barn. In the stalls.

As she neared the barn, she slid from Majesty's back and slapped her flank to encourage her to escape whatever or whoever was causing the disturbance. The mare took off along the path to the front of the house as Frances ran towards the barn doors, which stood ajar. As she pushed them open wider, she was horrified to see that a couple of men had managed to get Kapitan onto a lead rein and were walking towards the open doors. They were sunken-eyed and wearing remnants of what, at some time, must have been clothing.

Frances recognised them as displaced persons—belonging to the millions who, after the war, had found themselves in the wrong place or country and were striving to make it home, as Kristian had done, or find a place to settle. Many of them had turned feral over the year; they had lost all trace of humanity; their only thought now was staying alive. The Allied military had helped repatriate tens of millions, but still, they came.

"Take your bloody hands off my horse," she yelled, making towards the men until a third caught her from behind. She twisted in the man's grip, and he placed one arm around her neck, in an attempt to stop her from struggling. She kicked a foot backwards, catching the man on the shins, and he cried out and loosened his grip on her enough for her to lunge toward the other two men.

She repeated, "Take your hands off my horse. Let him go. Now! My husband is on his way, so you had better scram." One of the men, a tall, scrawny fellow holding the torch, held a large piece of wood, which he brandished toward her. His sudden movement freaked out Kapitan even more, and the third man, who was much smaller, struggled to keep hold of him as the animal picked up on Frances's fear.

"Keep back, lady, please," the scrawny one warned. "No one up at the house will hear us down here."

She faltered long enough for the man she had earlier kicked to grab her arm and pull her back so that once more, he had her securely in his grasp. She twisted and kicked as much as she could and shrieked, "He will hear. He's out walking the dogs. He will hear, and he'll get help."

She lashed out again at the man, and her nails found some naked flesh on his arm, which she tore into.

"Fucking hell, Braun, get this whore off me, for Christ's sake, will you? Knock the bitch down with your fucking stick."

The smaller man, holding Kapitan's lead rope, had managed to calm him and made for the barn doors, followed by the taller man who had raised the stick he carried to shoulder height, ready to bring it down on Frances. She readied herself for the blow as the stick moved towards her and stopped millimetres from her head.

"I can't do it," the scrawny man shouted above Frances's scream as she continued to fight and scratch the man who held her. "The woman's pregnant. I can't do it."

Frances was grabbed and hurled to the floor as the three men and Kapitan made for the barn doors. She fell awkwardly, twisting her ankle and banging her head on a metal bucket. It took her longer than she would have liked to recover enough to stand, and then she felt it. The warm liquid flowed down her legs, soaking her trousers. Her waters had broken.

CHAPTER 9

The pain in Frances's ankle was excruciating, as was the pain in her head, where she had hit the bucket, and together with those pains came the cramps in her uterus. She clutched her abdomen. These had to be the start of labour pains, surely. But would she have two healthy babies at the end of it or a further two little corpses to lay beside the one that was already at rest in the local churchyard?

She had to get back to the house for the sake of her unborn children, and Kristian would have to go and get Kapitan back. She looked around her in the gloom of the barn. Thankfully, no horses were in the stalls other than Majesty and Kapitan.

Her head was swimming, but she focused her eyes, which fell upon a broom. She limped over to it and tucked it beneath her arm, using it as a crutch to help her return to the house. Taking the path that led her through the gateway in the wall and back up the garden to the kitchen, she prayed that Anna would still be there and that she hadn't already left for the day.

Each step she took was agony, but at least the pain in her uterus had eased for the time being. By the time she got to the garden wall, she was soaked in sweat, and a feeling of faintness washed over her. She leaned on the wall for a while, trying to muster the energy to keep going. The cramp was starting again. Low down and in her thighs. She wanted to lie down. She was exhausted. The sound of a latch being lifted brought her back around. That was the back door, and someone was coming into the garden. It would most likely be Anna gathering a few herbs or putting food out for the birds to find the next morning.

"Anna," she breathed, disappointed that the sound that left her lips was so weak. She took several deep breaths and called out a second time. "Anna," and propped herself against the wall to give her the strength to stand as the pain increased and her abdomen tightened.

"Froggy?"

It was utter relief when she heard his voice and called, "Kristian." And before she knew it, he was through the gate, and she had fallen into his arms. He picked her up and carried her through the garden as she rambled away, trying to explain what had happened. But he was scarcely listening. He told her they all thought she had eaten her meal and gone for a lie-down and that he couldn't believe how bloody stupid she was to go out for a ride.

"It wasn't the ride, Kristian," she argued, but he wasn't listening.

"You have put our children at risk, and what for? Because you felt like a ride in the moonlight? How bloody selfish is that, for God's sake, Froggy?"

When they reached the back door, he called, "Anna, open this bloody door." When she did so, in the light, he could see Frances's state. He visibly paled, and she burst into tears.

"You're not listening to me, Kristian," she sobbed. "I didn't have a fall. Men were in the barn. I saw the light beam and heard a horse squealing; it was Kapitan."

"You went into the barn knowing something was going on in there. Bloody Hell, Froggy! Why on earth didn't you come and get me?" he asked, setting her down in a chair and squatting in front of her.

"I could hear him; he was in distress. They had a head collar on him, pulling him towards the doors. They've taken him away, Kristian. You have to get him back."

Anna pushed her way past Mueller with a basin of water and some lint.

"Look at me, girl," she instructed. Frances raised her face to Anna.

"You've got one hell of a bump on your head. How did that happen?" she asked.

Mueller stood. "Let me see," he said, pushing Anna aside and parting Frances's hair to get a better look at her injury.

"And what else is wrong with you, child?" Anna asked, noticing France's twisted features and hearing her gentle panting as another contraction began. She turned to Mueller. "I think you had better call the doctor, Kristian; your wife is in labour. I'll clean up her face, and then we will get her into the bath before he gets here."

Mueller turned to face Frances. "Are you?" he asked, brow knotted with worry.

"Yes. That is, I think so."

"Then I'll go and call Neumann."

"No! No! Bloody no! Please, just listen, will you?"

"What on earth is all this rumpus? Freya is already in bed and—" Peter's jaw dropped as he took in the state of the other three, particularly Frances. "Ladies first. Frances, what on earth have you done to yourself?" he asked.

They all began to speak at once, and he held up his hand to silence them.

As the other two quietened, Mueller said, "Frances is in labour, Pa. Could you please go and ring Dr Neumann? And then I could do with your help. It appears we have visitors on our land. They've hurt my wife and taken one of our best horses."

"The devil they have," spat Peter Mueller. "My God, I'm such a fool. I suspected for some time that there was a camp. I should have looked into this days ago, and then all of this could have been avoided," Peter said. "They'll be wanting the horse for food."

"Gypsies?" Anna questioned.

"Displaced persons, I should think. Have there been fewer eggs than usual, Anna?"

"Well, yes, now you come to mention it."

"Sod the eggs. What about my horse," shrieked Frances. She jumped up from the chair, ignoring the throbbing pain in her ankle and the soreness of her abdomen, hobbled across the kitchen, and grabbed Peter's arm, struggling to speak through her tears.

"You have to get him back. Go with Kristian, please, Peter. Please go, both of you. Bring my horse back home. They can't kill Kapitan; I love him so much."

Mueller glanced at her, set his jaw, and nodded toward his father. "Pa, even if they have killed the horse already, they attacked Frances, and we can't let that go." Peter nodded as Mueller continued, "Anna, you go and call Neumann. Before I leave, I'll get Frances upstairs, where, hopefully, she will behave herself and allow you to clean her up. Pa, there's something we need." Peter gave him a knowing nod. "You go and saddle up. I'll be with you in a few minutes."

Mueller disappeared into the house and returned to the kitchen moments later with two shotguns.

Frances looked at him wide-eyed. "I thought we gave up all of our guns."

"Clearly not." His answer was short.

"What are you going to do? How will you find them?" Frances asked.

"I'll decide what to do when we get there, and I have a good idea where they'll be," he replied.

"Kristian, please don't do anything stupid," she begged.

"No, I'll leave that to you," he snapped and then sighed, seeing how broken she was. He squatted again before her chair and wrapped his arms around her. "So, you approached these men and thought you could scare them off, did you?" he asked, gently lifting her chin and holding her gaze.

She nodded, and great tears splashed onto his hand. His face worked with consternation and worry. "Because you're so scary, of course, eh?" he finally said. She shifted her gaze and looked down at her hands, feeling very foolish.

"They won't have killed him yet, will they?" she muttered into her lap.

He shook his head. "I have no idea, but if he is there, I will bring him back home, I promise." He kissed her brow and straightened up. "Plus, the heads of the men who hurt you, eh? And now I'm going to get you up the stairs and then get going, or I will miss the birth of my children. Now, Froggy, promise me you will do what the doctor says. She nodded as he swept her into his arms.

As Mueller reached the stables, Peter walked out of Bismarck's loose box with the saddled horse. He handed his son the reins.

"I found Majesty down by the barn with a headcollar on. I'll grab her blanket and saddle and bridle, and we'll be off."

Peter walked to the barn, quickly returning with the necessary tack for Majesty. Once she was saddled, the two men mounted their horses.

"Where are you thinking?" Peter asked.

"Where would you go?" Mueller replied.

"Lake?"

"I think so," said Mueller. "They'll need water for sure, and it's nicely sheltered down there."

"Do you think the horse will still be standing, Son?"

Mueller shrugged. "Do you?" he asked.

His father gave the reply he was expecting. "It's doubtful," he said, and Mueller nodded in agreement. They headed off at a gentle canter, not wishing to give the encamped people any warning of their approach from the sound of galloping horses.

It was a mere fifteen-minute ride to where Mueller thought the camp would be. They crossed fields, climbed to the coppice, skirted around it, and went a mile further, dipping downhill towards the lake, which stood in a clearing behind a lightly forested part of the Mueller land. As they approached the lake, they kept to the trees.

Mueller drew Bismarck to a standstill. "Did you hear that?" he asked.

"I heard something," Peter replied. They both sat still and silent, ears cocked, until they heard the sound again.

"Children," said Mueller.

His father nodded in agreement. "How many of them do you think?"

"Three or four. Cheeky bastards haven't moved on then. We need to get closer to see how big the camp is. Stay here with the horses, Pa. I'll take a look and see what we've got here."

He dismounted from his horse and, keeping to the trees, made his way, as quietly as he could, down through the trees towards the lake. He stopped now and then to listen to the children's laughter, altering his path when he needed to put more distance between them and himself.

Mueller was unsure who had the more tremendous shock when he came upon a couple of the youngsters practising the art of being grownups. The young boy had his lederhosen around his ankles, and the girl he was fondling had her skirt pulled up around her waist. She saw Mueller first as he stepped out from between some trees. Mueller saw the shock on her face as she let her skirt fall and, turning, ran through the trees towards the lake.

She called out to the boy. "Eric, get yourself together. Run for it!"

Eric did his best to do as she said but got tangled in his lederhosen, which allowed Mueller to grab him around the waist and prevent him from following the girl.

"Ina, warn Papa. Tell him we've been tumbled," the boy shouted as he twisted in Mueller's grip. "Let me go, you fucking bastard," he shrieked, trying to lash out with feet and fists.

Mueller held him fast. "Keep still, you little shit, or I'm going to end up hurting you," he warned as he dragged and half-carried the child back toward the place where he'd left his father. They met halfway, hearing the commotion.

Peter Mueller made his way with the horses toward him. "What have you got there?" he asked as the boy berated them both with language that was blue and fought with every trick he knew until his boot made contact with Mueller's shin. Mueller momentarily let go of him but quickly grabbed him again, placing one arm around the boy's neck.

"Keep still, or I'll break your bloody neck," he threatened, putting a little pressure on the boy's throat as a warning.

There was shouting from the direction of the lake—a combination of men, women, and children. Mueller threw the boy onto Bismarck's back and quickly threw himself behind him. With reins in one hand and the other exerting a little pressure on the boy's epiglottis, Mueller and Peter made their way through the trees down to the lake. They found a small camp and a group of people in disarray. As they burst out of the trees, the people quietened, and Mueller thought he read fear on their faces rather than aggression.

A tall, lanky man stepped forward, his face full of worry. He turned sunken eyes onto Mueller as Peter raised a shotgun to his shoulder. "Please don't hurt my boy. I promise we'll be gone by morning," the man said.

Mueller scanned the rest of the group. There were three men, one of whom was elderly, five women, one who held a baby in her arms, and three children, all approaching their teens, other than the boy Mueller still had hold of.

"You hurt my wife," Mueller growled. He tightened his hold on the boy's throat, causing the lad to gurgle. "An eye for an eye. That's right, isn't it? What's my horse worth, I wonder?"

One of the women, who looked elderly, called out. "We have your horse here. He's unhurt. Give us the boy for your horse, and we will be gone by early tomorrow."

Another woman cried, "Where to, mother? We have nowhere to go. There's no food. How long before we perish, do you think?"

The woman's words bit into him. Mueller knew that feeling. It wasn't so long since he'd been just like them. Less than a year since he'd trekked across Europe as a displaced person with people like these, making his way home or somewhere. But these people had overstepped the mark, and he couldn't forgive them for their attack on Frances. However desperate he had become, he would never have attacked a woman.

"Where's the bastard that hurt my wife?" he asked. "He's the one I want."

"Gone," the lanky man said. "We kicked him out of the camp for what he did. We are not what you see before you. You look at us and see gypsies or rogues. Underneath our sunken skin, we are decent people just striving to survive the aftermath of this damn war."

* * *

Mueller left Peter with the horses and sprinted from the stables to the house, checking first at the front to see if Dr Neumann had arrived. It was with some relief that he saw his car parked near the front door. Bounding up the staircase, he had no idea what news would be waiting for him behind the closed door of his bedroom and Frances's. He pushed the door open and briefly caught sight of Frances lying on the bed with her legs pulled up and her knees apart before Anna steered him back out of the door.

"This is not the place for a man to be," she said in a harsh whisper.

"Neumann's in there, isn't he? He's a damn man," he retaliated.

Anna raised her voice. "You will have to knock me down to get in there."

"Tempting," he replied.

Anna hmphed. "Well, do you want to know if you're a father yet?"

He looked at her wide-eyed. "Of course, I bloody do," he said.

"You have a daughter," she announced with a smile that creased her entire face. "Come here, my boy." She threw her arms around Mueller's neck and planted a kiss on his cheek. For the first time ever, he saw the trickle of tears run down her face.

"So, I've missed it," he said.

He heard his mother shout out encouragement, "Come on, Frances, push. Give me your hand."

He then heard Neumann tell his mother to wait. "She's nowhere near ready to push yet, Frau Mueller. Wait for my instructions, please. The head is in a good position, so hopefully, there will be no complications. And if there are, I have the forceps ready."

"I'm going in, Anna," Mueller announced.

Anna blocked the door with her body. "Like I said, you'll have to knock me down. Why can't you go and join your father with the brandy bottle? You're not needed here," she said.

With that, Mueller picked her up, turned her away from the door, and pushed his way in, getting an immediate reprimand from his mother. "Kristian, what on earth are you doing in here? Get out now."

Mueller made his way to the side of the bed, seeing that Frances's eyes were closed. He thought how exhausted and pale she looked. She opened her eyes as he took her hand and rewarded him with a smile.

"You came," she said.

"As soon as I could. I had to fight my way in past Anna."

"Kristian," Freya said, "really, this is improper. You shouldn't be here. Dr Neumann, please tell my son to leave,"

Neumann looked over the top of his spectacles at Mueller. "It's not usual," he said, "most men wouldn't want to be here—"

"I want him to be here." Frances's tired voice stopped them all in their tracks. "I want Kristian to stay and hold my hand." She turned to Mueller, almost afraid to ask the question plaguing her. "Did you get Kapitan back?" she asked.

Mueller nodded. "I did, and he's fine."

"Thank you," she murmured and squeezed his hand.

The rest of the people in the room surveyed one another uncomfortably at the thought of a man other than the doctor present at such a time. Frances drew them back to the task at hand. "Come on, the rest of you, get a move on. Let's get this baby born, eh?" she turned to Mueller. "You haven't introduced yourself to your daughter yet. Don't you want to meet her?"

"I most certainly do. Where have you put her? I can't hear her crying."

"The other side of the room. Anna moved the crib as it was in the doctor's way where it was."

Mueller nodded. "Should I go then?"

"Of course." Frances chuckled. "Go on."

"I don't want to wake her up, you see," said Mueller.

"You won't; she's dead to the world. Go on," she encouraged.

Mueller walked across the bedroom to the crib and looked

down on his newborn daughter, wrapped in a white shawl. The feeling in his chest was intense and unexpected, and he felt his eyes fill with unshed tears.

"Why don't you pick her up?"

He straightened up, finding Anna beside him. "She's so tiny. I don't want to hurt her," he said. Anna bent over the cot, gently lifted the child, and laid her in Mueller's arms.

"How does that feel?" she asked him.

"Wonderful," he replied. He filled up with emotion that was threatening to tip over. "Bloody wonderful," he repeated. "How old is she?"

Anna looked at her watch. "About thirty-five minutes."

"Look how perfect she is, Anna. And she's looking right at me. I'd never have guessed."

Their conversation was cut short by Frances's raised voice. "I'm having a contraction, Doctor Neumann. Oh! Oh! Kristian?" she cried out.

Mueller placed the baby back in the cot and returned to Frances. The doctor propped her back up on several pillows, and Mueller saw that she was sweating profusely. Grabbing a chair, he moved it closer to the side of the bed and took Frances's hand. She had fallen back on the pillows, exhausted after the last contraction.

"What can I do?" he asked.

"Rub your wife's back," the doctor muttered between Frances's legs. "I can see the head." He straightened up and gave them all a smile. "Good," he said, "Now we wait for the next contraction, which shouldn't be long at all." He had one hand on Frances's abdomen and was watching her intently. The wait was short. "The contraction is coming, yes?" He looked over his spectacles at Frances, who was panting as the contraction built up. "Now push," he instructed and disappeared once more between her legs.

Mueller looked on, wide-eyed as his wife's face contorted, and she cried out with the effort she was making.

"Push, come on," Neumann encouraged.

"Now rest," he said, reappearing with a wide grin. "Head's out, you're doing just fine, and you didn't need any help from me."

Ten minutes later, Mueller joined his father in the study.

"So, one of each. That's the way to do it, hey?" Well done, Son," said Peter Mueller, topping up Kristian's glass. "Not a bad day's work. We've removed those people from our land and added a couple of Mueller's to the family."

Mueller sniffed. "I'm feeling a bit emotional, Pa. When are you going to see them anyway?"

"I'll wait until morning, when everything's been cleaned up, and Frances feels human again. So, what are they like, these new Muellers?"

Mueller's voice cracked with emotion as he answered, "Beautiful. One is a lot bigger than the other and has more hair. I think that one's the girl." He sighed. "They've knocked the stuffing out of me, Pa." He rested himself in an armchair. "We're lucky, aren't we? We've come through this war none too badly. You still have your business. I have two healthy children upstairs."

Peter Mueller gave his son a questioning look. "I can't stop thinking about those people tonight," Mueller continued. "They have nothing, and we know the crop will be poor again this year, which will mean the food shortage will be even worse. There's a good chance they won't survive. There's a baby there too. At least one."

"What are you thinking, Son?" Peter asked.

Mueller shook his head. "I don't know, that's the trouble, Pa.

How can we help them? They need food and shelter. And there's what? A dozen of them. That's too many to have here."

"We can't become a charity, Kristian. This next year will be tough for everyone in the British sector. I heard that food is being shipped over from Britain, and the British are not too pleased about it. I can't say I blame them. They've won the damn war, and they're not much better off than the losers. Believe me, Son, I feel sorry for the people we met earlier; I really do."

"You know it's only a year since I was sharing their fate. There were quite a few times when people with very little shared." He gave a harsh laugh. "There were times I received help. There were times when I stole. I was pretty self-sufficient. There were times when some bastard took my last crust, too."

The door burst into the sitting room, and Anna and Freya walked in with broad smiles, preventing Mueller from any further narrative.

"So, Peter, we are now grandparents," said Freya, bending to kiss her husband on the cheek. He grabbed her, and stood, picking her up and swinging her around as she shrieked with unaccustomed laughter.

"Doesn't this call for a proper celebration, woman?" he asked, putting her back down.

"Oh, how I wish we had some champagne," Freya said. "Do you think we will ever get any again?"

"It's there if you want to pay the going price," said Mueller. "I suggest we stick to brandy. I'll have one more with you all, and then I'm turning in."

"I made your old room up ready," said Anna.

"Don't know what for. I'll be joining my family," said Mueller.

Chapter 10

Mueller crept up the stairs to the matrimonial bedroom at almost two in the morning, a little worse for wear. He was surprised to see a strip of light showing under the bedroom door, indicating that the light was still on. In his head, Frances was worn out and wouldn't wake up until the next morning; he hadn't considered that she might be unable to sleep. He pushed the door open to find her sitting in a freshly made bed, peering into the crib that had been moved to her side.

"Kristian, come and see. Look at Paul, he's sucking his fist. Do you think he's hungry? Do you think I should try and feed him?"

Mueller sat beside her and looked at his children with wonder. There was a baby at each end of what was, thankfully, a large crib. One of them, who he assumed to be Paul, was sucking madly on his little fist; the other larger infant was sleeping soundly.

"He's going to eat his arm," he said. "How are you going to feed him?"

"You're going to have to help me. Maybe if you lay some

pillows across me and I hold him, sort of like that." Frances picked up a pillow to show Mueller what she meant. "What do you think?"

"I haven't got a clue, Froggy. You're going to try to—" He held his hands over his chest.

"Breastfeed, yes," she replied and laughed at his expression.

"You're going to do it now?" he asked.

Frances pushed herself up the bed and swung her legs over the side.

"What on earth are you doing?" Mueller asked.

"With your help, I'm going to try feeding him. He's hungry, isn't he?"

"Froggy, I think I should go and get help," he said, moving towards the door.

"Kristian, we can cope. Anna and Mutti must be worn out."

"How come you're not worn out?" he asked.

"I'm on a high; I was hoping you would be too. Come back here and sit down. You haven't even kissed me yet."

Mueller sat back down on the bed, bent forward, and kissed her on the brow. She looked at him wide-eyed.

"What's that?" she asked. "I want a proper kiss. Don't I deserve one? What on earth is wrong with you?"

He took her hand. "I'm feeling blessed," he said.

"You could have fooled me." He looked down at her hand and rubbed it gently.

"Thing is, Froggy, why should I be when thousands, possibly millions of others, are feeling desperate?"

"Is this to do with those bastards that took Kapitan?" she asked, watching him chew on his lip.

"There were children with them, you see, and a baby," he eventually said. "It's going to be a rough winter, Froggy. We are not expecting a good harvest. What will become of them, do you think?"

"You told me once that I shouldn't feel guilty to be one of the lucky ones, do you remember?" He shook his head, and she continued. "It was when I felt guilty about surviving. Same thing, Kristian. We are lucky. We shouldn't feel guilty about that, should we? We've both suffered enough in our way."

He sat for a while, lost in thought, mulling things over. "I need to go back to the lake, Froggy."

She huffed and then met his gaze. "I'll make a deal with you. Help me get Paul sorted, and then I'll let you go where you like."

"Deal. You'll have to tell me what to do then," he said.

"Get Paul out of the crib for a start, and when I've got this pillow sorted, you can pass him to me." She grabbed a pillow and laid it across her body as Mueller grappled in the crib for his son.

"Got you," he said, turning to Frances with the child dangling from his hands in midair.

"Kristian, you need to support his head." Thankfully, the child didn't seem to mind, and Frances laughed at Mueller's awkwardness as he quickly passed her their son. She moved Paul around until she felt both he and she were comfortable, with him lying across her on the pillow. She unbuttoned her nightdress and uncovered her breasts, which brought an expletive from Mueller.

"My God, when did that happen? I knew they were getting bigger, but—"

"But what?" she said with a frown.

He grinned at her, fixing his eyes on her chest. "But they're very nice," he said.

"Well, make the most of them because they'll probably return to being nowhere near as spectacular. Right, now I need this one to somehow latch onto my breast."

"He's got loads to go for," said Mueller.

She ignored his comment and lifted the baby's head, turning him towards her. She then pushed her breast towards his cheek, which caused him to turn his head further towards the conduit of his nutrition and to open his mouth wide. Frances lifted him awkwardly, and the baby took just her nipple.

She cried out. "Ouch. Kristian, can you take some of his weight, do you think? I can't get him quite high enough."

Mueller cradled the baby's body as Frances once again directed his head towards her breast; this time, Paul latched on perfectly and grunted with satisfaction as the milk flowed.

"Seems like he knew exactly what to do," Mueller said.

"Hmm, he must get it from his father," said Frances with a chuckle.

"Are you going to manage to feed both yourself, Froggy?" Mueller asked, and she shrugged. "I don't want you getting worn out, you see. Maybe we should look into some alternative?"

"Let's see how it goes, shall we?" said Frances. "Why don't you go to your old room and try and catch a couple of hours' sleep?"

"I can sleep in a bit tomorrow," Mueller replied. "I don't think old Konrad will expect me into work when he hears our news. I'm going back to the lake if you're all right with that. It should only be an hour or so. Do you think you can manage?"

Frances nodded. "Go and do whatever you need to do. I know you won't rest until you have. This little one seems more content now, and hopefully, the other is fast asleep for a while."

Mueller bent over and kissed the top of her head, brushed his hand over the baby's head, and then, with a quick look into the crib at his sleeping daughter, left.

Frances found it impossible to settle. Mueller had left, and she was on a high note from the evening's events. She sat on the side of the bed, almost unaware of the pains from having just given birth, unable to tear her eyes from the sleeping forms of her children. She felt an enormous wave of love sweep over her, taking her breath away. It was a new feeling. Not the feeling of love, she'd always had love in her life and the love she felt for Mueller overwhelmed her, such that she knew she would die for him. This love was different. It was primeval. If she had to, she knew she would kill for her children.

* * *

Frances made her way down to the stables. She was desperate to see Kapitan and Majesty. It had been more than forty-eight hours since she had given birth, and although sore, she felt fine. She had attempted to escape from the house the previous day but had been stopped by one or other of the Muellers or Anna, who told her that it was much too soon for her to be up and about.

"I'm not ill," she told them, "I've given birth, it's natural, isn't it?" She secretly confessed to herself that she did feel slightly wobbly that first day but thought that was due to her lack of sleep rather than the exhaustion of giving birth to two babies.

Konrad Adenauer had, as Mueller said he would, told him to take a couple of days off. The babies, having been born late on Wednesday night, meant that this day was a Saturday, which also meant that Mueller had the weekend at home before returning to his apartment in Bonn for the week. She would miss him. She hoped he would be back from his morning ride, something he insisted on doing every Saturday and Sunday. As she approached the barn, she noticed Bismarck's stable door was open and felt a pang of disappointment and envy, knowing it would be a few weeks before she could join him on a hack.

As she got closer, she became aware of movement inside the stable; someone was giving it a really good cleanout. Willie, she thought and made her mind up to sneak up on the boy and give him a turn. He was hardly a boy anymore, though, now approaching manhood. He was one of the lucky ones, having been called up to fight as a member of the Volkssturm, the home defence force made up of old men and teenage boys. He had escaped being involved in any active service. Frances was relieved about that. The boy had hung onto his innocence. He was still the gentle soul he had always been. Creeping up to the stable door, she was surprised to see that it wasn't Willie but Kristian cleaning out the stable. She watched for a moment, confused not just by the fact that he was doing the mucking out but also by how he was doing it. His body was rigid; there was anger in it. She called out his name.

"Kristian?" and he swirled round and faced her. She read the expression on his face. Something was amiss, but he quickly walked towards her, holding out his arms to embrace her. She rushed into that embrace, and he pulled her close.

"Should you be here?" he asked. She stepped back a little and lifted her eyes to meet his gaze. He blinked and looked away.

"I managed to escape for a few minutes. With Anna's help, I have fed both of our children, and they are now asleep. Hopefully, they will remain asleep for an hour or so. Anna will soon come and get me if I'm needed."

He replied with a grunt, and she stepped away from him. She hadn't seen him since the night before. He had got up early, she assumed, to take his Saturday morning ride.

"Did you have a good ride?" she asked.

"No," he answered her with a single word.

Where did you go? Where have you put Bismarck out?"

"Froggy, stop. Bismarck hasn't been put out to grass. He's gone." She was incensed.

"Gone where? Those people have taken him?"

"I took him to them. They needed food," he said. There was a loud intake of breath as her hand flew to her mouth.

"He was your horse, Kristian. You loved him." Mueller looked into her eyes and sighed.

"He was a bastard," he said through a forced smile.

"But he was your bastard," she replied as tears tumbled down her cheeks. She spoke through her tears. "It should have been

Kapitan, shouldn't it? You sacrificed Bismarck because of me. Couldn't you have given them one of the cattle?"

"Don't you think I thought about that? I'd have struggled to move one down there, through the woods. And I think Pa would have been more than a little pissed off. He told me we are not a charity. It had to come from me, you see. Something of mine."

"But surely not Bismarck." She grabbed his arm and asked, "Do you think those people will come back again?"

"No. I think they know they have been lucky. The man who hurt you has left the rest of the group. They are decent people, Froggy. We could get others coming here, though, who may not be, so perhaps we should ride around our land regularly. I'll make sure I do it each weekend," he said.

"Isn't Peter going to be mad about Bismarck? I know he rates his bloodline."

Mueller gave her question some thought. "Sometimes it's good also to breed for temperament. We should look to Kapitan for that. In another year, he'll lay down more muscle, too. He'll make a fine stud for us. Have you visited him yet?"

She shook her head.

"Come on then," he said, "let's go and give him the good news."

* * *

On the way back to the house, a little more than an hour later, they bumped into Anna in the garden. "I was coming to look for you," she said. "Those children need their mother."

"Are they both crying?" Frances asked.

"They are. Freya and I have been talking. We think that maybe you should try some formula."

"No, I'm fine. I can feed them myself."

Frances knew she had snapped, and Anna didn't make it any easier by asking, "So, who are you going to feed first, huh?"

By the time she had been in the bedroom for five minutes, she felt totally frazzled. She tried lifting Karin to feed her first and was met by the fury of the other red-faced infant, who demanded that he should be the first. The enormity of being a mother to two babies suddenly hit her. The high she'd been on left her without a backward glance as the cries from two hungry babies increased. She didn't know what to do and was relieved when the door opened, and Freya walked in. Somehow, having another person in the room helped calm her a little.

"I don't know what to do, Mutti," she said. "I can't feed two babies at once." And with that, the tears started again.

Freya placed a hand on her shoulder. "This was bound to happen. You've been so up in the air since Wednesday that you had to come down to earth at some point. Better sooner than later. Jump up on the bed, and I will pass you one of these noisy little beings to feed while I try and calm the other, and then we can swap. I would give the one breast and save the other for baby number two. I'm struggling to tell them apart."

Freya passed Frances one of the babies to feed while she calmed the other by carrying it around the room. The crying stopped, and both women looked at one another with relief.

"This is Karin," said Frances. "See, she's bigger than her brother, and look, she has a little dimple on her chin?"

Freya nodded. "I haven't noticed the dimple before." She sat down on the side of the bed. "I have news," she announced.

"Good news, I hope."

"I think so." Freya's face lit up with a smile. "We have an invitation to a wedding," she said. Frances shrieked with delight, setting Paul off crying again, which earned her a shake of the head from Freya.

"When, Mutti?"

"December 29th. In town. New dress, I think, don't you?"

"Oh, most definitely. When are they home? Oh, I have missed Sara so much. Do we know anymore?"

"For the moment, no, but I think I might drop in for coffee and a chat with Eva. Why don't you come with me? I know Eva would love to see these babies."

Freya and Frances took the babies to visit Eva Kohl on the following Monday afternoon. As Eva and Freya cooed over the babies, Frances thought about how empty the house felt without Sara there. She was excited when Eva told them Sara and Jack were expected to return with Jack's brother, Tom, before Christmas.

"That's brilliant news, isn't it, Mutti?" said Frances. "I can't wait to see them, and I can't wait for the wedding either."

"I have something to ask you, Frances—a request from Sara. I hope you don't mind," Eva said.

"Of course, I don't mind. I would do anything for Sara. What is it?"

"She would love you to play at the wedding, both at the ceremony and the reception. We hope you don't think it's a bit of a cheek."

"Eva, that would be an absolute honour. I'd love to play, though she needs to let me know what she wants, both for the ceremony and the reception. I hope there is going to be a good dance band."

"Jack," said Eva, "and his brother, who plays piano. Jack thinks he can round up a few boys still serving from the American sector to make up a pretty good band."

"That's marvellous. I'll tell Peter to polish up his dancing shoes. I can't wait," said Freya.

"And neither can I." Frances agreed.

The wedding plan wasn't the only good news that Frances heard that week. When Mueller returned home on Friday night, he informed his family over dinner that he had decided to give up his bachelor flat in Bonn and return home to Schonen Felder each night.

"I don't know why you moved into that flat anyway," said Freya. "Your home is here."

"I needed time out Mutts. I needed time to come to terms with what I was feeling."

"About me?" Frances asked.

"No, everything other than you, Froggy. You were the one thing I was sure of. But I messed up. I was messed up. I didn't know if I would ever find you again, and I wasn't sure it was right to even look for you and expect you to return here. But I did find you, and you are here with our children. And for me, it's the best thing that's ever happened. So, you're stuck with me all week. It will mean an early start in the mornings, but at least I will be at home in the evenings to help out. I want to be part of what's going on. I don't want to miss anything. I want to be around like Pa was for me and Karin. Sometimes, I might have to stay over, but I can sleep in my office or stay at a hotel now and again. I think there will be visits to Paris, too."

"I hope we can all go," Frances said.

"Wherever possible. I don't see why not. If we stay in Neuilly, it will save Konrad money. And now most of the rail lines are open again, it will be even easier."

Frances thought it was wonderful news. They would be a proper family. Something she had only dreamt of. They went to bed early, knowing they would be woken up at least twice during the night, possibly three times.

Once in bed, Frances snuggled up to Mueller. "I love that you're going to be around for us, Kristian," she whispered.

"He pulled her close. "Now I'll be around, I can help. Why don't you agree to the formula, Froggy? It would free you up, you see."

"How could you help?" she asked, forgetting to keep the volume down.

"We could feed one each," Mueller suggested. "That would take the pressure off. It would be like having just one."

"But one would get the formula, and one would get breast milk each feed."

"Then we could give one just formula and one just breast milk. It would be an experiment. We could see who did best."

Frances was horrified. "Kristian Mueller, are you really suggesting that we conduct experiments on our children?"

"Shush, no, alright. We can discuss this in the light of day. Shall I turn off the lamp?"

"Yes," she snapped quietly. Then, a few minutes later, she whispered, "Will you hold me?"

He threw out his arm towards her, and she rolled towards him, burrowing into him and laying her head on his shoulder. He smiled in the darkness. It was the way she liked to fall asleep. Once she had nodded off, he would untangle his body from hers so that he could sleep, too.

He lay awake for a while, wishing that he hadn't mentioned the damn word 'experiment' to her. It was thoughtless, and he hoped it wouldn't interfere with her sleep. She needed it more than ever now, with two children to look after. There were still times, though not often, when he would find her curled up on the floor, asleep or soaked in sweat from a bad dream. Then he would lift her back into bed, and she would mutter like she just had, "Will you hold me?"

He had other news to give her, and he didn't think she would be happy about it. He would have to choose his time.

* * *

Mueller was impressed when he returned home the next weekend. In the week he had been away, his wife had become a breastfeeding expert. She didn't need his help with the feed, though she suggested he might like to help with the nappy change. He'd seen enough blood, guts, and shit over the last few years and didn't think a dirty nappy could be worse than that, so he agreed to give it a go when the next feed was due.

He groaned when the crying started. Surely it couldn't be three hours since he turned off the damn lamp, and yet the clock was telling him it was. As he struggled to come around, he thought that maybe he'd been dreaming—no such luck. Frances was also telling him his three hours were up. She was shaking his arm and whispering that he should turn on the lamp on his side of the bed, away from the babies, so that they didn't get too much light to wake them further. He rolled over and stuck his hand out, feeling for the light switch. Frances was up and had made her way to the crib in virtual darkness.

"My God," he mumbled.

"Welcome to my world," she said. "I'll feed Paul, and then you can change his nappy while I feed Karin."

"I need help, Froggy. You'll have to show me."

"Let's do it first, then. You need to watch."

Frances expertly showed Mueller how to remove a dirty nappy, where to put it, fold a clean one, wrap it around a baby, and secure it with only one safety pin. She put the baby on the bed, clambered beside Mueller, and fed Paul.

"How long will it take to top him up, do you think?" Mueller asked.

"Fifteen or maybe twenty minutes, I hope."

"The nappy should take me five?" he asked. Frances nodded. "Then, can I talk to you for a minute or two?"

She nodded, and Mueller sat down on the side of the bed.

"I have something I need to tell you, Froggy,"

Half asleep, she missed the seriousness of his tone. "What?"

"You know the doctors and medical staff that carried out experiments and worse have been rounded up?"

"For trial at Nuremberg again. Yes," she said.

Mueller noticed her jaw set as she continued, "Hopefully, they will hang the lot of them. That would be just, don't you think?"

Mueller pulled his hand through his hair. It was going to be difficult; he knew it would be. He was going to have to choose his words carefully.

"Maybe for some, yes. But the world is watching, and justice must be done."

"And it would be if they all hung."

"Only if the evidence is there, Froggy."

She snatched her eyes to his. "Careful, Kristian, your inner Nazi is beginning to show."

She might as well have slapped him in the face. Her comment cut into him as much as if she had, and being tired, he retaliated. "And so is your warped idea of justice," he said, immediately wishing he hadn't.

They both sat on the bed in silence for some minutes, stunned and hurt by each other's comments.

Eventually, Mueller puffed out his cheeks, exhaled noisily, and said, "That was tiredness that made me say what I said. I'm sorry."

There was a silence until Frances said quietly, "I'm sorry too. After all, you did for me, too. Getting Kapitan back. I don't deserve you."

Mueller started to chuckle. "I hope you mean that in a good way," he said.

Frances was prevented from answering as the quiet of the night was ruptured by Karin, who had every right to complain as she hadn't been fed or changed.

"Feed first," said Frances, "otherwise the other one will wake up again."

"Agreed. Have a think about this formula stuff. It really would help to free you up."

Frances took Karin from the crib and put her to the breast. "I still don't understand why Konrad wants you to go to Nuremberg, you know."

"To see they have a fair trial."

"Why should they have a fair trial? People in the camps and ghettos didn't have a fair trial, did they?"

"No, they didn't. Think through, Froggy. These people will be judged much more harshly by folk if they've been seen to have had a fair trial and are found guilty. Surely, you don't want to sink to their level. And remember, there will be a few decent men amongst them."

"I don't think so," she spat.

"There are. I can tell you one from the first trial."

She scoffed. "Who?"

"Karl Donitz. My Godfather. Speak to Pa about him. You wouldn't be here if it weren't for him."

CHAPTER 11

Once a routine was in place, Frances found life got a little easier again. After the first month, she agreed to try out the formula for some of the feeds. She had to admit that the babies took it well, and she could enjoy a little more freedom by passing the feeding over to Freya and Anna now and again. They were only too happy to assist, and now and again became pretty regular. However, due to running the house, Anna felt she was getting the short straw as Freya had much more time with the children.

After six weeks of doing little other than sorting out her offspring and pottering down to the stables on her own or with the pram, Frances decided it was time to start riding again. She told Freya and Peter one morning over breakfast.

"Are you sure it's not too soon?" Freya asked.

"No, really. I'm fine, but I wouldn't mind some company," she said to Peter. "Just to be on the safe side."

"My pleasure, my dear," he replied. "So, what shall we say, ten thirty at the stables? I have a little business I need to sort first."

"Marvelous," Frances replied. "That will give me time to make sure the twinnies are settled and beg Freya to keep an eye on them."

Freya replied with a smile. The children had given her a lift and something to cherish, and she felt helpful at last.

"You needn't rush back, and you needn't inform Anna either. I'm quite capable of managing on my own for a couple of hours or so, you know," she told Frances.

"Ah, now that will get me into trouble," Frances replied. "I must tell Anna. I'll have to let her do the same on another day."

"Huh," said Freya, rising from the table. "She sometimes forgets who the grandparent is. And so do you."

She turned to leave the room as Frances stood and took her arm.

"Mutti, I never forget that you are the twinnies' grandmother, but I can't forget the love and kindness that Anna has shown me, even if it has been in a somewhat military fashion. I love you both, you know. Please don't make things difficult and never ask me to choose between you."

Freya sniffed and tossed her head a little as she walked towards the door, and Peter called after her. "Freya, my dear. I hope you were listening."

She didn't reply. As she left the room, Frances turned to Peter and sighed. He smiled at her and patted her hand across the table. "Ten thirty at the stables. We can both escape for a while, huh? And I happen to know that Freya has an appointment tomorrow morning at the hairdresser, so why don't you ask Anna to look after the children for an hour or so then, and if I have no business to sort, we can ride out again?"

"That would be brilliant, Peter. What I really need is a little time to get the old fiddle out of its box. I'd better go and sort out my children. I don't want to be late for our date," she said, kissing him on the cheek.

Time in the saddle with Peter beside her. She had wanted that for weeks. Her conversation with Mueller regarding Karl Donitz had stayed in her mind, and she wanted to check out this Donitz chap with Peter.

She made her way down to the stables. The weather was warm, and she was dressed in jodhpurs and a shirt. Turning up a few minutes early, she found Willie cleaning the loose boxes.

"Have you seen Herr Mueller?" she asked him.

"No, Frau, not today." They both turned as they heard the pebbles crunching on the pathway. It was Peter, the dogs were at his heels.

"Sorry, sorry, I got held up," he called as he reached them and ruffled the hair on the top of Willie's head. "So, are we all tacked up?"

"No, I haven't long been here myself."

"Come on then. Willie, give Frau Mueller a hand tacking up, and I will see you in five minutes. I'm ready to go. Come on, dogs."

Frances felt the life force running through her as soon as she mounted Majesty. She joined Peter in the yard, and they set off towards the lake. It was somewhere that Frances hadn't investigated, as she tended to keep out of wooded areas, preferring to take off across a field at a gallop and feel the breeze lashing against her skin and through her hair. Today, though she held back, she wanted to chat with Peter about something that had been playing on her mind. Peter was mounted on his enormous Hanoverian stallion, Saxon. They rode side by side to the gate of the first field.

"Are you up for a little canter?" he asked her.

"Yes, in a bit," she replied. "I need to ask you something first."

"Ah. I thought you had something on your mind. You have had, for a few days, I would say. Have you and my son been arguing?"

"No, no," she denied. "Konrad has asked Kristian to do something, and I'm a bit annoyed. Actually, Peter, I am bloody annoyed. Has he mentioned anything to you?"

"No, I don't think we mentioned his work last weekend, though I could detect that there was a little heat between you two."

"This has been sitting uneasily for a few weeks, if I'm honest," Frances informed him.

"Ah. Come on, then. Tell me."

"He's been asked to go to Nuremberg,"

"Nuremberg again?" Peter repeated thoughtfully and shook his head.

"The doctors' trial? Konrad wants him to attend the trial and report back to him on the way it's handled."

"To see fair play, I suppose," said Peter.

"But they don't deserve a fair trial, surely, Peter."

"Frances, my dear, everyone deserves a fair trial, but I can wholly understand why you wouldn't think so. That court will overflow with evil men, but a decent man or two may be amongst them. Men who are not guilty and who perhaps deserve saving."

"You sound just like your son," Frances accused.

"Then I must have brought him up with the right values. What exactly did Kristian say to you?"

Frances took a deep breath and exhaled. "I told him the whole lot of them needed hanging as none of them were good men. He told me Karl Donitz was a good man, and if it wasn't for him, I wouldn't be here, and I should talk to you about him. How can the man that was put in charge of Nazi Germany by bloody Adolf be a good man, for God's sake?"

Peter Mueller bit his bottom lip thoughtfully. "Ah," he said eventually. "So, Kristian is worrying about Karl. I'm not surprised. Karl has always been good to him. Our families were close for many years. Karl's two sons and Kristian saw a great deal of each other at one time."

"I see. How did you and Karl meet?" Frances asked.

"First World War. He was already in the Navy when war broke out, and we both ended up at the submariners' school in Flensburg-Murwik. We passed at the same time. January 1917. Both became watch officers and then U-boat commanders. On top of that, we married around the same time and had families, though Kristian was a little older than Karl's sons. After the war, I returned to farming, and Karl, who, as I said, had joined the navy before the war, upped his game and eventually became Grand Admiral in 43. Sadly, he lost both of his boys in battle, you know. One early that summer."

"That's when Kristian found me at Dachau," Frances said.

"There, you see. Grand Admiral and the death of his boy in the U-boat arm, and he still had time to look into finding you for Kristian. That's the man I admire. However, Karl is a bit of an enigma. There appear to be two Karls."

"What do you mean?" Frances asked.

"I said I admire the man who looked out for Kristian. I do not admire the man who worshipped Hitler as some demi-god. Something changed him, Frances. Maybe it was losing his boy—"

"You said he lost both of his sons."

Yes. He lost Peter, my namesake, in 43, as I said. Adolf had a policy, which was one of the better things he did. If a senior officer lost a son in battle and had other sons in the military, the latter could return to civilian life. So, Klaus was retraining as a naval doctor. It was his birthday, and he and some mad friends thought it would be exciting to go on an E Boat raid on Selsey—"

"Selsey Bill, England?" Frances asked.

"I assume so if this Bill place you speak of is coastal."

"It is. What happened?" she asked.

"A French destroyer sank the boat," Peter replied.

"So, the poor man lost all of his children," Frances mused.

"He had a daughter, Ursula. She was the eldest, more Kristian's age. They were a lovely family when we were close to them. Close enough for us to ask him to be Kristian's godfather. He took the job seriously; he was very religious. He cared too, I think, about his men. Kristian held him in high regard, and it sounds like he still does."

"Do you, Peter?" Frances asked. "Is he a good man like Kristian says?"

"Without a doubt, he was a good commander. If Adolf had listened to him, who knows, the war may have had a different outcome. I believe something turned him. He gave Hitler his undying love when he was promoted to Grand Admiral." He shook his head and continued. "I never knew him to have racist beliefs, yet I hear he has made slurs against the Jews. He was loyal to Hitler to the end when many left him, and in what I suppose was gratitude, Hitler made him his successor. A wiser choice than Goring or Himmler, though a poisoned chalice, I would say, to be the sole representative of an imploding German Reich. Strangely, he fled to Flensburg-Murwik. I remember reading in the newspapers during the last trial that he denied referring to the poison of Jewry, and he made a point of saying none of his men would be violent to Jews."

Frances had a flashback to UBA. There had been one man there that had shown himself to be antisemitic. The others could scarcely tolerate him. "So, is Donitz good or bad? Peter, do you think? Is Kristian right?"

"What do you think?" he asked.

"I don't know. I want your opinion. Kristian asked me years ago if there was good and evil."

"And what did you say?"

"I said there wasn't. There were only men."

Peter Mueller drew his horse to a standstill, and Frances followed his lead, reining in Majesty. He turned to her and held her gaze.

"Perhaps we are all made up of both, to some degree or other. What do you think?"

"Once upon a time, you liked this Donitz. Perhaps that is good enough for me. Maybe there is the odd, good man amongst those on trial."

A smile crept across Peter Mueller's face. "Time for a damn good gallop," he said. What do you say?"

"I say I bet I can beat you across this field." She laughed and dug her heels into Majesty's flank, and they flew.

* * *

When Mueller arrived home the following Friday evening, he found his wife had changed. There was a lightness in her that hadn't been there for a few weeks. When he had mentioned the doctor's trial and Konrad's request that he attend it on behalf of the Democratic Union Party to see fair play, he could understand her reaction. She believed these men to be evil through to the core, and he agreed that many of them were, but as a lawyer, he had to believe in a fair trial before justice could be carried out.

She ran out of the door when he drew up in front of the house that evening and threw her arms around his neck before giving him an exceedingly sensual kiss. "I've missed you," she said, taking his arm and leading him across the hall towards the staircase.

"I should just put my briefcase in the study," he said, trying to guess her mood. She took it from him and tossed it across the floor towards the hall table. Then she grabbed his hand and led him up the stairs to their room, pushing the door open and pulling him inside. He had a pretty good idea what her mood was by then and quickly turned, slamming the door shut with a bang and flattening her body back against it, seeking her mouth with his own. He had missed her, not just for that week but since she'd given birth to his children. It was suggested they should refrain from sex for six weeks at least and that she should take time to recover and heal. As she unbuttoned his flies, it seemed that time was now over.

He undid the buttons down the front of her dress, and she let it fall to the floor, surprising him with her nakedness beneath it and the beauty of it.

"Are you sure you are ready for this?" he asked, his voice thick with passion. "I don't want to hurt you, Froggy."

She led him to the bed, walking him past the crib he had totally forgotten about, and a quiet laugh left her lips as she reacted to his double take.

"We're making love with them in the room?" he questioned, looking sheepish.

"Yes, unless you want to wait until we move them into their room in another six months."

"Well, bollocks to that!" he replied, sweeping her off her feet and depositing her on the bed as she shrieked without thinking that she might ruin the moment if the babies woke. Mueller sat down on the edge of the bed beside her, and she pushed herself up onto her knees and, leaning forward, unbuttoned his shirt, slipping it from his athletic frame. She wrapped her arms around his neck, and he kissed her hard and pushed her back onto the bed, where he ran his hand over the new contours of her body. Her breasts were more significant but still firm, and her hips had widened slightly, giving her a womanlier curve from her waist to her thighs. "You're more beautiful than ever," he breathed.

She smiled, stretched her arms to him, and opened her legs. "Come here."

He rolled over and lowered himself onto and into her with a sigh. "I suppose this has to be a quickie then, does it?" he asked.

Her eyes flashed wide. "Not blooming likely. I've missed you, Kristian Mueller. Let it be as long as it takes. Longer even. They're quiet. Let's make the most of it."

"They're stirring," Mueller remarked sometime later, stretching and yawning. "I suppose that's it. We need to move. They will all wonder where we are."

"Not yet. Stay put for a while longer. And I'm sure they know where we are. I love it when you hold me; I could stay like this forever." Mueller sighed in agreement. "I spoke to Peter about your Donitz, you know," Frances continued.

"Good," said Mueller. "And what did he say?"

"Oh, he told me all about the family and that you spent much time together with his children when you were younger."

"Hmm. We had good times. They were a great family."

"I feel so sorry that both sons died. Peter said his youngest son died on his birthday around the time you asked him for help to find me."

"An accident that shouldn't have happened," Mueller muttered. "Anyhow, do you agree that Donitz is a good man?"

"He is a Nazi, isn't he?" Frances reminded him.

"So, they say. Maybe he felt driven into joining the party. A bit hard not to when you're rubbing shoulders with the top man regularly."

"Perhaps. But he did make comments about the Jews, I read—"

"Which he denied in court," Mueller argued.

"Well, he cannot be considered a good man because of that. However, I will agree that he probably isn't a bad man. And I agree that someone needs to be at the doctors' trial to see they are tried fairly, even though I still think the bastards should all be hung."

"That's good news. I'm glad you agree. I have some news that you may not like."

Frances pushed her way out of Mueller's embrace and sat up. "What?" she asked. "What won't I like?"

"I've kissed goodbye to my flat. I'm coming home every night starting next week."

CHAPTER 12

NOVEMBER 23, 1946

Things had settled down nicely at Schonen Felder. Kristian was now commuting. They had taken a trip to Paris as a family, too, and Frances had found time while she was there to sort out her banking and the rental of her aunt's apartment within the city. She toyed with selling it, but Mueller talked her out of it.

"The apartment brings in a good rental, and the tenants are dependable," he said. "Maybe sometime in the future. See how it goes. If the present tenants want to move on, perhaps think about selling it then."

She let him persuade her on that but was determined not to let him persuade her out of stopping breastfeeding. "Half my day is taken up by sitting with a baby stuck to my breast or my lap," she told him. "I think I am going to put them onto formula completely. It will free up my day considerably, and I have noticed that when I substitute formula, they are more satisfied for longer."

He surprised her when he agreed that it was a good idea. The bugbear came later when she told others. Freya accepted that breastfeeding two babies was time-consuming, and she knew that by feeding formula, she would have even more significant input into her grandchildren.

It was Anna who hit the roof. Frances told her when she brought in mid-morning coffee for herself and Freya. "I'm surprised at you. What can be more natural than giving a child the milk that its mother supplies?" she asked, which made Frances have momentary doubts; she felt like a bad mother.

It was Freya who came to her defence. "Well, since you're so against Frances giving up the feeding herself, you won't want to poke your nose in, will you?" she said, giving Anna a smug look. Frances looked on as Anna's mouth worked. She tried to think of a comeback, but then her face buckled, and she sped back to the safety of the kitchen. Frances lifted her eyebrows and gave her mother-in-law a look.

"What?" asked Freya.

"You know what," said Frances. "I won't have any fallouts; I told you that before." Her mother-in-law hmphed. "I mean it, Mutti," she said as she left the room to be greeted with the sound of crying children from upstairs. Should she start with just the formula now, she wondered, or gradually cut back on breastfeeding?

"You'll be wanting these then." Anna's voice stopped her dead, and she looked towards the kitchen door. Anna was framed there, holding a couple of bottles of ready-made formula. "I can help if you want it. If you want me, that is."

"Come on. I'm not proud," she replied. "I'll accept help from wherever."

"Even from me?" Frances swung round as the sound of that voice she loved rang through the hallway. Sara Kohl's laughing form confronted her, and she gave an enormous shriek of joy. The two women flung themselves into each other's arms.

"When?" asked Frances.

"Yesterday afternoon. We would have come over yesterday,

but we were both tired after all the travelling, and to be honest, Mutts and Pop were so pleased to see us. Well, you know.”

“So, what have you done with Jack?”

“He’s talking to Kristian. I don’t suppose we will see either of them for a while. Anyway, Frau Mueller, do you want my help or not? Those babies can probably be heard at the Kohl residence. I can’t wait to meet them.”

“I’ve told them all about their Aunty Sara,” Frances said, taking Sara’s arm and leading her to the staircase.

“So, you don’t want my help now.”

Frances had forgotten entirely about Anna, who was still standing in the kitchen doorway, clutching two bottles of formula. She walked over to her, took the formula, and kissed Anna on the cheek. “Aren’t you going to welcome Sara home?” she asked.

“When she acknowledges my presence, then I might. Perhaps.”

Sara strode across the hall and grabbed Anna, kissing her too. “What’s wrong with you, you old misery?” she asked.

“Freya’s what’s wrong with her. Take no notice,” Frances said, taking Sara by the arm and leading her upstairs.

As they reached the bedroom, they heard Anna call. “It’s not just Freya; it’s you too.”

Frances closed the bedroom door and shrugged. “So, soon to be Frau Burton. What did you make of America?”

Sara leaned in close conspiratorially. “It’s very different to here,” she said. “And by the way, I’m Frau Burton already.”

“Well, Frau-Burton-already,” Frances said with a chuckle, “how are you at feeding babies their bottle?”

Frances passed Paul to Sara, plus a bottle, and fed her daughter herself. It gave them time to talk and catch up with one another’s lives. It was months since they had seen each other. Sara spoke of Jack’s parents and his brother Tom. She said they had welcomed her, and Tom was coming to Germany for the wedding, along with a lad they had grown up with, Bernie, who Sara said she wasn't too keen on. "He's a weasel," she said.

"What does that mean?" Frances asked.

"You'll find out. Jack's parents can't come as they are so busy on the farm. There's a lot to do before the weather gets bad. And boy, does it get bad. They showed me photographs. They've promised to come next spring, though," Sara said. "You'd like them, Froggy; they're down to earth like us. Hardworking. Typical farmers, I suppose."

Frances smiled as she listened to Sara rattle on. She had missed her more than she knew.

"You should see the size of the machinery they are using; it's enormous. I managed to ride while I was there. Their little mustangs are so hardy. They'd keep going all day."

There was a gentle knock on the door and Kristian's voice from outside. "Can we come in? Jack wants to meet our children."

Frances stood up and carried Karin to the door. Full of food, she drifted off and was ready to put down in the crib.

She opened the door with a shush. "Come in but keep the volume down. With some luck, we can all go downstairs and have a few hours of peace. Jack, how are you?" she asked as Burton entered the room. "Congratulations, by the way." She said, giving him a peck on the cheek.

"Thanks, Frances, and congratulations to you too. You look wonderful. Motherhood must be suiting you."

"It's getting a little easier, thankfully. I do not recommend having two at a time, however. If it weren't for Mutti and Anna, I would be totally worn out instead of quite a bit worn out." Mueller gave a slight cough. "What?" asked Frances.

"Don't forget the help I give you," said Mueller.

Frances reached up and put an arm around his neck. "Which is?" she asked.

"Morning nappy, and coffee and toast in bed. I suppose I will have a bottle thrust into my hand, too, now that the breasts aren't coming out anymore. I'm going to miss them."

Sara and Jack couldn't contain their laughter as Frances blushed. "I think we should get these two babies down for a couple of hours and have some grown-up time. I could really do with it, you know."

"That would be a boon," said Sara. "We still have so much to plan. We're hoping you can come up with a few suggestions."

"Most important is to get this civil marriage booked," Jack said.

"You're already married, aren't you?" Mueller questioned.

"Of course we are," Sara replied.

"As long as it was a civil ceremony, you don't need another here," Mueller informed them. "I'm assuming you have the certificate."

"Of course," said Sara.

"Well then, that's one job done already. Come on, Froggy, get those children down. We'll meet you in the study; we have serious planning to do."

* * *

"I'm so glad they're back," said Frances as she clambered into bed that night. She watched Mueller with a smile as he checked his offspring for the umpteenth time before joining her in bed. "Are they all fine then?" she asked him, unable to keep the smile from her face.

"Can't stop looking at them. You've given me the best gift ever."

"You played a part in it too, remember?" she said.

"A tiny part," he said, lying back on the pillow. She turned on her side to face him and pushed her hand between his legs.

"Now, Herr Mueller, I wouldn't say that at all," she replied.

* * *

Over the next few days, Frances spent considerable time with Sara at Schonen Felder and with Jack and the entire Kohl family at their residence. On a particular day, just weeks before the wedding, Frances and Sara were enjoying each other's company in the sitting room at the Kohl home. She had driven there with her children and was only too happy to relinquish their care to Sara's mother for a while. She watched with some amusement as Eva tore into her daughter.

"I can't understand why you're so chilled about everything, Sara," she said while jiggling both babies up and down on her lap. "We still have so much to sort. When are you going to deliver the invitations? It will take you a couple of days to do so. And there are others that aren't local that will need posting."

"Have you written them all?" Sara asked.

"I told you days ago when you got here that they are in the hall at the back of the table. For goodness' sake, girl. Have you given poor Frances any idea about what music you want her to play in the church yet?"

"No, she hasn't," Frances chimed.

"Well, I don't have a bloody clue about what music to have. You choose it, Frances; you'll be playing it."

"Are you giving me free rein?" Frances asked.

"Yes." Sara and Eva spoke together, and all three women laughed.

"Seriously, Frances, can we sort the music while you are here?" Eva asked.

Frances shrugged. "Let's do it then," she said. "How many pieces will you want? Are you having the bridal march? That is not a piece for the violin. Oh, and by the way, would you mind if I pass on playing at the reception?"

"As long as you play me in, I'll let you off with the

reception. I'll be nervous, but hearing you play will help," Sara said.

"I'll be nervous too, you know," Frances replied.

"Rubbish, you've played to thousands of people—"

"People I don't know, Sar. I will be nervous about playing at your wedding, for sure. This is why I will choose something easy for you to walk up the aisle to." The other two women gave her a questioning look. "Pachelbel's canon in D. It's hardly ever used these days, and it's gone out of fashion a little, but it's quite lovely. It would be nice to have a piano playing, too. Do either of you know a pianist?"

"Jack will know someone, I'm sure," said Sara.

"Where is Jack, anyhow?" Frances asked.

"With Pop. He's showing him the accounts and all the running," Sara said.

"We could ask the organist at the church," said Eva. The conversation had moved on, and Eva saw Sara and Frances's confusion. "To accompany you, dear," she said to Frances.

"That's probably a better bet. Then, I can find time to practice. Now, what else do you need?"

"Something while the register is being signed and something to leave the church by."

One of the babies cried. "I think they are getting hungry," Eva said, jiggling them both even faster.

Frances ferreted in a bag. "I bought a couple of bottles; I thought they would need a feed. Shall I pop to the kitchen and warm them?"

"I'll go," said Sara. You and Mutti can carry on choosing the music."

Frances laughed as Sara left the room. Paul was crying, and Frances took him from Eva and sat him on her lap beside her as they waited for Sara to return with the bottles.

"So, Frances, are you enjoying motherhood?" Eva asked.

"I'm tired, I must admit, Eva, but yes, I love every minute. The changes I see even from day to day are wonderful."

"They will soon grow up, my dear, so enjoy them as babies while you can. Your life will never be the same again. The highs will be higher, but sometimes there will be lows too." Eva laid her hand on Frances's cheek and looked deeply into her eyes, drawing a wide smile from Frances.

"What?" she asked.

"You don't appear depressed, I must say," Eva replied.

"That's probably because I am getting so much help. Freya and Anna are almost coming to blows over whose turn it is."

And what is Kristian like as a father?"

"Doting. He's lovely with them. He comes home every night now and struggles to tear himself away and go to work in the morning."

"He should be helping Peter on the farm," Eva said.

"He will when he feels the time is right. Should I go and look for Sara? We need to sort this music out and feed these little people."

"She will probably be gabbing in the kitchen. I don't think that girl is interested in the wedding ceremony. She just wants the party." Eva gave a shake of her head. "Let's just sort it between us."

"If you are happy, I can come up with some suggestions," Frances said.

"Please." Eva sighed. "Let's just get it sorted."

"Now then, I have given it some thought already. How about the Schubert's Ave Maria for the register signing? And because it's Sara, what about something up-tempo to leave the church by? I am thinking something English."

"Well, we are in the British zone, I suppose," said Eva.

"Elgar, then. Salut d'amour. Greetings of love. Fitting, I think. I will need that pianist, however."

Chapter 13

The harvest of 1946 was, as Peter Mueller had forecast, very poor in Germany and across Europe as a whole. Food was in short supply, and as winter approached, Frances thanked her lucky stars again that she and her family were in the envious position of being farmers. They did have to give a considerable amount of what they harvested to the government, but that still left them plenty compared to others. There were the eggs and meat from chickens, beef from cow slaughtering, and fresh vegetables from Frances's greenhouse. She had talked Peter into buying what she called an experimental greenhouse, not too big but big enough to supply the household with a range of fresh food. It had proven successful, and she reminded Mueller of that daily.

As December approached, he prepared for his trip to Nuremberg, which he secretly dreaded. He had seen photographs of the city's devastation, which had occurred almost two years ago. It looked even worse than Berlin if that were possible. The RAF and US Army Air Force had destroyed 90% of the city in under an hour, killing almost two thousand people and making a hundred thousand civilians homeless. He still couldn't get his head around the Allied bombings; he thought it was no way to fight a war. But what of these men was he going to watch being tried? They had killed and maimed not thousands but millions, so it was said. They were his countrymen. He'd probably met some of them briefly and thought what decent chaps they were. And that was the difference. Even in the Great War, there were acts of decency. Decency now, it seemed, was a thing of the past.

Frances could see that the closer Mueller came to having to leave for Nuremberg, the more screwed up he was getting. "I don't know why you don't just tell Konrad that you don't want to go," she said. They were seated in the sitting room a few days before he was due to leave. Enjoying one another's company while the babies slept, "I'm sure if he knew how much it was upsetting you, he would find someone else to take your place. And I would be happy with that."

"The peculiar thing is, Froggy, that I'm touched that he has asked me instead of someone else. I think it shows he trusts my judgment."

"I'd like to make a bet no one else wanted to do it," Frances said.

"Well, thank you for that, sweetheart. There was me thinking that Konrad appreciated my judgement." Frances huffed. "It will be good to get these things over with. I am so tired of this sodding war. It's over, thank God, but go into one of the cities or even our little town, and you can see how people still suffer because of it. If the weather turns, there will be another death toll." He reached out and took her hand. "You know, sometimes I wish we had stayed in Paris. The more I go there, the more I like it."

"Ah, and that, my love, is the magic of Paris, though I believe if you lived there, you would soon see it for what it is."

"Which is?" he asked.

"Superfluous, arrogant, vain, shallow—"

Mueller cut in. "Enchanting, romantic, artistic, magical—"

"Timeless, alluring, unforgettable, and if we lived there all the time, you would hate it. Your children would grow up as Parisians."

"So?"

"It's expensive. And I happen to know that you wouldn't leave Schonen Felder."

"You know me too well. Are you happy here, though, Froggy? Living in Germany, I mean." he asked.

He watched as Frances gave the question a little thought before nodding. "Yes. I'm happy. And why wouldn't I be? I'm with the man I love, and I wouldn't change that for anything." She reached up, cupping his cheek with her hand, looking deep into the blue of his eyes. "I also have two wonderful children that you've given me. It's tough at times, but it seems it's tough for everyone, and compared to most, we are living a good life."

She took his hands. "You wait and see, Germany will recover, I suspect, pretty quickly. It will be a good place to be, Kristian. I think we can safely have a little optimism. Konrad knows there is a way forward in joining up with the rest of Europe, so you tell me. Wouldn't it be wonderful if one day we could travel around as though it's just one country? No borders, no boundaries. Think of that."

"A nice thought," he said, "And now I must give some more thought to leaving. I have no idea how much of the railroad is working between here and Nuremberg. It could be a long journey."

"Maggie has sorted your hotel, though?" Frances questioned. "I am assuming there are hotels still standing."

"Bloody hope so," said Mueller. "I suppose the Yanks will have taken over the best ones. I think the hotel will be outside the old town. I believe there is very little of the old historical city left. So, I am guessing a daily brisk walk to the court is on the cards." He hugged Frances. "At least we have Christmas and a wedding to look forward to, eh?"

"Our first Christmas together," she said.

"Aren't you forgetting the one we had in 42?" he asked, raising his eyebrows.

She met his gaze. "Kapitan Leutnant Mueller, how could I ever forget the Christmas of 42? That's when I fell in love, and I've never doubted that love for one second. And, just in case you doubted me earlier, there is nowhere I would rather be than at your side."

* * *

DECEMBER 9^{TH,} 1946

Kristian Mueller took his place in the courtroom of the Palace of Justice in Nuremberg on December 9th, the first day of what was to become known as the Doctors' Trial. The British transferred a number of SS and military doctors to the courthouse so the United States could try the case. The courtroom was chosen as it had an adjacent prison for the 23 leading German physicians and administrators who were to go on trial.

Brigadier General Telford Taylor was the Chief of Counsel who gave the opening statement when the tribunal began proceedings.

"The defendants in this case are charged with murders, tortures, and other atrocities committed in the name of medical science. The victims of these crimes are numbered in the hundreds of thousands. Only a handful are still alive; a few survivors will appear in this courtroom. But most of these miserable victims were slaughtered outright or died in the course of the tortures to which they were subjected. For the most part, they are nameless dead. To their murderers, these wretched people were not individuals at all. They came in wholesale lots and were treated worse than animals."

During that opening statement, Mueller cast his eye over the twenty-three defendants. He didn't recognise any of them and, for that, he was thankful. The juxtaposition was that he could have done. They mostly all looked like good German men. The kind of men he'd mixed with at university and when training to be a U-boat commander. The sort of men he'd partied with on return from patrols or when on leave. He took a deep breath and settled himself. It was going to be a long haul until he got back home. The court would close for a Christmas recess in fourteen days on the 19th [of] December, all being well. He would be able to forget about the damn trial, enjoy Christmas and the wedding of Sara and Jack. Despite everything, he smiled as he thought about how manic it would be back home as preparations for the ceremony and Christmas would be well underway.

* * *

Things at Schonen Felder were manic, as Frances begged Anna for help to get to a rehearsal with the pianist who would accompany her when she played at Sara's wedding.

"Please, Anna," she pleaded, "look after the twinnies. I promise I will only be gone for a couple of hours, and then I will help you make a stollen and prepare anything else you want me to do."

"And who will be looking after the twinnies while you help me in the kitchen?" asked Anna.

"I can ask Freya," Frances said.

"You think Freya is going to help you if it helps me?"

"Oh, for goodness' sake. Isn't it at times like this that we should all pull together?"

"Well, you go and tell that to your mother-in-law."

"Tell me what?" Anna and Frances both turned to find Freya in the kitchen, standing a few feet behind them. "What? What have you got to tell me?" Freya repeated the question and eyed both women, who'd coloured up under her scrutiny.

"Well, it must be said, "Anna began, "I will need some help in the kitchen if you want to celebrate Christmas as you like."

"You've managed for years without help," Freya snapped. What's so different this year?"

"I'm surprised you haven't realised that this is the first year since I don't know when we will have your son home for Christmas, and there isn't a war to worry about. On top of that, it's your grandchildren's first Christmas. That makes it extra special in my eyes, and extra special means extra work, which means I need extra help. I am not as able as I used to be."

Frances looked from one woman to the other. This was one discussion she was going to keep out of. She wondered if they'd notice if she snook out of the kitchen and left them to it.

"Hah!" shrieked Freya. "I never thought there would come a day when you would admit you were getting older and needed help. So how long has it been, Anna, that you have felt that you couldn't cope?"

"Did you hear me say I couldn't cope?" Anna asked, her voice brittle. "I said I was not as able as I was."

"Well, thank goodness. At last. I'm happy that you are not as able." Frances looked on and saw Anna's face drop.

"So now you have an excuse to get rid of me, Freya," she muttered.

"No!" Frances's eyes widened, and she wondered if she should intercede.

Freya continued before she could say another word. "In light of your admission, Anna, I now have an excuse to come into the kitchen and involve myself with the running of this house. You brought up my son. You have managed the kitchen and produced food for us all for I don't know how many years. You clean up after us, and now you want to involve yourself with bringing up my grandchildren. For God's sake, woman, slow down and let me help you. Let me do something useful for the first time in an age."

There was absolute silence in that kitchen following Freya's outburst, and Frances wondered if she had heard it correctly. It seemed the two older women had backed themselves into a corner. Anna admitted she could no longer cope with cooking, cleaning, and stepping in to help Frances. And Freya admitted that she had little input into her son's upbringing or the running of the house. The silence seemed to drag on, though it probably lasted seconds before Frances decided someone had to say something.

"So, what are you going to do?" she asked.

Both women glared at her and answered in unison. "Who?"

"Both of you. Seems to me that you both want something the other can give, so why not come to an agreement." Frances pulled her hand through her hair and cast her eyes over them both. "No! Wrong word. I suppose that expecting either of you to agree with the other is asking too much. Why not just call it—" The sound of babies crying reached the kitchen, and Frances gave both women a filthy look. "Oh! For goodness' sake, she said. "Just come to a bloody arrangement, will you?" She walked out of the kitchen and left them to it.

CHAPTER 14

DECEMBER 20, 1946, LATE EVENING

Frances had just completed the twinnies' late-night feed and put them on either end of the cot when she heard the car crunch across the gravel and pull up in front of the house. Her heart leaped. It had been more than a fortnight since Mueller left for Nuremberg, the longest they had been apart since they had found each other again in April. The weather had taken a turn for the worse, with temperatures now being the coldest people could remember for a good while at minus 14.9 degrees centigrade. Peter had left to pick Kristian up from the station earlier that afternoon, preferring to travel one way, at least in the light. Thankfully, he knew the roads like the back of his hand and didn't foresee any major problems even though the roads were icy. Now, thankfully, he was back.

As Frances made her way down the staircase, the door was thrown open. Mueller was framed momentarily on the threshold before dumping his cases and rushing towards her. She flung herself down the last few steps of the stairs and into his arms, stupidly surprised by how cold his lips felt when she kissed him.

"How was it?" she asked. He shook his head.

"Can I just hold you for a while, Froggy?" he asked. Frances

140

was aware that Freya had joined them in the hall, and Peter gently led her back to the lounge to give Kristian and herself a little space.

"Don't you want to take your coat off and get to the fire? You're freezing," Frances said.

"In a minute. For now, I want you in my arms. That's all right, isn't it?"

"It's more than all right," she replied, nestling into him and sharing her warmth as he kissed her neck, sending a shudder down her spine.

"And how are my offspring?" he asked.

"Asleep. Let's leave them for now and see them when we turn in, shall we? I don't want to rock the boat by possibly disturbing them. I'm greedy, I want you all to myself."

Freya passed them in the hall a second time and returned a couple of minutes later with a pot of real coffee and some sandwiches that Anna had left prepared. "Come on, both of you. Come and settle in the lounge for a while. You need to relax, Kristian, or you won't sleep," she said.

They followed Freya into the lounge. Peter was on his hands and knees, stoking up the fire to fight against the freezing nighttime temperature, which the heating system in the house was struggling to cope with. Frances glanced at Mueller and could see that he was worn out. She led him to the couch and sat beside him, snuggling herself into his body.

"What time did you leave Nuremberg?" she asked him.

"Seven this morning. Fourteen bloody hours to get to Bonn. It was a hellish journey. I couldn't relax because it was so damn cold. We stopped briefly at Fulda. At least, I think it was Fulda. I was so bloody tired by then; it could have been anywhere. At least I could grab some food and get a drink, thank goodness." He turned to Peter. "You know I've never been gladder to see my father," he said. He kicked his shoes off. "Feel my feet, Froggy. They're still bloody freezing."

He lifted his feet onto her lap, and she rubbed them. Peter passed his son a large brandy, which he gratefully accepted. He gave his shoulder a fatherly rub before passing a drink to Frances and Freya.

He then sat on one of the armchairs, giving Mueller a long look before asking, "How was it, Son?"

"Rough. There's not much left of Nuremberg, much less than Berlin. The old town is completely in ruins. The station was in a bit of a state, too," Mueller replied through a tired yawn.

"And the trial?" Peter questioned.

"Has gone well so far. The prosecution has nearly finished giving their evidence. There will be a few more days before the court gets to the defence."

"But Kristian, what are these men actually being tried for?" asked Freya.

"What are the actual indictments? Can you tell us?" Peter asked.

"I can't see why not," Mueller replied. "I'm sure it will all be posted in the newspapers soon. So, there are four indictments. Conspiracy to Commit War crimes and Crimes Against Humanity. War Crimes. Crimes Against Humanity. Membership in a Criminal Organisation."

"What's the difference between the second and third," Frances asked.

"So, the second, which is just War Crimes, are crimes against persons protected by laws of war."

"Such as?" Frances questioned.

"People like prisoners of war," Mueller explained.

"And Crimes Against Humanity?" she questioned again.

"That's crimes against persons not protected by rules of war."

"Like in the camps?"

He nodded. "The case is the United States of America against Karl Brandt et al."

"But why is just Brandt mentioned? I thought there were more than twenty of these men on trial," Freya said.

"The et al. means and others. It's a shortened way of recording it, Mutts, so you don't have a long list of names."

Freya carried on questioning. "But why name Brandt then? Wasn't he Hitler's own physician?"

"He was involved in the euthanasia program, Mutts, among other unpleasant things. Do you think we can leave it there? I'm really very tired. I want to relax and enjoy Christmas and that special wedding. Frances stood and took Mueller by the hand, pulling him up.

"I'm going to get your son to bed, Freya. We'll see you in the morning, although I suppose I will be up in a couple of hours feeding those twinnies."

* * *

Unusually, the babies didn't wake until six a.m. Hearing them crying, Freya knocked on the bedroom door and quietly asked if Frances needed any help.

Her son answered, "We're all right, Mutts; I can help. Frances is already down in the kitchen sorting out the bottles. Get back to bed for a couple of hours, and when you see Anna, tell her I'll grab some breakfast later."

When Frances returned to the bedroom, Mueller was kneeling before the fireplace, lighting a fire. She walked across the room and kissed the top of his head.

"I'm so glad you're home," she said. He looked over his shoulder and smiled at her.

"It's still bloody freezing. We need to keep the fires in for the next few days," he said, getting up. "Let's get these horrors fed. Do you think there's any chance they'll go back off for a while?"

"Hopefully. I've put a bit extra in the bottle. "Let me sort the nappies. How are you feeling?" she asked.

"I'll be fine when I've had another couple of hours of sleep."

They sat silently, hoping the milk would do the trick and they could claim a little more rest. It worked, and Frances laid the babies head to toe in the cot and wrapped them up before clambering back into bed.

"Was there any mention of Mengele, Kristian?" she asked in a hushed voice.

"Only that the bastard appears to have disappeared," he replied quietly.

"He'd have made plans, I suspect," she continued. "He wouldn't leave anything to chance."

Mueller whispered, "Let's forget about Mengele, Brandt, and the damn trial until morning, eh? And get a couple of hours more sleep, shall we?" They snuggled under the bed covers, and Mueller turned off the lamp on his side, throwing the room into darkness.

"Will you hold me?" she asked him. And then, remembering that they hadn't been together for a couple of weeks, she added, "Unless?" She heard him chuckle.

"I'm back until well into the new year, Froggy. Plenty of time for lots of 'unless.' Come here and let me hold you, God, I've missed you."

He threw out his arm, and she snuggled close to his body and laid her head on his shoulder, but she had other questions that she needed answers to.

"How long do you think the trial will last?"

Mueller gave a tired sigh. "A long time. There are more than twenty medical crimes. The court is looking into each one to see which defendants committed which crime or crimes."

"How are there so many?" she asked.

"Think about all the different camps that have come to light. Different crimes were being committed in different places."

"Like what?"

"You know, like what? You told me what was happening in

Dachau: the freezing experiments and the high altitude. You know what Mengele was up to with his experiments on twins. Sweetheart, I don't want to talk about it anymore. Just know there were experiments with different chemicals and poisons. What you knew from Dachau and Auschwitz was just a part of it, Froggy. It's all too bloody horrendous."

She suddenly sat up. "Are you cross with me for asking?"

He wrapped his arms around her and pulled her back down onto the bed, close to his body. "Not cross with you. I am more cross with myself. I don't think I can ever forgive myself for choosing to believe you were mad when you told me about what was going on back in 43."

"We've had this discussion, Kristian. Lots of times. I understand, I do."

"I know. I know. This damn trial has thrown it all back up again."

"Well, don't let it. What do you think you could have done when I told you? You could hardly have acted."

"I could have spoken out."

"And been killed for your trouble. You've bided your time and believed in Justice. Come on, let's get some sleep."

Mueller sighed in agreement and settled down again. It came as a surprise when she sat bolt upright a second time. "This trial will all be over in time for my concert in Boston, won't it?" she whispered.

"I'll make sure it is. I told Adenauer about that an age ago. We have months until then. Sleep now, sweetheart. Please."

* * *

It was well after breakfast time that Mueller woke. Frances and the babies had gone, and he wondered where. The sound of crying informed him that they were not far away. He made for the bathroom, deciding to bathe before breakfast and spend the rest of the day doing as little as he could get away with. After bathing and dressing, he made his way down to the kitchen in search of something substantial for breakfast after having missed out on good food the previous day.

The sound of women shrieking with laughter stopped him dead in his tracks. It was a sound that he wouldn't normally associate with the kitchen at Schonen Felder, but there it was. He quickly identified Frances's laughter, but at least two other women were in there. He stood outside and listened.

"I swear it's true," he heard his wife say.

"I don't believe you. You little fibber." That was Anna, Mueller thought.

"Here, here, was it like this?" That was most definitely his mother. Her comment was met with more shrieks of laughter.

Mueller pushed open the door to be confronted by his mother holding bread dough shaped like a man's private parts, and Frances and Anna doubled over with laughter. As the door opened, the laughter stopped; Freya dropped the dough back onto the table, and Frances quickly rolled it into a ball. Mueller was at a loss for words. He stood open-mouthed and blinked at them. He noticed the pram at the end of the kitchen and wondered how on earth the babies had slept through the racket he'd walked into.

"What's going on?" he eventually managed to say.

"Your wife was just showing us how they shape bread rolls in Paris," said Anna, biting on her lip. Mueller turned his gaze to Frances and gave her a questioning look. She held his gaze, lips pinched together, desperately trying not to laugh and eventually succumbing. Once she had regained control, she said, "You can get penis-shaped rolls in the little bakery by Aunt Edie's. They're extremely popular. Next time we go to Paris, I'll take you there." She ended by grinning at him.

"No! It's fine. Why would I want a penis-shaped bread roll, Froggy?" he questioned, his brow knitted.

Despite trying to fight it back, Frances's laughter got the better of her, setting off Freya and Anna again, though Mueller noticed that his mother looked a little embarrassed. He puffed out his cheeks, exhaled noisily, and gave all three of them a disconcerted look. "I just came here for some toast and coffee," he said.

"Well, you know where it is," said Anna.

"Huh," Mueller grunted. "I remember a time when I got looked after."

While Mueller set about getting himself some breakfast, Frances and Freya quietly finished making bread, and Anna started on the stollen. Christmas was only two days away, and there was much making to do before then.

Mueller prepared his breakfast and strode over to the worktable. He grabbed Frances by the neck, put his hand in the flour bag, and rubbed it in her face. As she spluttered from the flour and indignation, he said, "That'll teach you not to spread rudery in this kitchen, woman." He gave his mother and Anna his best gap-toothed grin as he left the kitchen with a tray of toast and coffee.

"Do you think he'll tell his father?" asked Freya as the door closed behind him. The look of worry on her face brought more peals of laughter from Frances and Anna.

Mueller was making his way to the dining room when the phone rang. He was overjoyed to hear Jack Burton's voice when he answered it. "So, you're back safe and sound from Nuremberg then, fella? Sara and I were wondering if you and Frances would like to spend some time with us today. We thought you could perhaps come over here after lunch. I believe there is a lady who would love to do a bit of babysitting, too," he said, referring to Eva Kohl.

CHAPTER 15

The couple of days leading up to Christmas were special. It was Kristian and Frances's first proper Christmas together, and their new family made it all the more remarkable for Peter, Freya, and Anna, too. Additionally, Kristian and Frances developed a close relationship with Jack that they both believed would be lifelong.

Kristian had invited Jack along for a ride that morning. Due to the extreme weather conditions, it didn't last long. Both men went into the kitchen for morning coffee and found Frances and the children ensconced there again with Anna. They were in full fling, laughing, baking, and preparing for Christmas.

"It's a beautiful morning but bitterly cold," Jack told the women as he rubbed his hands together. He kissed Frances on the cheek before gazing into the pram and chucking the children under the chin. Frances thought it was lovely that he showed an interest in her children.

"So, did you enjoy your ride?" she asked, thinking how good it was going to be for Kristian to have Jack around. He had grown accustomed to male company during the war and lately had been stuck with a group of women.

Jack brought her back to the present. "I did enjoy my ride. It was certainly different. Those big guys compared to the horses on our farm…" He shook his head. "Well, they're ponies, in comparison. The power in these Hanoverians is incredible."

Kristian slapped him on the shoulders. "Ah, they were bred for sport, you see," he said. "Coffee, Jack, here. And if we're nice to Anna, she will produce some Christmas biscuits."

"Will I now?" said Anna as she disappeared to the pantry and returned with a tin. "I'm limiting you to two each, Kristian."

Frances put some on a plate and offered them around, but they were soon gone. It pleased her to see that Jack and Kristian were getting on so well, but why wouldn't they? They were both outdoor chaps, and their interest in farming and the outdoors would be a tremendous bond.

The babies were starting to grizzle, and she went to the pram to quieten them.

"Kristian, I could do with a little help," she said.

He nodded. "Another quick coffee with Jack first." He then raised his voice and searched the kitchen with his eyes. "More biscuits. Where's the old Harridan?" he shouted, grinning at Jack and Frances.

Anna's voice rang out. "I'm in the pantry. Watch your mouth."

Mueller winked at the others and shouted back. "What makes you think I meant you?"

"Because I'm the only old harridan in the house," came the reply, which made them all laugh. Anna exited the pantry, wiping her hands down her pinafore, and punched Mueller in the shoulder hard. "I don't think I've got time this year to make any more of your favourite biscuits," she sniffed. Frances turned to Jack and shook her head as Mueller wrapped his arms around Anna in a warm embrace.

"You have," he wheedled, "you'll find time for your favourite boy."

"Ah well, that's it, isn't it? I forgot to tell you that you have been replaced. You are no longer my favourite boy," she announced.

Mueller's hands dropped to his sides in disbelief. "I don't believe you. You could never replace me." Anna raised her eyebrows, forcing him to ask, "Who with?" as Jack and Frances chuckled away.

"Your boy, of course," said Anna. "Paul isn't rude to me."

"Not yet," said Mueller. "I still have to teach him that."

Anna gave a humph and pushed herself out of his embrace.

"You're a brave man, Kristian," said Jack. "I wouldn't dare approach our woman for a biscuit and certainly not a hug."

Frances held her breath, and Mueller laughed as Anna swung round and faced Jack. "Woman?" she questioned him, with a scowl that Frances thought might turn a lesser man to stone. She prayed that Mueller would put things right. She had seen that Anna was easily hurt by a thoughtless comment like the one Freya had recently made.

She held her breath when Mueller said, "She's not our woman, Jack." Frances's heart sank as she waited for Anna's comeback, but Mueller continued. "She's my favourite girl."

He picked her up and swung her around, and as he put her down, he deposited a sloppy kiss on her cheek.

Anna glanced at Mueller and caught Jack's gaze. "I don't recommend you treat your WOMAN like that, Herr Burton," she said, disappearing into the pantry for more biscuits as Mueller grinned at Jack and Frances.

"It's a shame we can't walk to you later," Frances told Jack.

"Much too cold for your little ones, Frances. It's bitterly cold out there. I don't think you would enjoy it; the snow will make it hard for you to walk it. Anyhow, while I'm here, you can make use of me. Give me a bottle, and I'll give you a hand."

"Really?" she asked. "Have you bottle-fed a baby before?"

"Nope, but it can't be hard, can it?" he replied.

"Ask Kristian, who seems to have disappeared. Boy or girl?" she asked him, wondering if he had a preference. She received a shrug and a smile in reply. She passed him Karin. "I think you're a lady's man," she said. Let's go into the lounge and find a seat with an arm and some cushions; it makes it much easier.

Jack gave Karin a broad smile as he lifted her towards the ceiling. In reply, he received a squeal and a giggle.

"You're a natural," said Frances. "Would you like children, Jack?"

"To be honest, I can't wait," he said.

* * *

"We'll drive to the Kohls at 2 p.m. Be ready and reasonably flour-free, please," Mueller told Frances that lunchtime. "By the way, I got a letter from Inga this morning, and there is one for you too."

"For me? Who's it from?" asked Frances.

Mueller laughed out loud. "How do I know? It's your letter," he replied.

"Well, what did Inga say?"

"She wishes us both a joyous Christmas and asks after us all, particularly our offspring. She says things are still pretty awful in Berlin, but people are acting communally with Christmas coming. I think she means sharing. That's a good thing, I think. She says things are better in the British than in the Russian sector. She has taken Johanne over there several times as chocolate is available if you're lucky." He pulled his fingers through his hair thoughtfully. "It seems things in the Russian sector are getting rather more spartan."

"So, are they staying in Berlin?" Frances asked.

"For the time being, I think."

"But they will be going to Russia?"

"Tell you what, Froggy, read the letter." He put his hand in his pocket and pulled out the folded paper.

"You don't mind me reading it then?" she asked.

"Why would I?"

"I don't know." She shrugged. "There may be private things in there."

Mueller shook his head. "There is nothing private between us, is there? Here." He passed Inga's letter. "And here is yours." He passed her a second envelope.

Watery winter sunshine reflected onto Kohl's drive as Mueller pulled up in front of the house. Before they were even out of the car, Sara came rushing from the front door, arms wide in anticipation of warm hugs. "Got something to tell you when we get inside," she announced to Frances as she got out of the car, leaving Mueller bent inside, grabbing hold of the carrycot.

"Tell me now," Frances wheedled.

"When we're inside. Come on, it's too damn cold to hang around. Let's get in by the fire."

Jack had appeared in the doorway. "Do you need a hand?" he called to Mueller.

Mueller shouted his reply, "I'm fine, thanks. Let's get inside. You'll freeze without a coat on. Where are the girls?"

"Inside already," Jack said, rubbing his hands together. "Let's get those little ones out of this weather."

The Kohl's woman was waiting in the hall to take the coats from them before returning to the kitchen. Frances had already made her way to the lounge, where she greeted Eva with a kiss on the cheek, noticing her colossal smile.

"Have you heard the news yet?" she asked.

"What? Tell me." Frances said.

"Don't you dare." Sara issued a warning to her mother from the doorway. "We'll wait for Kristian and Jack. Ah, here they are."

Sara walked into the lounge, followed by the menfolk,

including Sara's father, Gunter, who usually kept out of the way when Sara had friends call round.

"Come on then, spill the beans for these good folk," Gunter encouraged. "I've got things to do."

"Such as?" Eva questioned, throwing him a look.

"Shush, mother," said Sara. "Now, when everyone is ready, Jack and I have some news," Sara began.

Mueller interrupted, shouting, "Never," and received a thump from Sara,

"You should tell them, Jack; they might behave for you," she huffed.

"You must have guessed anyway, I'd have thought," Jack said, glancing at Frances and smiling.

Fed up with the wait, Sara made the announcement. "We're pregnant," she said.

Everyone was immediately up on their feet. Mueller grabbed Sara and pulled her into a bear hug, planting a kiss upon kiss on her face while she tried to fight him off. Frances hugged and kissed Sara's parents and, finally, Jack, who had looked on at the show of affection from the others with a huge smile. The hugs and laughter were cut short by the sound of crying babies.

"Oh no," said Frances. "If anything will put you off, babies, these two will with their howling."

"I'll sort the tykes," said Eva. "Where are the bottles?"

"Oh, I left them in the car," said Frances. "I'll fetch them."

Frances left the room searching for the bottles while Gunter opened one of his best bottles of port. She returned to find everyone with a glass in their hands apart from Eva who had a baby under each arm. Everyone was smiling and speaking at once, and Frances felt a warm glow wash over her. She passed a bottle to Eva, took Karin out of her arms, and immediately passed her along with the second bottle to Sara.

"Practice makes perfect," she said, kissing her cheek. "I can't wait to tell Freya your news. Should I let you or Eva tell her, though?" Frances asked.

"I'd like to tell her, I think," said Eva. "I'll call her later, and we can have a good old pre-Christmas chat."

Gunter crossed the room to Frances and passed her a large glass of port wine.

"I bet you can't wait to walk Sara up the aisle, can you, Gunter?" she asked.

"Aisle? No, no. I'm not involved."

"You're not walking your daughter up the aisle?" Frances questioned wide-eyed, and the rest of the group laughed.

She turned to Mueller. "What?" she asked.

"It's different here, Froggy. Something you didn't know, eh? Jack will walk Sara up the aisle."

"Really? So, you're not involved at all then?" she asked, turning to Gunter, who laughed heartily.

"I'm involved, all right, Frances, my dear. I will be paying the damn bill."

* * *

They left before the night drew in. It had started snowing again, and although they were literally only minutes away from Kohl's by car, Kristian was eager to get back into the warmth and relax for the night.

"I wonder what Anna's put together for dinner. I'm starving," he said as the car crackled up the drive. "Any clues this morning?"

"No, but everything she makes is good. I'm hopeful that our children will go down at a decent time. They've had a lot of stimulation. I was dreading them nodding off on the way home."

"Well, thankfully, they haven't. Do I get to know who your letter was from, by the way? Or is it from a secret admirer?"

"Oh, it was from Miriam, I forgot to say. I'm worried about

her, Kristian. She tells me she is involved with some organisation bringing war criminals to justice. She is still so full of hatred. It can't be healthy."

"Perhaps understandably, huh, if she has no support. You go and get yourself inside, and I'll bring these two in. We need time to talk and plan," he said, lightening the conversation.

"Talk and plan what?" she asked.

Mueller tapped the side of his nose conspiratorially. "Secret. I'll tell you later when these two are asleep."

She tapped hers back. "They won't say anything to anyone, so you needn't worry. Tell me now."

"Get inside, woman, before you freeze," he ordered. "Are these two having a bath? If they are, I'll take them straight upstairs."

"Yes, good idea, I'll go and run it."

Frances bumped straight into Freya in the hall. "Ah, there you are," I've been watching through the window. It's freezing out there by the looks of things," Freya remarked.

"It certainly is," said Frances. "Freya, I'm going to run a bath for these little ones."

"Can I help?" she asked.

"I was hoping you'd say that. You certainly can," she said. "I think Eva may call you later. She has some news?"

"What news?" Freya asked.

"I won't spoil things for Eva; she will want to tell you herself, but I would love some help getting the little ones down before dinner and then having a relaxing evening. Kristian's taken them upstairs."

✳ ✳ ✳

"You've been ages," Mueller said when she returned to the bedroom with two clean babies.

"We've been all of fifteen minutes," Frances replied, looking at her watch. "Will you help me with the bottles?"

Mueller nodded. "I've sent Mutts downstairs to sit with Pa. He doesn't seem quite himself lately. I need to have a chat with you about the wedding."

"I've told your mother you have plans, Kristian. She was worried you wouldn't keep it fun. Will you?"

"I promise. I'm an adult now," he said, unable to keep the grin from his face. "I'll go down and get the bottles. I need to see if we have any old clocks lying around?"

As the door closed, Frances lay back on the bed with her children beside her, wondering what on earth Mueller wanted with old clocks. When he returned minutes later, he found her leaning over the babies, sniffing them.

"What are you doing?" he asked.

"I just love the smell of them after they've had a bath. Come and have a sniff."

He joined her on the bed and passed her a bottle. He grabbed the nearest baby in his arms and gave it a tentative sniff. "See what you mean. Definitely better than usual." He stared down at the baby in his arms before asking, "Which one's this?" he pushed the teat of the bottle towards it, and the baby grabbed it greedily.

"Which one do you think it is?" Frances asked him.

"Well, it's got to be Karin or Paul," he replied. "Can't we fix something on them so we can tell the difference?"

"So, you can tell the difference you mean." Frances chuckled.

"Do you know what, Froggy?" Frances shook her head. "I can't believe Sar is pregnant and getting married. It seems two minutes ago that we were kids. We were never apart, you know."

"Are you jealous?" she asked him.

Mueller chewed his lip thoughtfully for a few moments. "Perhaps a bit," he said. "I like Jack, though he's a good sort. I like him a lot. I suppose Sar getting married is making me realise I'm getting old. Anyway, the wedding will be fun. I'm looking forward to it. Are you?"

"Once the ceremony is over and I can relax, yes," she said.

He looked long at her, holding her gaze thoughtfully.

"What?" she asked.

"You missed out on all of this, didn't you?" he said. "I didn't give you much choice, did I?" She gave him a questioning look. "About getting married, I mean," he said.

"You did have it all pretty well organised."

"I had to. I thought it best if I didn't give you a choice in the matter, you see. When you came up with the remark about whether it was necessary, I thought that was it. I was expecting you to refuse to go through with it."

"But I didn't, did I? And thank God I didn't." She reached up and laid her hand on his cheek. "I love you, Kristian Mueller. We have had a few trials of our own, haven't we? But we've fought through them, and I think we are stronger because of them."

Chapter 16

December 23rd 1946

Frances sat on the floor in the bedroom, surrounded by wrapping paper and presents. She kicked herself for leaving everything so late. She had no excuse; the presents had been bought on her last trip to Paris when Kristian had another little errand to run for Konrad. She was saving his office a fortune by having the house at Neuilly.

It had been an odd visit. The children had accompanied them. All the romance had been missing, and she wondered if it was due to the twinnies being there. In the past, when they visited, they had a devil-may-care holiday attitude. On this last visit, though, Paris appeared to her to be sad and dark, and even Kristian, who loved the city, said the only brightness was when the sun set. Perhaps on those earlier visits, the Parisians were still full of Joy de Vivre because the war was over, and they had their city back. Maybe now, reality had rubbed off. There were just too many reminders left from the occupation when Paris had been a fallen city.

But they were there. So, Kristian did a little sightseeing, and she did a great deal of shopping. What was the use of money if you couldn't enjoy it? She had mostly bought perfume as presents for Freya, Eva, and Sara, and if she had purchased a new dress for the wedding, so what? After the trials and tribulations of becoming a mother, she thought she deserved it and, thankfully, Kristian had agreed. She looked down at the floor, still strewn with presents. There was a food mixer for Anna, a scarf, and a new cap for Peter, and she had bought Kristian the latest Rolex watch.

How blessed they were. Despite all that she had been through, she was a wealthy young woman, and not just from money. The Muellers had also managed to hold on to the farm and were again starting to profit from it. This Christmas was one to be celebrated.

"Frances." That was Kristian's voice shouting from downstairs. She hadn't made a start on the wrapping. She had been too tied up in her memories and keeping an eye on Karin and Paul, whom she had propped up with pillows on the bed.

She ran to the bedroom door and called, "Up here," and he appeared at the bottom of the stairs.

"I'm going out with Jack to look for Christmas trees."

"Hey, Frances."

Frances recognised Jack's voice and called out, "See you in a bit, Jack?"

"Mutts said she is down here if you need any help," Mueller shouted again.

"All right. She can't come up. I'm wrapping presents. I'm okay; I can manage."

* * *

"Christmas Eve Froggy. Wake up."

Frances yawned and stretched before opening her eyes to find Mueller fully dressed, carrying a tray with toast and two steaming cups of coffee.

"I do believe we have had a good night's sleep," he said. "Up just the once. I can cope with that, and they're still sleeping." He walked across the room and drew back the curtains, letting in the beginning of the day.

Frances groaned. "You're not normal. You don't need sleep." She pulled the covers over her shoulders. "You don't feel the cold either." She turned over and looked towards the French door. "Ice on the inside again," she said with a frown.

"We'll get the fires going soon. Come on, drink your coffee while it's hot. Mutti said she is happy to take the children for a couple of hours if you want a Christmas Eve ride."

"Really? I'd love that." She sat up in bed and immediately regretted it as the cold hit her warm flesh. "My God. What temperature is it?"

"Warmer today. It's only minus nine," Mueller said, giving her that smile that warmed her right through, making her forget about the cold. "Come on, Froggy, up you get. That's a balmy heat compared with the other day. Come on, we've got lots to do. We've got the tree to decorate and the presents to open later."

Frances chuckled at Mueller's enthusiasm. Just a year ago, at a very different time, Anna told her how much he loved Christmas.

"Does Mutti want me to feed these monkeys first, do you think?" she asked.

"Tell you what, I'll go and get a couple of bottles while you wake them up and get dressed. Deal?"

"Deal but pass my clothes before you go. I'm going to get dressed in bed."

Mueller grabbed her clothes from the day before and flung them on her. "Get going, Froggy, or there will be consequences."

"Such as? she asked.

"No presents for you."

"You've got me presents?" she squealed.

"That very much depends on how soon you get your arse out of that bed and get it down to the stables."

Frances felt the icy kiss of a freezing Christmas Eve morning on her face and looked over her shoulder as she galloped across Mueller land. Even though he had given her a good start, Kristian was gaining on her. She was riding Majesty, and Kristian was exercising one of Peter's horses, Hawk, who hadn't been out for an age due to Peter not having the time, or so he said.

She knew Peter was feeling under the weather and wondered if she should mention it to Kristian when they were home. She decided that Christmas Eve was not the right time and pushed it to the back of her mind as he galloped his horse past her. He reined Hawk in. She watched the warm air of the horse's breath hit the cold air of the Winter's morning and materialise like magic as she reined in Majesty beside him.

"Well-ridden, Froggy," he said with a huge grin. "I'm proud of you."

She smiled back at him. "Race you back?" she asked.

"No, best not get them all sweated up a second time. Come and ride beside me and tell me if you've ever had a better start to a Christmas Eve morning than this." They walked the horses back side by side at a steady pace. "Well?" he asked. "Best ever?"

"How can it not be? Yes, best ever."

"So, coffee and breakfast, Christmas tree, lunch, church this evening, and my favourite, Christmas Eve dinner."

CHAPTER 17

Frances thought it had been the best Christmas Eve ever as she looked around the table and listened to the light-hearted conversation going on between everyone. The day had been perfect. Kristian and she had decorated the Christmas tree with some help from Freya, who had her ideas about what should go where.

Frances had to admit that Freya's input had perfected the tree, which now stood in the corner of the lounge and reached almost to the ceiling. It was now covered in glass baubles and lights resembling mini lanterns and large acorns. There had been a disappointment when Peter first turned on the power as none of the lights came on, but once the bulbs had all been tightened, on they came.

The twinnies had been mesmerised by them for some time, which had been a bonus and gave them all time to open their presents. And now it was getting on for midnight, and Christmas Eve would soon become Christmas Day.

Frances looked down at her hand yet again. At the ring Kristian had given her. He'd waited until everyone had opened their presents that afternoon, and then he had suggested that he and she make the coffee and start the washing up to give Anna a break. Once they were alone in the kitchen, he had taken her in his arms and told her he had something for her.

"But you have already given me presents," she said, referring to the large bottle of Balenciaga perfume, together with a fine pair of leather riding gloves and a silk scarf that he had given her earlier.

"I've something else to give you. I can't leave it at that. You've been so generous to everyone, Froggy."

She shrugged. "I owe your entire family for the love they've shown me, Kristian. I feel I truly have a family again."

He put his arms around her and kissed her forehead. "I should have given you this a long time ago," he said, holding a leather ring box in his hand. You missed out on all the romance, Froggy, and I'm sorry for that."

She opened the box and inside was a simple golden wedding band. Mueller took the ring and slipped it on the ring finger of her right hand. "For better or worse, Froggy, you're stuck with me. I hope people will see you as an honest woman now."

"You mean they didn't before?"

"I've noticed a few raised eyebrows in town at the lack of a ring," he told her.

"Really?" she said, and he laughed at the worried look on her face.

"Oh, you," she chastised. "How on earth did you get the size right?" She stretched out her hand and looked at the ring again.

"A piece of cotton, a pen, and you, asleep. Anyway, I haven't finished yet." His hand delved into his pocket, drawing out another ring box. Inside was a three-stone ring with a beautiful pale sapphire between two large cushion-cut diamonds. On the ring's shank, on each side of the central stones, was another cushion diamond and four smaller round diamonds. She looked at the ring and was speechless.

"You haven't said anything," Mueller said worriedly. "If I've got it wrong, we can change it, I'm sure." She'd shook her head. Struggling to speak from the emotion she felt inside, she swallowed several times.

"It's perfect," she muttered. Her eyes had filled with tears. "It's perfect, Kristian." She held out her hand. "Will you put it on for me?"

Since then, she hadn't been able to take her eyes off it for more than a few moments, and she made sure everyone else, family and friends, saw it, too, by sticking it under their noses and exclaiming, "Look!" with a broad smile on her face.

* * *

When the Muellers got to their bedrooms, it was almost 2 a.m.; the Kohls had left less than half an hour before.

Frances threw herself on the bed, fully clothed. "I'm shattered, and in four hours, we'll be up again, feeding these two," she said through a yawn, waving her arms towards the cot. Mueller threw himself down beside her.

"It's been a good day, though, hasn't it?"

"The best," she exclaimed. "I'm just worried we have another one to get through tomorrow. What time are we to be at the Kohls?"

"Not until early evening, so we can hopefully catch up with a snooze before we go. I'm looking forward to meeting Jack's brother and his friend."

"Bernie," said Frances.

"Yes, Bernie."

"Sar says he's a weasel," said Frances and Mueller screwed up his face.

"What's that supposed to mean?" he asked.

"I'm not sure, but Sar said I would know when I meet him. She certainly isn't too keen on him."

"Well, we'll see, eh? It's good that they will be here in a

couple of days for the Polterabend. Let's get some shut-eye, Frau Mueller.

* * *

Christmas day was for the families to be together in the evening, and the Muellers had been invited to dine with the Kohls. Anna was asked to join them, too. It had been Sara's idea, as Anna had been around for as long as she could remember, and she knew how fond the Muellers were of her. "If anyone deserves a day off, it's Anna," Sara had said to her parents. "At the end of the day, Anna is part of the Mueller family, and they had to agree.

Anna was very moved by the invitation but told Frances she wasn't sure she would accept it.

"Why ever not?" Frances had asked her.

"I won't know what to say," she replied.

"You don't usually have a problem with that, now do you?" Frances asked.

"But I'll be in company," she complained.

Frances took her hand and kissed her cheek. "Just be yourself, you silly old goose. We all love you. Of course you're coming."

Anna went along, and for the first part of the evening, she kept an eye on the babies. However, as she was plied with wine and relaxed, she was happy to join the conversation and provided them with many laughs.

When Mueller went to the kitchen for tea and toast the following morning, there was no Anna. They had dropped her at her cottage just down the drive to Schonen Felder at approaching midnight.

He checked his watch; it was almost eight-thirty a.m. She was an hour late, and he wondered if he should be worried. This was the first time he could remember Anna being late, ever. He looked out the window and was relieved to see her scurrying up the path towards the kitchen door.

He thought he would give her a turn, so he left the kitchen and waited until she entered the pantry to hang up her coat. Then he crept back in, grabbing her around the waist and shouting, "Where the hell have you been?"

He shouldn't have been surprised when Anna gave a loud scream.

Alarmed, the rest of the household ran to the kitchen to find Mueller being beaten with a large wooden spoon and Anna with tears coursing down her face from the fright he'd given her. It took a while to calm her, and Mueller tried to be apologetic through his laughter.

"You can stay in the kitchen for the rest of the day," Anna told him.

"But it's still Christmas, Anna," he argued, "and I need to be with my family."

"You can bring the family in here and have a good boxing morning cleaning the kitchen. If this is what happens when I am late for work, I will never be late again. I thought the devil had got me." She struck him again with the spoon. "And maybe he had," she said.

* * *

On December 27th, Jack's brother, Tom, arrived mid-morning, in plenty of time for the Polterabend. Frances couldn't get over the fact that he looked just like a slightly older version of Jack. Bernie the Weasel didn't show up and sent a message saying he'd met up with a real doll on the journey and would see them at the wedding. He told them he was bringing the doll and hoped it would be all right. The Mueller family had a day of rest, for which everyone was thankful.

Peter and Freya had agreed to host the Polterabend at

Schonen Felder on the afternoon of December 28th. The party was small, not one for fuss; Sara asked that it should be that way. There was just the Kohls, the Muellers, Jack and Tom, and the staff who worked for the two families.

Anna had liaised with the Kohl's woman, and they had a good clear out of their kitchens. They filled a large box with stoneware and porcelain kitchenware that had seen better times. The other staff members, some with family members, also arrived with a few items to smash.

The Polterabend was a merry affair that took place in the garden behind the kitchen. Anna had made a large bowl of hot punch to fight off the freezing air of the December afternoon, and Mueller had been out earlier with a shovel and a pot of salt and had removed most of the snow from the area just outside the kitchen. Once everyone had a glass of punch, Peter made a toast to the happiness and long life of Jack and Sara. There was a cheer followed by the breaking of the kitchenware. It was thrown onto the paved floor with gusto and a great deal of laughter and shouting.

Tom stood beside Frances, unsure what to make of the event and asked her what a Polterabend was and how it came about.

"Do you know, Tom, I haven't got a clue. Just another of the many traditions. Come on, let's find Kristian and ask him."

They found Kristian inside the kitchen with Jack. Each of them had one twin in their arms. "You're a natural," said Tom, laughing at his brother.

"I told him that yesterday," said Frances. "Where's Sar?"

"Probably smashing a few pieces of pottery if I know her." Mueller grinned. "Anyway, why aren't you joining in, Froggy?

"Tom asked me what the Polterabend was all about, and since I didn't have a clue, we came to find you."

"It's to scare off evil spirits that might be planning to ruin things for Sar and Jack," Mueller informed them. We can't have any of that, now, can we?"

"If the racket's anything to go by, all evil spirits in the neighbourhood will be long gone," said Tom.

"Surely. Jack, you should be outside with his intended, shouldn't you?" Frances remarked.

"Oh, I was, but I heard crying. I came back inside, and Kristian was already here, so I thought I'd give him a hand."

"Well done, both of you," smiled Frances. "So, Tom and I will go back out and keep Sar company. Is that all right?"

"Fine for a few minutes," Mueller said, "but could you come back in and take over while I introduce Jack to Alf and a couple of the other men? You're welcome to join us, Tom," Mueller said.

"After we've had another glass of punch, though, eh, Tom?" said Frances. She grabbed a couple of glasses, passed one to Tom, and took his arm. "Come on," she said, "let's smash a few things up."

They went back into the yard and, not beating about the bush, Frances asked, "So, how do you feel about your young brother flying the coup and coming to live in an occupied country, Tom?"

Tom raised his eyebrows and gave some thought to her question. "I guess, first off, I'm relieved that Jack survived the war. I felt guilty when he left home for the forces. I was exempted, you see, because I was a farmer. My Daddy would never have managed without my help. But seeing my kid brother go to war was hard."

Frances questioned him further. "And?"

"And I'm real glad he's met Sara, who is a great girl. Is that what you wanted to hear?"

"Tis." Frances smiled. "Come on, or there won't be anything left to smash."

The extreme cold meant the Polterabend lasted only about an hour, accompanied by a couple of glasses of punch. By four fifteen, Sara and Jack each had a broom to sweep up the broken crockery. Tom grabbed a broom to help until Freya took it from him. She did her best to explain in English.

"Unlucky Tom. It's job of errr das hochzeitspaar to—" She made a sweeping movement with her arms.

Tom looked at Frances for help. "Freya says the bride and groom must sweep up the mess, Tom," she explained.

Freya nodded. "Polterabend is to practice working together."

Chapter 18

December 29, 1946

On the morning of December 29th, nervous tension was present in the Mueller and Kohl residences. In the Kohl residence, Sara had risen early, unable to sleep, convinced she had forgotten to do something essential but unable to remember what it was.

"For goodness' sake, Sara, you will be the death of me," Eva complained. "Just calm down. If you carry on like this, we will all be at each other's throats by this afternoon. "Put your feet up in your room for a couple of hours, and do us all a favour, please."

Eva, usually calm, relaxed, and sensible, also reacted by accusing Gunter of doing little to help with the wedding preparations.

"My God," Gunter responded, "thank goodness this wedding will soon be over." He then shut himself inside his office.

Tempers were also frayed in the Mueller household. Jack and his brother Tom had stayed over the previous night, as it was, of course, unlucky for the groom to see the bride the night before the wedding. Peter, not at all his usual self, complained to Freya that Jack stayed over when he and Sara were already married. He

170

refused to enter the party spirit that the others had embraced that evening and was accused by Freya of being a killjoy. He went to bed, and by midmorning the next day, he still hadn't been seen other than by Freya.

"And he's still up there as miserable as sin, and I could have done with a lie in," Freya complained to Anna.

Frances had turned in by midnight and had drunk more wine than was good for her. She had a restless night sweating and tossing and turning, and when she finally dosed off, she was woken two or three hours later by Mueller, Jack, and his brother Tom, making what they thought in their inebriated state was a quiet ascent of the stairs. When Mueller finally bumped his way through the door, she was wide awake and suffering from a thumping headache.

"You could have been a little quieter," she complained in hushed tones.

"We were quiet, weren't we? I thought we were very quiet, Froggy." Mueller replied in not-so-hushed tones as he threw his clothes off into a heap on the floor, clambered into bed, and lay down with a sigh.

"Well, you weren't listening to you, were you?" Frances snapped. There was no reply other than a gentle snoring. Frances satisfied herself by kicking him.

Things were no better when the twins woke up at six, demanding to be fed. Frances still had a headache, and Mueller managed to stay asleep during the furore two hungry children were making. She took herself downstairs and prepared a couple of bottles, desperately hoping the babies would go back to sleep after a feed. While she was up, she rummaged around in the medical cabinet in the kitchen, relieved to find some aspirin, which she took with a large glass of water, and then returned to the bedroom, angry with herself for not showing restraint with the amount of wine she had consumed the night before. She was somewhat surprised when she returned to the bedroom to find Mueller up and changing Karin's nappy.

"How are you feeling?" he asked.

"Not brilliant," she admitted. "What about you? I didn't expect to find you up."

"Not too bad. I had a good drink of water and took some aspirin before bed last night. We all did, in fact. Important day today, Froggy. I'm excited."

"Good for you," she muttered as she picked up Paul and gave Mueller the other bottle.

"Hey, you'll be fine after a couple of more hours."

"I hope so. Thank goodness the service isn't until late afternoon. I wonder how Sar is feeling this morning. I hope Jack and Tom had a good sleep. If they're under par, we will get the blame.

They managed to get another couple of hours of sleep after feeding the twins, and Jack and Tom joined them for breakfast at 9 a.m., feeling reasonably well-rested. Anna produced plenty of fresh bread, butter, and slices of sausage.

"Has Pa already eaten? Mueller asked her when she brought in two steaming pots of coffee.

"I haven't seen hide nor hair of him," Anna said.

"Ah, he'll be out with the horses or chatting to Alf," said Mueller.

"Your mother says he's still in bed," Anna informed him.

"Unusual," Mueller remarked.

Frances looked away. She couldn't meet his eyes, knowing that she should tell him Peter had told her he was tired weeks ago. How could she bring it up on the day of Sara's wedding? And anyway, she had promised Peter she would keep it to herself.

"Jack, is there anything you'd like to do this morning? A bracing walk round the Mueller estate or a drive into town?" Mueller suggested.

"A brisk walk would do us good eh, Tom?" he said turning to his brother.

"Your day, you say, Bro," Tom replied.

* * *

It was almost 2.30 p.m., and Frances was nowhere near ready to leave for the wedding ceremony. She had bathed, changed her underclothes, and put the twins into their Sunday best, hopefully not too soon, and she had passed them to Anna for the day. That was as far as she'd got. She had managed to grab an hour's rest late morning, while the men were out for a walk and the children had another nap, but instead of giving her the energy burst she expected, she felt even more tired and was lounging on the bed when she heard male laughter downstairs.

Seconds later, the door to the bedroom burst open, framing Mueller. He was already changed into a dark blue suit with a white shirt and blue tie. Frances's heart lurched as always, and she thought how handsome he looked. He raised his eyebrows when he saw her.

"Not ready yet, Froggy? We can't make Jack late for his own wedding." She grunted. "Are you all right?" he asked.

She sighed. "Tired. I just wish I hadn't stayed up last night."

"Your choice. You didn't have to stay up and flap your eyelids at Tom all night, did you?"

"I didn't flap my eyelids at Tom. We were talking about Sar being pregnant. And Tom's disappointed he won't get to know his niece or nephew well, and he is worried his parents will miss out too. It's a shame." Mueller raised his eyebrows and gave her a questioning look. She repeated, "I did not flap my eyelids."

"You Jolly well did, you little flirt," he replied.

"Anyway, I like Tom," she said.

"I like Tom too, Froggy, but I don't bat my eyelids and flirt

173

with him. I would spank you for your flirtatious behaviour if we had time."

"You wouldn't." She giggled.

"Wouldn't I?" He looked at his watch. "Maybe I can make time." He took a step towards her, and she shot across the bed to the other side, but Mueller was faster. He grabbed her round the waist, sat on the bed, and put her across his knee while she shrieked with laughter, all tiredness forgotten. "Hmm, now let's see how many times should I spank you, huh? One for not being ready, two for staying up late, three for not knowing your alcohol limits, and several more for your appalling flirtatiousness." She struggled against him, trying to sit up, but he held her fast.

"Come on, let me go now, Kristian. I really need to get ready," she said, trying to control her laughter.

He bent forward, swept her hair aside and kissed the back of her neck, watching the shudder run through her body and hearing the little sigh escape her lips. She pushed her head forward in an invitation for him to do it again, which he did, and then followed up with a hard slap onto her buttocks.

"Ouch! That damn well hurt," she said as she jumped to her feet. Mueller stood, too, wrapped his arms around her, and kissed her on the cheek.

"Now get ready. A nervous man is being kept waiting, Froggy. The sooner we get to the church, the better."

"Don't know why Jack is nervous when he's already married anyway," Frances chimed.

"I don't mean Jack. I mean me," he said.

Chapter 19

Frances's eyes were fixed on the church door from the far end of the balcony. She was waiting for Sara and Jack to appear. The church pianist was seated in the church knave, where she could watch for her signal to play the Pachelbel Canon. She had given Sara and Jack orders to wait at least for a count of eight before entering the church. By that time, if everything went as planned, the violin would have joined the piano in the opening bars.

"Now, the piece lasts about 4 minutes," she told them both, "so you do not have to rush up the aisle. In fact, you could wait a minute or so before even entering the church."

She was waiting now for the doors to open. All the guests were seated, and she had a clear view of the Muellers in the pew behind Sara's parents and Tom. Kristian looked up at the balcony every so often, making eye contact with her and causing her to smile.

She hadn't lied when she told Sara that playing for people you know is more nerve-wracking than for an entire concert hall of people you don't know. As she breathed in the church's scent of old wood, stone, and a hint of incense, she wished the doors would hurry up and open so she could get on with the music.

There was a loud clunk of metal as the church doors were pushed open from the outside, framing Sara and Jack. The sight of them both, he in his uniform and Sara in her wedding dress, took her breath away.

She signalled the pianist to begin, and the church resounded to the opening bars of Pachelbel's Canon as the congregation turned to watch Sara and Jack slowly walk to their place at the front of the church, where the pastor was waiting and where the vows would be made.

From the back of the church, Sara couldn't resist raising her eyes to the balcony and giving Frances an enormous grin, which she managed to return despite playing.

Frances sat during the vows, and her mind wandered. She imagined walking up the aisle on Kristian's arm and the vows they'd have made to one another if things had been different. But if things had been different, they wouldn't have met, and she'd have remained married to Steven.

She wondered about Kristian. Who would he be with? Sophie Heyne, maybe Meena, or even Inga. The world had been turned upside down, and she, a French/ English girl, was married to a German, and Sara, a German girl, was marrying an American, and all because of a war that none of them wanted. It was all preposterous and made her wonder whether anyone had any say in how their life would pan out or whether everything was preordained.

The pastor coughed to attract her attention. She grabbed her violin and stood up to play the Schubert's Ave Maria while the register was signed. Kristian caught her eye; he knew she hadn't been concentrating.

Following the ceremony, once Jack and Sara had walked back down the church aisle, Frances shot to the pew where the Mueller family was sitting.

"How are your nerves now?" she asked Mueller, giving him a wide smile.

"Better, thank you," he replied, returning her smile with a grin. "You played beautifully, Froggy. We were all so proud of you. Are you feeling better now?"

"Yes, yes. But doesn't Sar look beautiful? That dress is just —" Lost for words, she shrugged. "Stunning. Sar looks stunning."

Peter Mueller touched her on the arm, and she turned to him. "Well played, Frances," he said. "We are all proud of you. The choice of music was just right."

"Do you really think so? Not too sombre?" she asked.

"Not at all sombre. I loved the last piece."

"The Elgar. Yes, it's lovely." She glanced at the rest of the company making their way out of the church. "We should move out to the porchway and congratulate the happy couple." She looked around for Kristian, who had disappeared. "Where's Kristian?"

"Already gone. There are people he will want to speak to, I suppose," Peter replied. "You get going and join him, and I will try and prise Freya away from all of these people she hasn't seen for a while."

"Good luck with that," Frances said, smiling at him. She then made her way down the aisle to the large porchway where most people had gathered to give their congratulations to Sara and Jack.

Frances saw Kristian was deep in conversation with three women, one of whom was very fair and reminded her of Inga Werner. She was unsure whether she should join him, and had just decided to when a hand was laid on her shoulder. Turning, she expected to see someone she knew and was confronted by a small man with ginger hair and pale eyes. She'd never seen him before but guessed who he was even before he introduced himself.

"Bernie Schneider," he said, taking her hand, kissing it, and not letting go. "Doll, that was some playing," he said, sidling up to her so close that she could feel his breath on her face. "How about we get together later and make some music of our own? If you're staying for the party, that is. And if you're not," he continued, "I could come with you wherever you're going, and we could make a night of it."

Frances pulled her hand from his and blinked at him. "Excuse me. I need to find my husband," she said, walking away toward Kristian, who was still talking to the three women. Before she reached him, however, she caught Sara's eye and gave her a horrified, wide-eyed look. Sara was immediately at her side. "I've just met the weasel," Frances said, collapsing with laughter. "Someone should tell him he needs to work on his chat line."

Sara joined in with her laughter. "Did he make a few suggestions?"

"Yes, he blooming well did."

"He did me, too, the first time I met him. Even after I was introduced to him by Jack as his intended."

"My God, he must be desperate," giggled Frances.

"That wasn't very nice, Froggy," Sara said, holding Frances's gaze and looking hurt. She struggled to contain her laughter as Frances looked so horrified.

"Oh, Sar, I didn't mean it like that. I'm so sorry. What a dreadful thing to say and today of all days."

Sara let go of her laughter and shrieked, drawing a great deal of attention. "I know exactly what you meant. Come on, let's find Jack and Kristian."

"I know where Kristian is. He's with a group of women. He's been talking to them for ages."

"Old school friends, nothing to worry about, apart from maybe one of them."

"The blond?" Frances asked.

"Look, you do not need to worry. You're stuck with Kristian; you know you are. Anyway, I haven't thanked you for the music. I'm tone-deaf, as you know, but even I thought it was beautiful." She hugged Frances.

"And I haven't told you how lovely you look," Frances returned.

Sara leaned in conspiratorially and said, "I'd prefer to be wearing a pair of jodhpurs."

"I know you would," Frances smiled. "You look lovely in those, too. I haven't told you how nervous Kristian has been leading up to today, have I?"

Sara pushed her arm through Frances's. "You can tell me now while we round up him and Jack. I suppose we should all stay together. I suspect someone will try to organise us soon for some photographs."

"First, tell me how on earth Bernie became a friend of Tom and Jack."

"It's just bad luck, I think," laughed Sara. I think he was the kid next door, and being their closest neighbour, I think it just happened, and they were stuck with him. The parents are all really close, too. Do you think there's another side to him?"

"Yes, probably a worse one," said Frances.

Someone did organise them, and photographs were taken first of the bride and groom, then of the bride and groom with their best friends. In this case, Tom and Kristian. Frances heard Bernie complaining that he should have been in the photograph, as he had been Jack's friend for many years, whereas Jack's friendship with Kristian was only recent. She took it upon herself to explain that Kristian was in the photograph as Sara's greatest friend and that the bride and groom could have their best friend in attendance, regardless of whether they were male or female.

"What! He's the bloody matron of honour then, is he?" he said, laughing at his own joke.

"Kristian is Sara's greatest and best friend, and I wouldn't do or say anything that might upset either of them. I certainly wouldn't refer to Kristian as the matron of honour. As his wife, I can tell you he wouldn't laugh."

"In effect, that's what he is, isn't he? What are you doing with him, doll? He's a bloody kraut and a loser."

Frances was relieved when the photographer's voice asked, "Can we have a shot of everyone together, please?"

Everyone moved just outside the church for the picture to be taken, and Frances joined Kristian, standing just to the left of Sara. Bernie managed to find a place in front of them, completely shielding Frances, as he intended. Just as the photograph was to be taken, he called out, "Hang on, there's a girl we need to get to the front.

The photographer drew Frances to the front line next to Bernie and said, "That's better. We don't want anyone hiding." Just as the photograph was taken, Bernie pulled Frances in close. She stamped on his foot and searched for Kristian, who laughed when she told him what had happened. After that, several more photographs of Sara and Jack with their friends were taken, and Frances ensured she stayed close to Kristian and Sara throughout.

* * *

Once the photographing had finished, and friends and neighbours had caught up with one another, it was almost six p.m. The eighty or so guests gathered at the hotel entrance, where Gunter Kohl addressed the wedding party.

"Good friends," shouted out Gunter. "Let's get inside to the warmth and enjoy our meal."

It was time to sit and enjoy the traditional wedding soup: chicken broth with noodles, pieces of chicken meat, and Eierstich. This secret ingredient was made from butter, eggs, herbs, and spices, all cooked together. Glasses were filled with good German wine, but before the meal began, Gunter called on everyone to stand, apart from Sara and Jack. All eyes turned onto the couple.

"Let us now raise our glasses to the young couple and wish them a long life full of love," said Gunter; following these words, he raised his glass and shouted, "Zum Wohl."

"Zum Wohl," everyone replied.

Frances and Kristian were at the top table, along with the Kohls and Tom and Jack. Frances was relieved to be there, as she felt safe for the time being from Bernie's attentions and intentions. The meal consisted of various meats and vegetables, followed by numerous and a wide variety of sweet dishes. The eating time was interspersed with speeches and one or two stories about Jack and Sara. Frances was amused and impressed that everyone was entering into the storytelling, which was utterly ad-libbed. This encouraged Tom to abandon his written speech and speak from the heart about his younger brother. His German wasn't good, but if he got stuck, Jack jumped in to help him. They stood side by side, two peas in a pod, Frances thought. They are two good men. Both were tall, well-built, and handsome. They had a host of anecdotes about their youthful adventures, which kept everyone amused, and Frances was touched by how close the brothers were.

Mueller didn't have a written speech to do away with; he fully intended to speak from his heart when he began talking about his relationship with Sara. He spoke of the times they shared as children. How Sara had had a knack for getting him into trouble, "Particularly with the parents, both mine and hers. It was more me that got up to the idiotic things," he said, "Sara just made the suggestions, and stupidly I did as I was told."

"We want to know what you were told to do," someone shouted, and a few more voices joined in. "Come on, Kristian, spill the beans. Tell us what you got up to?"

Mueller glanced at Sara. "Should I?" he asked. She was

laughing, and he thought how beautiful she looked and how wonderfully happy she was. He raised his eyebrows in question, and she nodded. "I won't bore you with them all," he said, "but there are three that jump to mind. Like the time, Sar bet I couldn't stand in the lake in the middle of Winter, starkers."

There were whoops of laughter, and someone shouted and asked Mueller if he still had a John Thomas.

"I can vouch for the fact that he has," Frances shouted back, and there was more laughter. Mueller bent down and planted a kiss on Frances's head.

"Thank you, sweetheart," he said before continuing. "Then there was the time during one Hexennacht. Somehow, we managed to lose the parents and find the fireworks. Sar thought it would be a good idea if we helped ourselves to a few and had a display all our own. We tore open the fireworks and tipped out the powder. She had matches in her pocket. Of course, she did. It wasn't unusual as often she would turn up with a couple of Gunter's cigarettes, and one time, I remember cigars. We both thought it would be fun to light the powder, but Sar encouraged me to do it. I was given the matches and—" He turned to Sara.

"Do you want to tell them?" he asked. Sara was laughing so much she was unable to speak and mutely shook her head. "I lit the powder all right and lost my bloody eyebrows and eyelashes in the explosion. Mueller said. "I think we both got a good spanking for that, didn't we?" Sara managed to nod through her laughter, and everyone else joined in. Mueller waited for people to quieten before he carried on.

"You see, this continued into adulthood. She'd always have some say as to who I should and shouldn't be dating. And what I should and shouldn't be doing. I think, Sar, you know me better than I know myself." He held Sara's gaze for a few moments, and for that time, the laughter left them both.

"I wasn't in a good place after the war, it has to be said. Like many men, not just German, I didn't know myself anymore. I didn't like myself and lashed out. I lashed out at Sara. She could have walked away. I'd have deserved that, but she didn't. She gave me a bollocking and told me what I needed to hear." Mueller chewed on his lip thoughtfully before giving a sniff and carrying on. "A couple of days after I returned, Sar encouraged me to break into the British Officers Club in Bonn." There was a shriek from Freya, which brought forth a great deal of laughter. "Don't worry, Mutts, I didn't get shot," Mueller shouted above the laughter.

"But you could have done," Freya said with a scowl.

Mueller smiled at her and nodded. "But I didn't, did I? I met Jack for the first time that night. There was this big Yank in uniform, and I thought I'd had it. He and Sara dragged me through an upstairs window. The reasoning behind this madness was that I should profess my undying love to this beautiful woman sitting next to me." He laid his hand on Frances's shoulder, and she tilted her head and smiled at him. "She had other ideas and flew the coup. It took me another four or five months to track her down and talk her into coming home. During those months, Sara was my rock. She was there for me whenever I needed her, like she was when I lost my sister.

"She's always been there to rub balm into my wounds, whether those wounds were accidental or, which was more often the case, self-inflicted. Sar, you've been my rock and best friend forever and always will be. Come here." Sara stood and Mueller took her in his arms. "I bloody well love you," he said as they hugged one- another.

The two clung to each other for some time until Mueller let her go and turned to Jack. "You'd better make her happy." He told him as the room continued its applause.

"That was beautiful, Kristian," Frances said as he sat back down.

Chapter 20

Frances was in a rush to get back to the wedding party from the Ladies' room. Whatever Kristian was going to get up to was going to happen now, and she was determined to be part of it. After she had washed her hands, she took a brief look in the mirror, reapplied a little lipstick, and left, bumping straight into Bernie.

"Are you lurking?" she asked him with a frown.

"Might be," he returned.

"You know most men would be embarrassed if a woman asked them that. You don't appear to have any shame at all."

"Well, most men aren't me, doll. I'm on a mission, see."

Intrigued, Frances had to ask, "A mission? What mission would that be?"

"To save you from the kraut you're married to."

"You want to save me from my husband?" She struggled not to laugh. "I must tell you that I don't want to be saved from him."

Bernie shook his head sadly.

"What?" she asked.

"You must know, surely," he replied. "Perhaps not; maybe you're too cute to realise."

"Bernie, stop pissing about and just tell me what it is that I'm supposed to know, will you?"

"It's probably not so obvious to you or Jack, but everyone else knows."

Frances shrugged.

"They're screwing. Your old man and the piece that poor old Jack has just married."

"Sara?" Frances collapsed into laughter. "Did you listen to my husband's speech, Bernie?"

"I sure did."

"Then you'll know that they have been best friends for years. They grew up together."

"Exactly, doll. They grew up. Experimented and—"

"Oh, I'm absolutely sure they did that. We have all laughed about it together."

"Well, there you go," said Bernie. "Their feelings in that room were clear to everyone."

"Exactly that. It was clear that they have a great love for one another that goes back to their childhood, and Bernie, I have no problem at all with that." Frances snapped despite trying not to.

"See, it's getting to you. You know I'm right."

"You're what's getting to me, Bernie. I don't believe you've ever loved anyone other than yourself. It's not always about sex, you know. I have a friend, Miriam, who I really love, and Sara, for that matter. And don't you dare go putting ideas into people's minds with your nasty, sordid gossip. And especially, you keep away from Jack, or I will fucking well kill you!" And with that, she turned and walked away.

"Hey, doll, that's some temper you've got," Bernie shouted after her. She stopped in her tracks but didn't turn around.

"That's not temper, Bernie. That's love."

* * *

"Ah, there you are," Frances said with relief.

Kristian broke off his conversation with the friends he was talking to, took her by the arm, and led her out of earshot to the corner of the room.

"Where have you been?" he asked. "You've been gone ages."

"Bernie," she said with a grimace. "He is an absolute arse, you know."

"It hasn't gone without notice. Has he been annoying you? Because if he has, I'll sort the little bastard out."

"I don't think he can be anything other than annoying," said Frances. "Anyway, what are you up to?"

"We up to," Mueller corrected her. "Come on, we have to go and find Gerda."

"Who the hell is Gerda?"

"She's on the desk. I've left the clocks with her, and she's agreed to let us into Sara and Jack's room. Come on, we don't want to be gone too long; we need time to kidnap Sar." He strode off toward the desk, and Frances followed him, shaking her head.

The woman, Gerda, passed Mueller his bag of clocks that he'd left with her at the reception desk. She agreed to let Mueller and Frances into Jack and Sara's room but insisted upon accompanying them. Once in the room, Mueller set each alarm clock to go off at different times, roughly every hour from 2:00 a.m.

"Now we have to hide them," he said, grinning at Frances and Gerda. Both women started to chuckle.

"Why don't we make an apple pie bed too?" Frances suggested.

"Good idea," Mueller agreed. "You girls sort out the bed, and I'll hide the clocks."

Less than five minutes later, they left the room, and Frances and Mueller returned to the reception party, and Gerda returned to her desk with a smile.

"Come on, tell me where you hid the clocks. I saw you put one in the bedside table drawer and another under the bed; what about the other three?" Frances asked.

"One behind the toilet, one inside that big vase, and another inside the wardrobe pushed to the back on the shelf."

"You are a dreadful man," Frances stated.

"Says the woman who suggested the apple pie bed," Mueller returned. "Come on, or we'll miss Sar and Jack's first dance."

When they returned to the reception, the tables and chairs had been moved to the sides of the room, leaving a good-sized dance floor for everyone to enjoy. The small band was in place, tuning up, and Sara made her way across the room to them.

"Where have you two been?" she asked.

"Nowhere," Mueller told her.

"Fibber," she exclaimed. "Honestly, you two, you can't keep your hands off one another, can you? And don't try to deny it because you were seen coming down the stairs together, looking very pleased with yourselves."

Mueller turned to Frances and winked. "We're not going to deny anything, are we, Froggy?"

"You caught us out, Sar," Frances said, struggling to hold on to her laughter.

The musicians began playing a waltz, and Jack walked across the room to claim the first dance with his new wife. As everyone looked on and clapped, he took her in an informal hold, arms around her waist. Sara placed hers around his neck, and they held each other close.

They moved as one, and Frances thought what a beautiful couple they made. They received rapturous applause before opening the floor to all who wished to dance. Mueller held out his hand to Frances, and she took it with a smile as he led her forward to join the other dancers. The band played a slow foxtrot, and he pulled her in close.

"You're not going to run out on me again, Froggy, are you?" he muttered into her ear.

"That depends on how often you stand on my feet," she replied.

"Are you doubting my dancing prowess?" he asked her as the music changed to an up-tempo quickstep. He took a step back from her and took her in a formal hold, taking complete control of her as he led her across the dance floor, throwing in a few twists and turns, keeping her on her toes until the music stopped and they came to a standstill.

"Impressive," she said.

"I've surprised you?" he questioned.

"Well, yes, I think you have," she agreed. "I don't understand how someone who understands the dance music so perfectly can have such a disability when it comes to singing."

"What's that supposed to mean?" he asked.

"You're tone-deaf."

"I thought I was quite a good singer, he said, finding her gaze and looking hurt.

"Are you joking? You must know that your crew—"

"My crew, what?" He interspersed and still, she noticed, had that hurt look. The thought came into her mind that he genuinely didn't know how bad his singing was.

"It doesn't matter," she said, looking away, not wanting to wound his ego.

"My crew, what?" he asked a second time. His voice was light, and he laughed at her when she turned her eyes on him. He knew damn well, she thought, and was just winding her up.

"You crew thought," she paused and started again. "I think that you sing like you have two left feet."

"Hmm, an interesting simile, Froggy." He sniffed.

"Something I must work on. How about I wake you at six each morning and serenade you?"

She fixed him with her eyes. "How about you don't?" she said. The band launched into the next number.

* * *

Following German custom, Sara was later kidnapped by the younger members of the reception party and taken to a Gast Haus on the other side of town. It was down to Jack to find her, pay the bill for the rest of the revellers, and take her back to the reception to cut the cake at midnight.

By the time Jack, Tom, and Bernie found Sara and the others in the Kaiser Gast Haus, it was past eleven thirty. Then, they were talked into sampling the German beer on offer before Jack was awarded the bill.

"I might have had second thoughts about this wedding had I known I had to pay for you," he teased.

"Then you would have missed out on what comes later," she said, throwing her arms around his neck and kissing him whilst the rest of the party cheered.

All the younger folk returned to the hotel, and the not-so-young folk who had chosen to stay at the reception, drink coffee, and chat in the warmth.

"My god, it's freezing," Frances complained. "Let me get back inside."

"Not yet. Hold on, Froggy," said Mueller. "It looks as though folks have been busy here while we've been drinking." He drew her attention to a large log laid across two cross-member supports. "We can't go in until Jack and Sara have sawn through the log, you see."

"What? I'm frozen, Kristian."

"Why on earth didn't you bring a sensible coat?" he asked.

"Because it wouldn't look right with my outfit, and I didn't

189

expect to be stuck outside for what could be a long time looking at the size of that log.”

“Then I suppose I will have to share.” He unbuttoned his coat, held it open for her to walk into, wrapped it around them as best he could, and took her hands in his. “I have confidence in Sar that we won’t be out here too long, though,” he chuckled.

Chapter 21

Mueller was right. Sara was no beginner with a saw, and with Jack's additional knowledge and strength, the sawing of the log was over within several minutes. Everyone returned to the reception, rushing to get in from the cold and ready for the cake to be cut.

As the guests looked on, Tom caused great laughter when he produced the saw a second time and asked Sara and Jack if they needed it for the cake. There was a gasp when it was brought in, as it was a rich-looking chocolate cake, and chocolate following the war was still a rarity.

"How on earth did they get hold of all of that chocolate?" Frances asked Mueller.

"Sar would kill for a piece of chocolate. I suspect that Jack managed to get hold of a load from the army stores."

Jack picked up the cake knife and laid it on the top of the cake, ready to cut it, and Sara placed her hand on top of his, which ended in more hilarity, as in Germany, the partner who lays their hand on top of the other is the person who will be in charge in the relationship.

"Which of us would have had their hands on top, do you think?" Mueller asked Frances.

"Me, I should think," she replied with a toss of her head, "and if you'd tried to change that, I suspect I would have used the cake knife as a weapon."

"I suspect you would have done back when we first married. Which one of us is in charge now, do you think?"

Frances gave the question some thought before answering. "I like to let you think you are."

Mueller planted a kiss on her head, which she ignored as hotel staff carried plates of chocolate cake to the guests and poured coffee. "Shall we sit down?" Frances suggested.

"Let's go and join the parents, shall we? I feel we've neglected them somewhat. I was surprised not to see them on the dance floor, to be honest." Mueller said.

"I suppose they've been enjoying a good old natter with Eva and Gunter."

* * *

"Gone midnight, the cake and coffee were put away, and there was beer and wine galore to be had. The more that was drunk, the wilder the dancing became. Almost everyone was on the dance floor, young and old alike. Frances noted that Peter wasn't. She ran over to him while Mueller grabbed another couple of drinks.

"You haven't danced with me," she accused. He smiled and held out his hand to her, and she thought how tired he looked.

"I'd better put that right then, hadn't I?" he said, taking her hand. "Thank goodness we have a waltz," he said. "Are you enjoying yourself, my dear?"

"I am," she said, "but I have a feeling you're not."

"Well, that will all change when you dance with me." He took her in a formal hold and led her away into a waltz.

"Are you all right?" she asked.

"Nothing to worry about. I feel tired lately, as you know, that's all."

"Have you told Mutti?"

"No, and don't you. I don't want her worrying about anything. And don't tell Kristian either."

"But they ought to know."

He gave her a severe look. "Frances, their worrying isn't going to help me."

"Well then, what would? Have you seen the doctor?"

"I've seen the doctor, and I know that you will not back off until I tell you what he said."

"Which is?" coaxed Frances.

"He told me I was suffering from an attack of old age. There, you have made me say it." He looked her in the eye and shook his head sadly.

"And I don't believe it for a minute. You're not old, Peter." The dance ended, and the band immediately played a quickstep. "Are you up for this?" she asked.

"I wish I were, my dear, but forgive me, I will sit this one out. Go and find Kristian. I can't see him."

"Oh, I know exactly where he'll be," she snapped without intending to, and Peter Mueller raised his eyebrows in question. She continued, "Chatting to those three girls he said he was at school with."

"Of you go and get him then. Maybe he needs rescuing."

"Oh, I doubt that. Your son is a flirt, Peter."

"Then, go and find a good-looking young man and do a bit of flirting of your own. Guaranteed to get Kristian to your side in no time."

"Hmmm," she said with a smile and headed for Jack Burton's brother Tom.

Peter was right. After a couple of dances with Tom, Mueller

walked over and, with a smile, asked if he could dance with his wife.

"You sure can, Kristian. She's all yours," Tom said, taking her hand and passing her over to Mueller. See you guys later; I'm off for a drink."

They watched him walk off to the bar as the band began to play the following number and launched into a Lindy Hop. The younger guests cheered their readiness for the upbeat tempo.

"Do you Lindy Hop, Frau Mueller?" Mueller asked.

"Of course I do. Why shouldn't I?"

"I thought you might be a little too refined for this," he said and swung her round hard and then pulled her back into his body. He raised his voice over the music. "You are, you know," he said.

"Are what?" she asked.

"All mine." He gave her one of his best boyish grins. "Can you double break?" he asked her.

"I don't know, show me," she replied, grabbing hold of his enthusiasm.

"Come on then, follow me, and let's show them how it's done, eh?"

She tripped the light fantastic with another Mueller who surfaced that night and who she hadn't yet encountered. She recalled Christmas of forty-two when he told her he loved dancing and would usually go into town and party into the small hours after dinner on Christmas night. That was before his dreadful injury when he was shot in the thigh, and he came close to losing his leg. And here he was, dancing, leading her around the dancefloor as though it had never happened. But then he was, and had always been, very active and rarely mentioned any pain in his leg.

As one swing dance followed another, she glanced at the clock on the wall, noting it was already 1.15 a.m. It seemed the night was still young, even for the older guests. Out of the corner of her eye, she caught sight of Bernie Schneider; he had partnered with the blond girl that she thought Mueller had been making too much of a fuss of. She had to admit Bernie was a damn good dancer; his moves were light and quick. He was heading for them now, promenading and flip-flopping around them with the blond in tow and preventing themselves from making full use of the floor, circling them, predatory.

"Little fucker," Mueller muttered under his breath. "Hold tight, my girl. We're going to fight back, and it will get bumpy."

"Kristian—" She intended to suggest that they remove themselves from the dancefloor and go to the bar instead, but Mueller had other ideas, and the dance became a game of cat and mouse, with neither couple knowing whether they were the cat or the mouse. Mueller used his body as the battering ram when he got close enough to Bernie, who then retaliated, not caring whether he or his partner did the bumping.

After several bumps, the blonde tore herself away from Bernie with a huff and returned to her friends.

"Good for Meena," said Mueller, and he gave Frances a broad smile. "She's put pay to Bernie's antics, anyway."

Mueller spoke too soon. Bernie Schneider didn't need a dance partner to show off his skills on the dance floor. He decided to perform solo and bait Mueller by dancing too close to him and Frances.

"He doesn't know when to stop, does he," Mueller remarked, and Frances could hear the anger in his voice.

She stopped dancing and said, "Come on, let's just call it a day and go and get a drink. He's not worth bothering with, is he?"

As they left the dance floor, Bernie followed them, gesticulating to Mueller to stay and dance some more. Other wedding guests picked up on what was happening and shouted for Mueller to accept Bernie's challenge. He shook his head, and then the chanting began,

"Come on, Mueller."

"Kristian, show him what you're made of,"

"Kristian, Kristian!"

Mueller looked at his friends and nodded. "This is where I make a complete arse of myself," he said to Frances. He took off his jacket and tie, gave them to her, and opened the top button of his shirt. "Ah, well," he said, "I suppose I must do it for Germany,"

Frances watched as he walked back to the dance floor. Freya joined her. "What on earth is going on?" she asked Frances.

"He's going to dance, Mutti. He says he's doing it for Germany," Frances told her with a frown.

"Well, I do wish he wouldn't," she replied as the band began to play Rockin' in Rhythm. Bernie immediately entered the swing of things, and Frances had to admit he was good. Mueller seemed a little lost, and rather than move, he watched Bernie for several bars of the music before joining in. Steady initially with a few basic Charleston moves. It had been a while, and he was now in his early thirties. Bernie was a good few years his junior.

Things were heating up as Mueller got into the swing. It was some years since he had danced this way. Peter joined Frances and Freya with a massive grin on his face.

"I had no idea, no idea," he said.

"He's pretty good, isn't he," Freya observed. "Of course, he gets it all from me."

The music changed to the more up-tempo number 'Tailspin. Both men were giving it their all now. There were turns and shuffles, swings, and shakes. Windmills, scissor steps, jigs, and all manner of variants, twists, and enhancements to those moves. The wedding party was rocking with delight.

Frances felt a tap on her shoulder and turned to find the blond girl behind her.

"Hi, Frances, isn't it?" she said. Frances nodded. "I'm Meena. An old friend of Kristian's. It's wonderful to see him after all this time. He's still one hell of a dancer. We all wanted him to partner with us at the dances. Your music at the wedding was wonderful, by the way."

Frances had to know and immediately wished she hadn't asked. "Are you married?"

"My husband's a POW in Russia. At least, I hope he is." Frances watched as the girl's eyes filled with tears. "I've heard nothing for months. At one time, he was allowed to write home regularly."

"Frances took Meena's hand. "I'm so sorry."

"Thank you. But look at me, crying at Sara's wedding when I should be joyful to be here. And look at Kristian; he's wiping the floor with that little yank."

Frances turned her attention back to the dancefloor. "Do you think so?" she asked.

"Sure. The other guy is good and precise, but his moves are sudden and short, whereas, well, look at Kristian; his moves are measured and elegant. Just gorgeous in comparison."

The music had stopped. Bernie had grabbed the microphone wire. "Time to limbo," he shouted and received wild applause. Two men held the wire, the band played, and Bernie and Mueller did the limbo until Mueller got caught up. "One to me," called out Bernie.

"Hold on, "Mueller shouted above the band. "Come here, Bernie. Come and stand by my side, eh?" Bernie did as he was asked, and Mueller drew attention to Bernie's height. He was more than fifteen centimetres shorter than Mueller. "I'd say you have an unfair advantage on the limbo."

"He does," shouted Freya, and then looked embarrassed when people greeted her comment with laughter.

"Come on, band. More dancing from these boys," someone shouted out.

"That's enough, surely," Mueller replied.

There was a chorus of *no*'s, and the band immediately struck up with a good old thirties number, 'That's you, baby.' Mueller looked at Frances with a frown; she could see he'd had enough. Sara picked up on that, too.

"One last dance for me, Kristian," she called out. "You can't refuse me on my wedding day." He shrugged and joined in again with Bernie, but halfway through the number, he stopped, pulled his shirttails from his trousers, and prayed he wouldn't make an utter fool of himself. He took a deep breath and finished with a perfectly executed cartwheel towards the bar.

A male voice called after him, "Come on back, Kristian, the exercise will do you the world of good."

He laughed and shouted, "I'll eat some spinach instead, thanks."

Freya met him at the bar. "Goodness, Kristian. That was superb. Where did you learn to cartwheel like that?"

"Hitler Youth Mutts. Old Adolf was good for something, it seems. I'm surprised and relieved I can still do them. Can I get you a drink?"

"I think your father is ready to go home, Kristian. I wish we had booked a room like you. But we should go home and give Anna a break. Don't be too late back tomorrow. Those children will be missing you."

He bent and kissed her cheek. "The night's still young, Mutti."

"It's gone 2 a.m. I must go, or your father will not be pleased," Freya said.

"Say goodnight, will you? I must go and find my wife."

CHAPTER 22

F rances had lost Kristian and wondered whether he was speaking to the woman at the reception desk. She didn't find him there, but she did find Bernie.

"Are you still lurking, Bernie?" she asked him.

"No," he denied. "The first time, yes, I followed you, but this meeting is purely by chance. I promise." He gave her a tentative smile and said, "So, I think your man outperformed me in the dancing."

"Oh, I think my husband could outperform you in every way," she said, dropping her eyes and looking him straight in the flies.

He replied with an "Ouch."

They both jumped when Mueller asked, "Are you all right, Frances? Do you need any help?" He was heading for the men's room.

"No, I'm fine. I was looking for you."

"And she found me instead," said Bernie. "I must take back what I said to you earlier, Mueller."

"What's that then?" Mueller asked a little too sharply.

Bernie gave his head a little shake. "You're no damn loser,

Mueller. You outdanced me, and you've got the girl. I hope you know what a lucky guy you are. She's something special. I wish I could get a doll like her. Have you got any advice for me, Mueller?"

"My advice at this precise moment is to ask Frances. If I stay here talking with you, I will end up pissing on you both. I hope my English was good enough for you to understand."

And with that, he quickly disappeared into the Men's room to the sound of Frances and Bernie's laughter.

"Seriously," said Bernie, "I guess I've behaved like an idiot."

"You have," Frances agreed.

"Maybe it's time for me to grow up then. I could do it with some proper advice. See, I always end up with the sort of girl I'm not looking for. All the nice ones walk out on me pretty damn quickly."

"Really?" Frances struggled not to sound sarcastic. "Well, the first advice I would give you, Bernie, is not to refer to a girl or woman you want to get to know as a doll."

"Really?" he asked wide-eyed.

"Really. I think most women would hate it!"

He laughed in her face. "Good joke, doll," he said as he walked off, leaving Frances blinking thoughtfully after him.

* * *

"Oh," gasped Frances. She looked across the breakfast table at Mueller and thought, from his expression, that he felt as bad as she did. He was yawning and looked to her after a good stretch.

"It must have been a good night, Froggy, because I feel shit."

She gave a weak laugh. "Me too. I wish they would hurry up with the coffee; I need one badly."

The door was thrown open, framing Meena and the other two girls she attended the wedding with. They stood momentarily, blinking, trying to focus on their surroundings. As Mueller burped a good morning, they frowned at him and made their way to their table. The scene repeated several times as other guests who had stayed over made it to their breakfast tables.

The kitchen door swung open, admitting two waitresses carrying pots of coffee. They went to the various tables, smiling their good mornings and receiving grunts back for their trouble. Mueller picked up the coffee pot, poured himself some, and then turned to Frances.

"Coffee?" he asked. She nodded and pushed her cup towards him. It fell onto its saucer with a clatter, resulting in a shush and a scowl from him.

The door opened once more, revealing Sara and Jack. "Morning all," they said in unison, sounding horribly bright.

They walked over to Frances and Mueller. "Can we join you?" Sara asked, giving them a victorious grin.

"Don't know. That was a filthy bloody trick, Sar," said Mueller. Sara and Jack burst into laughter.

"I knew you'd try to get away with the clock trick." Sara said, "We found them all but one and thought we'd return them to you, Kristian. The receptionist was very obliging. The clocks were all so nicely wound up with alarms ready set."

"We didn't want to waste them," said Jack. "The apple pie bed caught us out, though."

"When in hell did you manage it?" asked Mueller.

"Oh, "said Sara, "we turned in early, just before three; everyone else staying over was still in full swing. No one noticed us leave; if they did, they kept quiet."

She took a seat and pulled Jack onto another. "So come on, how much were you given towards your Paris honeymoon?" Frances asked them.

Mueller sat up in his chair. "You can't ask them that, Froggy."

"Why not?" Frances asked. "We're all good friends, aren't we?"

"Some people may think it's rude, that's why," Sara said, eyeballing Frances and pretending to be shocked.

"We'll be able to go for a couple of weeks," Jack told them.

"That's no good at all. You need at least a month to get to know Paris." Frances said.

"Says the rich lady," Sara said with a chuckle.

"You do, which is why—" She put her hand in her pocket and drew out a key, which she dangled in front of them. "I'm giving you the key to our house in Neuilly for a whole month."

"What?" screeched Sara, standing up and grabbing Frances in an embrace that nearly throttled her and delivering multiple kisses to the top of her head. Sara moved on to Mueller, who warded her off with his hands.

"I knew nothing about it," he said. "This has come entirely from Froggy."

"Frances, what a wonderful gift. Thank you." Jack bent over and kissed Frances on the cheek.

"Just make sure you enjoy yourselves. I'll tell you the best places to eat and write out a grand tour for you. You need to let us know when you want to go, or you could end up sharing the house with us and two noisy children. Oh, and I just remembered all this is dependent."

"On what?" asked Sara.

"On you having our offspring for a couple of hours at some point today so we can catch up on some much-needed sleep."

"I'd think about the offer very carefully before you accept," Mueller said with a chuckle. "It may not be worth two hours of purgatory."

"We'd love to help, wouldn't we, Sar," Jack said.

"Yes, but ensure they're handed over in clean nappies."

"So, what are Tom and Bernie doing?" Mueller asked.

"They've gone away for a few days sightseeing," Jack told him.

After breakfast, it was a quick tidy-up and packing, and then it was back to Schonen Felder. Frances and Mueller bumped into Meena again on the way out of the hotel.

"It was lovely catching up, Kristian," Meena said, "And Frances, the other girls and I meet up regularly for coffee in town; why don't you join us sometime?"

"I'd love to," Frances replied, giving Meena a quick peck on the cheek. "Have you something to write on? I'll give you our phone number."

"Oh, I probably have it at home somewhere. Do you still have the same number, Kristian?" Meena asked.

"Yes. I don't think anything's changed for years. Take care, Meena. I'm sure I'll see you around. Come on, Frau Mueller, time to face the music with the twinnies, eh?"

* * *

As they drove up to the front of the house, Mueller recognised the doctor's car parked there. He pulled up behind it and quickly went indoors, followed by Frances. No one was in the hall to greet them, and he immediately felt worried. With relief, he heard the children in the kitchen and Anna singing to them. He opened the door, expecting to find his mother there, too.

"Why's Neumann here?" he asked Anna. "Is everyone all right?"

"Thank goodness you are back, Kristian. It's your father. Neumann is with him now."

"What's wrong with Pa? I'm going upstairs."

Anna grabbed him by the arm. "You'll just be in the way," she said. "Let the doctor do his job."

"Tell me what happened then," he ordered.

"He fainted, and Freya got straight on the phone. The doctor was here in minutes. And your father was round before he got here. Freya and I got him upstairs and into bed before Neuman arrived."

"He's tired, Kristian. He told me some time ago," Frances said.

Mueller swung around. "And you didn't think to tell me. What the hell, Frances."

"He told me not to tell you. He didn't want to worry you. I didn't want to worry you, with the trial and all."

"And you think it was right, keeping it to yourself, do you?" snapped Mueller.

"No, I…I promised I wouldn't…"

As tears sprung to her eyes, she left the kitchen and ran upstairs to their room, feeling guilty that she hadn't even greeted her children. She wanted to go back down but didn't want to face Mueller. He was cross with her, and she thought maybe he had every right to be.

The outcome of the doctor's visit was that Peter Mueller had suffered a minor heart attack, which the doctor told him was a warning to him to slow down. He also suggested that Peter cut out the occasional cigar and the brandy he enjoyed and adjust his diet. However, his feelings were that the resulting heart attack was probably due to too much hard work and stress. Kristian promised that he would take on horse breeding and farming as soon as possible and step back from his post with Konrad. However, Peter assured him it was unnecessary as other workers could take on most of the physical work he was involved in.

Mueller delivered the twinnies to Sara and Jack to give everyone a bit of a break, who said they would return them by late afternoon in time for bedtime. It seemed everyone in the Mueller household was tired from the wedding party and the shock of Peter's illness. They all used the few hours of relief Sara and Jack had given them and used the time to catch up and get some sleep.

Frances went to bed as soon as Mueller left home to deliver the children; she was exhausted and immediately fell asleep, only to wake up an hour later to find that Mueller hadn't joined her for a rest. He still hadn't forgiven her for keeping Peter's secret. She was in a quandary as she hadn't forgiven herself. Still, if she had told him, she would be in the same situation and wouldn't have forgiven herself for going against Peter's wishes. She knew exactly where to find Mueller. He would have retired to his old room on the next floor. He was being childish and making her suffer, she thought. She also felt that she owed him an apology; if the boot had been on the other foot, she would be angry at him.

The house was silent, and she hoped that Anna was resting, too. She tiptoed to the next floor and opened the door to Mueller's room. He was stretched out on the bed and looked to be in a deep sleep. She lay beside him, unsure of his reaction—whether he would still be angry. He groaned softly and stretched out his arm, wrapping it around her. "Where have you been?" he murmured. "I've missed you. I love you, Froggy."

She nestled against him, and they both fell into a deep slumber.

Chapter 23

January 15, 1947

Mueller felt decidedly fed up. Christmas, Sara's wedding, and having Peter back almost to normal had left him on a high, and maybe, he thought, that was why he now felt so down. He had been seated in the courtroom for the last fortnight. He had listened to more evidence of the pseudo-medical experiments supposedly carried out in the name of science by his countrymen, most of whom had been highly thought of as scientists and doctors. After listening to the evidence over the last few days, he had no doubts at all that mostly these men were degenerates and criminals.

It was all about Polygal and Phlegmon on his return after Christmas. At the start, he hadn't got a clue what that was. After hearing the witness's reports, he felt he knew too much. Sigmund Rascher, under the patronage of Himmler, had carried out experiments on Polygal, a blood coagulant made from apple pectin and beet. He predicted that the preventative use of Polygal tablets would reduce bleeding from gunshot wounds or surgery. Mueller had thought that could be positive until he learned that Rascher had given his subjects a Polygal tablet and then had them shot through the chest or neck or had removed limbs without anaesthetic. The bastard had also been involved with the high altitude and freezing experiments that Frances had mentioned years before. At least Rascher was one of the guilty who truly got what he deserved. Frances had said that hanging was too good for some people. In this case, he found himself agreeing.

The man had made a fool of Himmler by staging three pregnancies with his wife, who supposedly had given birth to three children after the age of forty-eight. He was found out when his wife was arrested for trying to kidnap another baby. Himmler had been furious and had them both arrested. He was sent to Buchenwald and later Dachau, and she was sent to Ravensbrück. They were both put in special cells. Mueller could only imagine what a special cell might be. Rascher was shot through the food delivery door of his cell only three days before Dachau was liberated. Himmler hadn't liked being made a fool of.

Following the Polygal were the mustard gas, typhus, and other vaccine experiments. He listened for days to the prosecutors and witnesses, barely able to listen to some points at all. When it got too bad, he would fill his head with images of those last few days he'd had at home. The rides out with Frances.

He was proud of her; she had become an impressive horsewoman. Christmas with his family and the Kohls. Reliving the fun of Sara and Jack's wedding, hearing the laughter, and feeling the love of family and friends. He looked around the courtroom occasionally. There were others, he was sure, trying to block out some of the horror of what they were being told. You had to.

Following the vaccine experiments, the evidence had gotten even worse; the prosecutor had spoken of biological warfare experiments, and then on the 10th of January, worst of all—if you could choose any of them—the euthanasia program.

He struggled to listen to the witnesses, who were still talking.

He pulled his hands through his hair, thinking there would be only two more days until another ten-day break on January 17th. Everyone in that courtroom, including the defendants, would be glad of it. He wondered what they were feeling. He'd also been present at the first Nuremberg trials and had witnessed the arrogance of many of the men on trial. Fat Herman, in particular, came to mind.

He became aware of movement within the court. People were standing. The man at the desk beside him was standing and wishing him a good evening. He nodded and smiled before gathering his papers and putting them into his briefcase. He looked at his watch; proceedings had stopped a little earlier than most days, and he was glad of those few minutes. The night would be drawing in already, and he had a fifteen-minute walk back through the ruined city to the hotel that Maggie, Adenauer's secretary, had managed to book him into for the duration of the trial. It wasn't what he had been used to, but hotels were at a bit of a premium in bombed-out Nuremberg, and the Americans had quickly taken the best ones.

He at least had a bathroom and a reasonably comfortable bed, and dinner and breakfast were provided, though sometimes he wished they hadn't been. And now he felt guilty for thinking that, as he knew while he was eating, there would be those souls out in the cold again for another night with scarcely enough food to stave off the grim reaper.

As he walked out of the building, he was relieved it was warmer than anticipated. There had been a smattering of snow that morning, and it had all melted away, making the walk back to the hotel a little easier. It may have been warmer, but it was a gloomy afternoon, made gloomier still by the walk through the remnants of what had once been one of Germany's jewels in the crown. Nuremberg had housed the annual Nazi rally, and the infamous Nuremberg laws, which institutionalised racial discrimination, had come out of her courts. A model city and one of the most important sites of Nazi propaganda. Once upon a time. That seemed like a lifetime ago, but it was scarcely more than a year.

He pulled his coat around him, feeling a chill, and he wasn't sure it was down to the weather. The trials kept the horrors of the war alive in people's minds. Nuremberg was a cold city, for sure. He was approaching one of the badly bombed-out areas where there didn't appear to be a soul about, but he was damn sure there was.

The chill went down his spine, and he felt he was being watched and followed. Hadn't he felt that for a few days? Tonight, he felt it, almost from when he left the court. But he had put it down to tiredness and an overactive imagination. No! Just to the front of him, to the right, in the wreckage of a building, he picked up the sound of movement coming from more than one. He speeded up his steps, the quicker to get past that building, but they leapt out of the gloom before he could. Two of them, and he didn't think they would ask him for a light. He thought he should make for the road. There would be a few passing car lights there, maybe enough to freak these bastards out of whatever they intended. Subconsciously, he put his hand over the Rolex watch that Frances had bought him for Christmas. As he swung his body to move to the left, a crippling blow from behind sent him crashing onto the pavement.

He tried to rise, but whatever had hit him had come down hard, and he was still reeling from the blow. Making it to his knees, he felt the leather of his briefcase crash into his face, and as he hit the floor once more, he felt the toe of a boot make excruciating contact with his right kidney. He groaned.

Now, in a state of semi-consciousness, he felt himself being dragged. He needed to know where they were taking him and forced open his eyes enough to see the debris of a house. Two of the men had one arm each. He was being taken into the remains of the interior. Somewhere, he heard the third man speak, and he willed his brain to make sense of the sound and turn it into words. He wished he hadn't.

"Get him down the cellar. Victor won't be long. We can have a beer or two and watch a nice little hanging with some luck."

He felt himself being rolled over towards a door that was open and recalled their words, 'Get him down the cellar," as a foot made contact with his body and gave him a shove. He felt the harsh coldness of the first few steps and thankfully passed out.

* * *

When he came round, he was tied to the leg of what would have once been a quality dining table. Now, though, it was standing splintered and ruined, a bit like himself. He fought to focus his swollen eyes on the place in the cellar a few feet away, from where he could hear a hushed conversation. Through the flickering light of a lantern, he thought he saw four of them, or maybe there were only two, and he was seeing double. Every part of him was in agony, but worse than that was the dryness in his throat. He had to drink. He decided if he didn't ask, he wouldn't get. It was obvious their mutterings were about him; they'd look across at him occasionally and then continue their talk.

He wondered who the hell they were. His first thoughts were that they were more displaced persons, but if that were the case, he'd have been knocked down, robbed, and they'd have left. These people seemed more intent on him, not what they could take from him.

The newcomer must be Victor, he thought. This man was wiry in build and not very tall, but the others were treating him with respect. He was wearing a knitted hat pulled low on his brow. The face was in shadow. Mueller coughed to attract their attention, and all four turned their eyes to him.

He forced his mouth to form the words caught in his throat as he spoke to them. "I need a drink," and added as an afterthought, "Please."

"Why should we give a shit what you want?" asked the largest of the three men. A mean-looking ugly sod, Mueller thought. The man who jumped him and probably the one who had been following him.

"How about Christian decency?" Mueller said and gave a ragged chuckle. The big guy moved towards him, grabbed his hair, forced his head back, and then crashed it into the table leg.

"Did the bastards you are defending show any decency to the ones they experimented on?" he asked. Mueller held the man's gaze with a struggle, one eye scarcely open.

"You think I'm a defence lawyer for those men standing trial?"

"I know you are. I've been watching you for days, you Nazi turd."

"And what have you watched me do? Eh? you fat fucker." The man grabbed him by the jaw. Mueller knew that the fat boy could break his neck with one twist of his hands. He readied himself to meet his maker.

"Lisha, let go," Victor instructed, and the man obeyed immediately. Victor then asked, "What did you see this man do?"

"He was there every day writing everything down that the prosecution said. Getting ready to work on the defence."

"Whose defence?" Victor asked.

"It will be in his notes."

"No mention of defence, Lisha. Look for yourself. Just notes on the crimes and a report on the prosecution."

Victor threw Muller's notes across the floor to Lisha. The man grabbed them up and made for the table to leaf through them. Mueller watched with interest as Victor gave Lisha several minutes to look. "Well?" he asked. Lisha replied with a shrug.

Victor crossed the floor to the table, and Mueller looked at him closer. He was scarcely more than a boy, yet the other men were clearly wary of him. He would have been good-looking, but he'd received some damage to his face somewhere along the line. Victor confronted Lisha. "You stupid bastard," he muttered. "You've fucked up again." He raised his voice and glared at the other two men. "All three of you have fucked up again. How many more times, eh? How many more fucking times, you stupid fuckers?" Victor turned towards Mueller. "So, what have you been doing there every day?"

"Seeing fair play, which you clearly know all about." For his sarcasm, Mueller received another kick in the ribs from one of the other men, earning Victor's immediate reprimand.

"David, enough." Victor glanced at Mueller. "And now we're fucking stuck with you."

"And he knows who we are," said David.

"And where we are," Victor added, clasping his head with his hands for several seconds. "I'm going to have to report this to the boss," he eventually said. "I'll come straight back." As he walked past Mueller, he kicked him in the thigh. "One of you get him some water," he said and then left.

The man, David, approached Mueller with a tin cup of water. He held it to his mouth long enough for Mueller to take a couple of mouthfuls, then deposited the rest on his head before returning to Lisha and the third man, whom Mueller heard the other two refer to as Samuel. The three muttered together, casting more looks in his direction. It didn't fill him with any confidence that they would all become good friends. They were right; he knew who they were and could recognise them if given the opportunity. He had a damn good idea exactly where he was too.

If he got away, it would be easy enough to show the military police where they were hiding. As it was, he didn't think there was much chance of him escaping; the bastards had tied him tightly to the table. Victor was his only chance. Once he was back, he would tell them exactly why he was at the court. Tell him of his work for Konrad. Surely, he'd have heard of Adenauer. He'd tell him of Frances and his children and appeal to his better side, and he hoped to God that he had one.

* * *

Mueller wished he could check his watch. Victor had returned to the cellar. He must have passed out and come round when the cellar door opened, and a chilly blast of air crept across the cellar floor. Victor crossed to the other three men, and the muttering intensified enough for Mueller to hear their conversation.

"What did the boss say," asked Lisha.

"We have to get rid of him. We can't risk him leaving. One of you will have to shoot him. You can do it when I leave. We can discuss who if you want, or you can sort it between you."

In his aching brain, Mueller wondered if he should tell them he wouldn't give them away to the authorities. They could rely on him to say nothing about their mistake. He would walk back to the hotel and tell them he'd been in a hit-and-run accident. Would they fall for that and let him go? He didn't think so. They were so full of hate. He laughed inwardly at his predicament and was surprised when Victor cast a look his way.

"I'm glad we're keeping you amused. Do you want to share the joke?" he asked.

Mueller nodded. "Just thinking. I got through six years fighting in a war, and I get shot by some fucking vigilantes who are trying to make themselves feel better."

"We're no vigilantes. We're members of the Jewish Brigade," snapped Victor.

"My arse," rasped Mueller in reply. "The Brigade is a British regiment. They're organised. They don't make random killings. They certainly don't fuck up."

Victor grabbed a gun from the tabletop and put it on Mueller's head. He felt the cold metal on his temple and, raising his eyes, found Victor's gaze. He thought he had seen something like regret there.

"Make it quick then, Victor, eh? At least from there, you can't mess up. As a dying man, I have a last request, though."

"We don't do last requests."

"You're killing me because of your man's fucking mistake Victor," spat Mueller. You owe me a note to my wife and family, surely. I have to let them know I love them. Then do what you like."

Victor gave a shake of his head, but didn't pull the trigger. He made his request again, gently this time. "Please. They should know I'm not coming home. I need to tell them I love them, you see."

Victor sighed and lowered the gun. "You've children?" he asked.

Mueller replied, "Twins. A boy and a girl." and Victor nodded.

"So many children are still waiting for their parents to return home. They should know you're not coming back. Samuel, pass some paper and a pencil here and untie his hands. Let him write his note and then get rid of him. I'm going out."

He made for the door, and Mueller called out, "Victor, I need to know. Will you send it?" Victor turned and nodded again.

"Put the address on the top of the note and leave it on the table. I'll send it; you have my word."

Mueller was left to write his note while the three men huddled to discuss his demise. He wondered if he had time to undo the rope around his ankles and make for the door, but Lisha had tied his ankles so tightly that he knew the idea was a non-starter. They'd be sure to notice. He sat for some minutes thinking about what the hell he should write as his final letter home.

It was a strange feeling; he wanted to say so much but couldn't find the words to say any of it. He couldn't explain what had happened; any mention would mean the letter wouldn't get sent, and Frances would spend the rest of her life wondering and waiting for him to walk back through the door. He didn't want that for her. It was better, she knew, so that she could make some life for herself and the children without him. That thought hit him hard. He wasn't going to be around to see his children grow up. He wouldn't see Frances ripen into old age by his side. He took some deep breaths. This was something he had never considered. And why would he do it when they were all so full of life?

"Have you got your fucking letter written?" Lisha smirked when he shouted over.

"No," he replied.

"Well, get a move on, shithead. You've got a date with death."

Mueller wrote just a few words; he couldn't bear to write anymore. Each word tore at his heart, and he was almost relieved when he finished. He wrote:

Dear Froggy,

My wonderful girl. I will no longer walk this earth when you receive this. My luck has run out, sweetheart. Something has happened here that is resulting in my death. It had nothing to do with the trial, just bloody bad luck. I beg you to make a life for yourself and our children without me and know that in my final moments, you are filling my head and my heart, and with you there, I can face anything.

I love you.
Kristian. X

The letter was complete, and he scribbled the farm's address onto a second piece of paper.

"Here," he said, holding up the paper. Just do it. Make it quick."

"Why?" asked Lisha, "I watched men like you commit murder daily at Buchenwald. They didn't make it quick."

"Oh, for fuck's sake, I know nothing about Buchenwald; I don't even know where the bloody place is."

"Isn't that what they all say?" Lisha said, turning to the other two men. They nodded in agreement. "Fucking Kraut", he continued, "Oh boy, we're going to take it nice and slow."

"Victor said to shoot him," Mueller heard one of the other men say, but he wasn't sure which.

"Is Victor here, Samuel? The last thing I heard Victor say was to get rid of him. Get me a rope and tie this bastard's hands back together while I make a noose."

Mueller was mesmerised as he watched the man slowly winding the rope to make a perfect noose; he appeared to be an expert, which didn't make him feel any better. He'd prepared himself for a bullet to the head. That at least would be a quick end, but now? Lisha was going to make it slow. There would be no drop, nothing to break his neck. A slow death by asphyxiation. He thought he should at least try appealing to the other two men.

"Hey, Victor said shoot me, didn't he? Do you want to risk his anger?"

Samuel and David looked at one another. Mueller thought he was getting to them. "What about the boss? I bet he's a mean one," he continued, watching the two men get more ruffled and feeling a spark of pleasure and hope, which was immediately dowsed by a hard punch to the back of the head.

* * *

When Mueller gained consciousness, he was lying on the floor in the middle of the cellar. The first thing he saw when he opened his eyes was a beam over which the noose had hung. He strained against his bonds, but he'd been tied fast. His movement caught the attention of Lisha, who raised the mug he was holding in salute.

"To those who are about to die," he said, then turned to the other two men. "See, here he is, our main player." He crossed to Mueller and kicked him in the ribs. "You've kept us waiting. Let's get on with it. No need to hang around—oh, sorry about the pun."

He leaned over and grabbed Mueller's clothing, pulling him up to stand easily, even though Mueller lashed out with his feet and twisted in his grip. The man was a mountain. Mueller couldn't see any way out. Hadn't he been in this position many times on UBA? He'd kept his cool even when the adrenalin had kicked in, telling him to run as it was now. He'd always been able to control and overcome it by thinking his way out of a situation, by outthinking the enemy.

The enemy now had a distinct advantage, and even though his pulse was thumping away in his temple and his brain desperately searched for a solution, there was none. He broke into a cold sweat as panic ran through his body. Run, run, but there was no way out this time. Lisha had him in a vice-like hold, and it was crushing the breath from him, crippling him. He heard him call out.

"David, get over here and put the noose around this Nazi fucker's neck."

David made his way over reluctantly and opened the noose, slipping it over Mueller's head. As he tightened it, he muttered, "Sorry," and made his way back swiftly to where Samuel was standing, staring wide-eyed. As Lisha pulled on the rope, Mueller felt the roughness of it as it tightened around his throat, pushing on his larynx and making him gasp for breath.

He was pulled onto the tips of his toes, until they were the only part of him making contact with the floor. Lisha then tied the rope up at that length, leaving him suspended. As he made to move away to join the other two men, he kicked Mueller's legs from under him with a laugh. The rope tightened further, resulting in Mueller kicking his legs around madly until his feet found the ground again, finding stability, which gave him a little relief. But not for long. After a minute or so, Lisha was back, knocking him off his balance for a second time, laughing in his face as he went through the same grotesque dance until he re-found his balance.

This happened another three times; each time, Mueller felt himself weakening; his breaths were coming in short gasps, and the pulse in his neck was growing weaker. He closed his eyes, wanting to die, but his hearing was still astute. He heard Samuel say, "Lisha, I've seen enough. Put the bastard out of his misery."

And Mueller wished he would.

And then he heard David back Samuel up, "Stop it. We are not animals, Lisha. Even if this is what happened in Buchenwald, it doesn't make it right. Shoot the poor sod."

"What, and spoil my fun? Let's have a bet, eh? Let's bet on how much longer he can last. What do you say? We can time him on his watch." He walked over and kicked Mueller's legs from under him for a fifth time. Mueller felt the pulse in his neck grow weaker still, and then he felt the warm flow of urine down his leg. The pulsing stopped, and everything went black.

Chapter 24

Someone was shaking him hard. He could hear a voice somewhere distant.

"Mueller, for God's sake. Mueller, can you hear me? Open your damn eyes! Mueller! Come back, for God's sake. I had no idea, I promise you. God, Mueller, please."

He felt happy where he was. There was darkness there, but he didn't mind it. He was out of pain, which had to be good. And now some bastard was shaking him, and the pain was returning. He was struggling to breathe, and he needed to puke.

Miriam felt utter relief as Mueller's eyes shot open. She saw they were bloodshot, but he was looking straight at her. She was sitting astride him with the back of his neck cradled in her hands, and as she pulled him more upright, he wretched, and she quickly turned his head to the side to assist him.

Afterwards, he went limp, and she felt panic course through her, thinking he had succumbed and was dead. But when she laid him back, his eyes were still open, and they were searching her face for recognition. A husky laugh caught in his throat. He fought against the pain of his injuries to speak, only managing a hoarse whisper.

"Victor. How about you give me that bullet, eh?"

Miriam gave a shake of her head. "You're not getting a bullet, Mueller. We're going to get you well; you'll be fine. I'm Miriam…. Miriam, Frances's friend."

Mueller studied her briefly before muttering, "Frances," and replying, "You're Victor. I won't forget you. You set that bastard Lisha on me."

"I'm sorry, Mueller. You can forget Lisha, he's gone. He's unable to follow orders. I've contacted Frances. She'll be here tomorrow. Now we'll get you to your hotel and find you a doctor. Try and stay awake until he's seen you."

* * *

Mueller was unable to stay awake, exhausted by pain; he passed out when David and Samuel moved him from the cellar on a stretcher to the back of a battered German army vehicle. Miriam had been joined by her partner Simeon, who was known to others as the boss; he was worried that Mueller could still slip away during a loss of consciousness.

"We can't let that happen, Sim," Miriam said. "This man is the husband of my dearest friend. I caused her to miscarry her child, and somehow, she found it in her heart to forgive me. I don't think she will be so forgiving if I'm responsible for the death of her husband, too."

"Lisha's responsible for what's happened," Simeon said.

"Hah, think about it: Lisha saved him. Mueller would be dead for sure if he'd carried out orders and shot him, which is what I told him to do."

She took Simeon's arm and led him away from the other two men. "What are we going to do with Lisha, Sim."

"I'll get rid of him later when we've got Mueller to the hotel. The man's a liability, Miriam. He enjoys killing people a bit too

220

much, and he's shown us time and time again that he can't follow orders."

"He has children, Sim. What will become of his family?"

* * *

Mueller woke up sometime later and found himself cleaned up and in bed in his hotel room. He groaned from the pain he was in, and the three people who were grouped together and speaking in hushed tones turned and faced him.

"Ah, my patient is with us now," said a small, wiry man whom Mueller thought was probably in his late fifties. He walked to the side of the bed and laid his hand on Mueller's forehead. "I'm Doctor Henk. I need to check you over now that you're awake. It's easier if you tell me where you hurt rather than me poking around and trying to guess the extent of your injuries. I will be as gentle as I can."

He gave Mueller a weak smile and pulled back the bedclothes. As he saw the extent of the bruising to Mueller's body, his eyes widened. "Just as well, these two good people found you along with a card from the hotel in your pocket. If you'd been left much longer—"

Mueller was aware of the shake of the head that Miriam was giving him. It was a warning to keep quiet. Now that the hat was removed, he saw that the dark hair that framed the face most definitely belonged to a woman, and he thought she was almost pretty. The man standing at her side was tall and a little on the gaunt side. He was also dark, and his face showed a few days of beard growth. He nodded at Mueller and gave him the ghost of a smile.

"Well, now, let's begin, shall we?" The doctor raised Mueller's arm and winced at the bruising down his left side while running a practised hand over him. "Your ribs are badly bruised, and I would

221

say that there are at least two that are broken." He did the same to the right, tutting at the bruising. "Not quite as bad on this side, but probably a few cracked. By the looks of things, you have a broken ankle and a broken big toe. Your legs are bruised but nothing more —a couple of broken fingers on your left hand and deep ligature wounds on your wrists. I will bandage up the breaks and wounds before I go. Now, your face. You don't look too pretty at the moment," he said with a comforting smile, "but most of these cuts are superficial and will heal. Your eyes are bloodshot and swollen."

He tilted Mueller's head back and gave a horrified bark. "Good God, man, someone has tried to hang you and pretty nearly succeeded by the looks of things. I'll put some iodine on these wounds to stop any infection. What the hell did you do to deserve this kind of treatment?"

Mueller swallowed before replying, "I think I was just in the wrong place at the wrong time." The doctor looked at him through worried grey eyes.

"I think I should report your injuries to the police. We can't have people on our streets who can do this to another human being. For God's sake, have we learned nothing from the last six years?"

Mueller noticed the movement across the room as Miriam and Simeon looked at each other, troubled.

He shook his head and forced his voice into a little more than a whisper so they could hear. "Leave it, doctor. I'll hopefully be on my way home tomorrow. My wife is coming to collect me, you see. I want to go home and don't want to wait around here while the police investigate. I can't give any evidence; I was jumped on from behind, knocked out, and strung up. That's all I could tell them."

The doctor held Mueller with a steady gaze for a while. He looked doubtful. "Well, come on, let's get you bandaged and bathed, and then I'll give you a shot of morphine. You could do it with a good night's sleep, I think. I'll call back tomorrow around lunchtime and give you another shot."

The doctor was gentle and practiced it took him minutes to bathe Mueller's wounds and make him more comfortable. "You must surely realise, young man, that you won't be going home with your wife tomorrow; you will be in a good deal of pain. I would suggest you wait at least a few weeks before you travel, but I suspect you will ignore my advice entirely. I hope your wife has a little more sense than you." He took out a syringe and a bottle from his bag and injected Mueller in his thigh.

"Let me know what I owe you, doctor," Mueller said.

"I will when my treatment has finished. Now I will leave you and return at lunchtime tomorrow, as I said. Have a good rest, my friend."

The doctor left.

"We'll stay with you until your wife arrives," Simeon said. "Do you think he'll go to the police?"

Mueller gave a painful shrug, and his eyes felt like they were spinning. "If he does, I'll keep—" Mueller sighed and fell into a much-needed drug-induced sleep.

* * *

"How are you feeling?" Mueller opened his eyes to find Simeon leaning over him.

"I've felt better," he rasped. The pain in his throat was almost unbearable. "Is that food I can smell?"

"It is. I ordered you some scrambled eggs. Do you think you can eat?"

"I'm bloody starving," Mueller admitted. "But how the hell I am going to swallow—" He shook his head.

"Well, you must try, my friend," said Simeon. "Miriam has gone downstairs to see if this place has any ice. Try the eggs. I'll give you a hand, and Mueller, for what it's worth, I'm sorry this happened to you."

There was a knock on the door, and Miriam's voice was from the other side. "Are you decent? Can I come in?"

Simeon crossed the room and opened the door, and Miriam entered carrying a tray with an ice bucket, several glasses, and a water jug. She gazed at Mueller before putting the tray on the table and walking to his bedside.

Leaning over, she said, "You look like shit,"

He winced as he bit on his dry lip. "I feel like shit," he replied.

He held onto Miriam's gaze briefly, looking deep into her eyes. He made her uncomfortable, and she turned away, making for a trolley on which there was a breakfast. Toast, a small amount of butter, and some solid-looking scrambled eggs. Miriam dealt some of the egg onto a plate, grabbed a spoon, and returned to Mueller's bedside. "Simeon, try to sit him up a little, can you?"

Simeon took Mueller behind the shoulders and pulled him to near sitting as Mueller groaned miserably. "What time is it?"

"Coming up midday. Come on, open up." Miriam instructed as she lifted the spoon towards Mueller's lips.

"I can do it myself," Mueller complained. "I don't need your help."

She pushed the spoon towards him. "Well, you've got it, anyway."

He met her eyes and opened his mouth, taking the egg. Miriam watched as he worked the food around his mouth before trying to swallow it and gagging. Passing the plate to Simeon, she quickly poured a glass of water and threw in a couple of ice cubes. "Drink," she instructed, "wash it down Mueller. You have to eat and drink." She proffered the spoon several more times, and he managed to eat most of what she'd put on the plate, though with some difficulty. "Well, that's a start. Do you need the bathroom? Sim will help you."

"At this moment in time, no." He forced a harsh laugh and wished he hadn't as it caught in his throat. "God knows what Frances is going to say," he rasped.

"About me being here?" Mueller shook his head. "What then?" asked Miriam.

"About me pissing myself and puking the first time I meet her great friend Miriam." Brown eyes investigated bloodshot blue. A smile played on both their faces. Miriam broke into laughter first, followed by guttural chuckles from Mueller, who begged her to stop because laughter was painful. It was one of those moments when the more you try to stop doing something, the harder it gets. It ended with Mueller coughing uncontrollably and Simeon grabbing another glass of iced water for him to drink, having no idea what was funny.

The doctor arrived as he had promised at lunchtime to give Mueller another dose of morphine. He found him propped up in bed, conversing quietly with Simeon and Miriam.

"Have you managed to eat and drink anything?" he asked Mueller.

"A little, yes. Some scrambled egg," Mueller croaked.

"You need to start eating as soon as possible, and not just eggs. Try some steamed fish, but make sure the bones are all out, for goodness' sake, and some vegetables. Get them pureed."

"Have you been to the bathroom?"

"Not since last night, no," replied Mueller, drawing a laugh from Miriam. "But I think I could probably make use of a visit now. The iced water is soothing, thank you."

"I'll go and get some food for when Frances arrives," Miriam said, leaving the room, and Simeon volunteered to get Mueller to the bathroom.

He placed one arm around Mueller's shoulder to assist him in sitting, causing Mueller to groan in pain.

"Just a minute," said Henk, "I'll give you a hand."

Between them, the doctor and Simeon managed to get Mueller to stand.

The doctor suggested he sit on the edge of the bed for a while. "I have some crutches in my car. They may be too short for you, but they may help. Later, I will drop some larger ones here for you. I think you will need them for a while, my friend."

As the doctor left the room, Mueller turned to Simeon.

"You seem to be an intelligent man," he said, "so what the hell are you doing?"

"Ridding the world of garbage," Simeon replied.

"You're committing murder, Sim, and making mistakes along the way. If they catch you, it will end badly. Stop while you can."

"You don't understand, and why would you?"

"I'm not one of them, Sim. I'm a German, I'm not a Nazi, and I do understand. What you're doing, though, is wrong. I explained to Miriam that you would get greater support for your cause if you let these men be found guilty through the justice system. Taking the law into your own hands makes you as bad as them."

There was a knock on the door, and the doctor returned with a pair of crutches. Mueller had a difficult choice between taking his weight on his broken ankle or his broken toes. He plumped for the toes, and with the doctor's and Simeon's help, he made a harrowing visit to the bathroom. Once back in bed, the doctor reassured him that the next time he got up, he would know what to expect, and it would be easier. He wasn't convinced.

* * *

Late afternoon, there was a gentle tap on the hotel room door. Miriam stretched. She had slept on the sofa for the last couple of hours since Mueller had been given his morphine injection. He was asleep within minutes, and she saw her chance to catch up on some sleep herself while Simeon went to check on what was going on in the cellar. She opened the door expecting to see Simeon standing outside but found Frances, suitcase in hand.

"Frances, thank God," Miriam said with relief. Frances kissed her briefly on the cheek as her eyes dated around the room.

"Where is he? What's happened?" she asked, going over to the bed. She clasped her hand to her mouth when she saw the state of Mueller and gave a guttural cry. "Who the hell would do this?" she muttered as tears surged.

Miriam laid a hand on her shoulder. "I'm sorry. It…it was an accident. We…we made a mistake."

Miriam stumbled over her explanation as, eyes wide, Frances asked, "You are responsible for this?" She sat on the bed, cradled Mueller's face in her hand, and blanched when she saw the ligature marks around his neck. "You tried to hang my husband, and you tell me it was a mistake?" she asked, jaw clenched. "What the fuck Miriam? You can't have done this alone."

"I didn't do it at all. Frances, just listen, will you? I can explain."

"Oh, I doubt that," Frances spat.

"I've been working with a group. We've been Nazi hunting. We've found loads of them, Frances. Made them pay the ultimate for what they did to us."

Frances's breath came short and sharp. "And how many more mistakes have you made, eh?" she asked. She raised her voice. "When will you stop, Miriam? When will you rein in your hatred and return to being a normal human being?"

"Never. Not while there's any of them left."

"And how many innocent people have you killed already, do you think?"

The door opened, and Simeon came into the room. He looked at both women. "Miriam?" he questioned as Frances swirled around to face him.

"Get out," she hissed and turned to Miriam. "Get out, both of you. Now."

Frances let go of a torrent of tears as the door closed behind them. She felt incredibly useless as she looked down at Mueller, who hadn't moved during the altercation with Miriam. She wanted to kiss him but didn't want to disturb him. He was in some pain, that was obvious, as he winced and groaned even in his sleep. His right eye and lip were severely swollen, and there was a multitude of further cuts and bruises over his face. She hadn't had a clue what to expect when she received Miriam's phone call the day before. Not this, that was for sure. Miriam had told her that Mueller had been involved in an accident, and he needed her in Nuremberg. She had a multitude of questions to ask her, but the line had been poor. Or had it been? Miriam had told her she couldn't hear her well. Now, she thought it more likely that she didn't want to answer her questions.

She walked over to the window, which looked out onto the street below and yawned. The journey had been long and tiring, and the argument with Miriam on top of it had left her shattered. She decided that while Mueller was resting, she should catch up with some rest, and she climbed onto the bed and nestled into him. He groaned in his sleep; her nearness clearly made him uncomfortable.

She rolled away and eventually managed to forget her anger enough to find some hours of sleep.

Near midnight, there was a gentle knock on the door. Frances woke and, for a few moments, wondered where she was. Mueller stirred, which served as a reminder, and she padded across the room to the door, dreading finding Miriam on the other side. She felt drained and exhausted and didn't want another fight. The man on the other side of the door clutched a pair of crutches and introduced himself as Doctor Henk, and with relief, Frances invited him in.

"So, you are Frau Mueller. I'm glad you're here. How is our patient?" he asked politely.

"He's been out of it since I got here, so I don't know," she replied. "He will be all right, won't he, Doctor? He will pull through?"

The doctor took her hand and gave it a fatherly pat. "It all looks worse than it is, my dear. Your husband is young and strong and should make a full recovery, though the ligature wound may leave some scarring. The breaks will mend, the bruises will fade, and most cuts will heal perfectly. However, I can see why you would be worried, as he looks quite a mess. Thank goodness to those who had been looking after him until you arrived. Have they gone now?"

"Yes, they have, Doctor," Frances replied as she thought good riddance.

"A shame. You could do with some help, my dear. You are rather slight to be heaving someone around if you don't mind me saying. Your husband is going to rely on you for a few days yet."

"We'll manage," yawned Mueller. He was awake and trying to get himself into a sitting position on the bed. The grimace on his face told the doctor all he needed to know.

"Take things steady," Henk said as Frances raced to Mueller's side and kissed his forehead. "How are you feeling? Dreadful, I would guess." Henk remarked.

"I have felt better, it has to be said. I thought I would do without an injection, doctor, now my wife is here."

"You'll do as you're told, Kristian," Frances cut into the conversation. "If Doctor Henk thinks you need another injection, you will have one."

"And that would be my advice, too," Henk said with a chuckle. "I suggest you listen to your wife, Herr Mueller. The night will be long if you can't sleep. We can see how you are tomorrow lunchtime. Have you eaten?"

Mueller shook his head. "Just the eggs, whenever that was."

"Too long ago," Henk turned to Frances. Go and see what you can get from the kitchen. It needs to be soft and nourishing. Get something for yourself, too. While you're away, I'll check Kristian over and redress any wounds that need it. And then my parting gift will be a good night's sleep."

When Frances returned, she found Mueller washed and his wounds freshly dressed. The kitchen had closed hours ago, and she had to beg the night staff for food and a drink. She returned with two bowls of porridge, a pot of coffee, and more ice.

"Perfect," Henk said. "I'll call in tomorrow lunchtime again. Frau Mueller, make sure you get some good food down your husband and yourself. Insist that the staff understand that he needs fresh food that's easy to swallow. His throat looks less swollen. The good thing about mouths and throats is that they heal quite quickly. Not so the broken ribs and digits, I'm afraid. Now get some porridge down you, both of you. I'll wash my hands and pack my bag."

Henk disappeared to the bathroom and returned a few minutes later to find two empty dishes and Mueller sipping at iced water while Frances downed a coffee.

"That coffee will keep you awake," he said to Frances as he fished around in his bag again for the morphine and a syringe.

"I don't think anything will keep me awake tonight, Doctor.

Henk threw her a smile as he gave Mueller an injection. He looked at his watch. "One a.m. My wife will be wondering where I am. Sleep well, both." He picked up his bag and left.

"What a lovely man," Frances said as she locked the door behind him. She turned, expecting Mueller to agree. He was already enjoying the effects of the morphine and was snoring gently.

* * *

Frances yawned, stretched, and checked the clock on the bedside table. It was eight a.m.

"Hello." She flipped onto her side to find Mueller watching her. "I thought I'd dreamt you when I first woke," he said. She leaned over and kissed him.

"How come you're so sexy even when you look like something from a Boris Karloff horror movie?" she asked.

"My natural charm, Froggy, and don't make me smile because it hurts."

"I should think everywhere hurts, doesn't it?"

"It's playing havoc with my dancing." He chuckled. "So, how is everyone back home?"

"Worried about you, of course. Mutti is beside herself, and Anna and your father want to kill a few people, and so do I."

"And the children?" he asked.

"Are fine. They can both almost sit up without support and smile and giggle endlessly."

"Good, I miss them. Now, give me your hand," he said. She held out her hand, which he took. "I've found somewhere that doesn't hurt." He gave her an even more lopsided grin than usual that ended up as a leer as he thrust her hand beneath the bedclothes, and she felt his hardness. "Come on, Froggy, climb aboard; I need to see if part of me still works."

She raised her eyebrows. "Kristian Mueller, you are incorrigible," she said. Relief flooded through her. He would mend.

CHAPTER 25

JANUARY 20, 1947

"I do not understand why we can't go home, Kristian," Frances said, pulling a hand through her hair in consternation.

"You can go home; you should be with the children. I've a job to do, Froggy, you know that." He was sitting in an armchair beside the bed with his foot raised.

"But you can't do it in your present state, can you?" she argued.

"I have another week to get well," he argued. "The court doesn't convene again until January the twenty-seventh."

"And you think you will be fit enough by then, do you?"

"I think I will manage, yes."

"You think you will be able to sit all day in a courtroom with broken ribs and a broken foot?" She looked at him and shook her head. "Look, how about you come home for the week and take it easy. Your children need to see you, and so do your parents. Anna will be jumping up the wall, too."

"It's easier if I stay here," Mueller replied awkwardly.

"It may be for you, Kristian, but I am missing my children."

"Don't you think I am missing them, too? Go home to them.

I'll be fine." She turned her back on him and walked away, looking out the window onto the ravaged city.

"Are you so determined to see it through?" she asked him.

"It's not determination."

"What then? Konrad said to come home. He can send someone else here."

Mueller sighed. "Come here. Look at me. It's not determination. It's a need. I have to try to make sense of it. Then maybe I can let go of this guilt."

"There is no sense in it, Kristian. Haven't you at least realised that?" she snapped and then immediately wished she hadn't. "Look, I understand that you want to see it through. I do. But how can I leave you here like this? Can't we reach a compromise?" He raised his eyebrows.

"Compromise, Froggy? Now, that's a new word for you."

"Perhaps I don't use it often because you're so bloody awkward," she snapped and shook her hand free. They glared at one another for a moment until Mueller started laughing.

"What?" she asked.

"I shall tell the doctor you've been mean to me, Froggy." She turned her eyes on him.

"The doctor knows what an awkward sod you are."

"How? I'm always on my best behaviour when he calls."

"I've told him what you're really like," she muttered, and then walked over to the bed and sat beside him, taking his hand, making him wince. "See, you're still in a lot of pain," she said, and he hmphed as she continued. "Come home with me, Kristian, please. Come back and see your folks and the children, and if you must come back here on the 27th, I won't make a fuss. I promise. I can visit every few weeks if you're unable to return home for a while. Mutti would agree to have the children if I were with you."

She could see him thinking things through and forced home her argument. "You should go home and see your father, anyway.

There may be things he needs you to take care of. He needs you."

They sat quietly with Mueller, deep in thought, until he said, "I could do with a change of clothes. And you won't make a fuss when I return on the 26th?"

"27th," she said.

"26th, the court reconvenes on the 27th. I need to be back by then."

"Then I will have you home for six days."

* * *

Frances struck while the iron was hot and arranged for them to travel home that day. She contacted the doctor, thanked him, and let him know he didn't need to call for a while. She also ensured that the hotel would hold onto Mueller's room. Then, she ordered a taxi to take them to the station, hoping that Peter would be well enough to meet them at the other end of the journey and take them the rest of the way to Schonen Felder. And, of course, he was there.

The journey hadn't been easy, as Mueller was still in a great deal of pain, and Frances wondered if bringing him home was the right thing to do after all. But at least the train ran, and the holdups were minimal.

There was a very emotional welcome, and many tears were waiting for Mueller when they reached Schonen Felder. Freya and Anna ran to the car when it drew up as near as Peter could get to the front door.

"Oh, oh! "Freya exclaimed once Mueller had managed to clamber out of the car with Peter and Frances's help. She saw the extent of his facial injuries. "What have they done to you, Kristian?" she sobbed.

She threw her arms wide, waiting to embrace him, but Mueller backed away. "Mutti, don't grab me, for goodness sake.

Every damn part of me is hurting after the journey. Let me get inside and get comfortable, and then we can talk," he said.

Anna stood back, and Frances noticed the tears in her eyes, too. She rubbed her arm as she walked past. "Come on," she said. "I know a boy who could do with a coffee and a piece of your fruit cake."

For the few days he was home, he was treated like a king, with Anna, Freya, and Frances on hand to ensure his rest and Sara and Jack visiting to ensure his laughter. There was extra laughter, too, with the children who were now developing their own characters as they approached their 6-month birthday.

* * *

"You know, Froggy, I have to admit that you were right. Making me come home for a break has done me good," Mueller admitted after being back for three days. They were sitting together on the sofa in the front room with the children propped up with pillows and cushions on the floor in front of them, just in case.

"Of course I was right," Frances replied. "It was obvious you'd be more relaxed once out of Nuremberg. The place gives me the shivers. For all of its destruction, even Berlin had a nicer feel. It must be all those evil people in one place."

Mueller turned to her with a grin. "Here was me thinking it would be a nice place for us to move to," he said.

Frances moved closer to him and leaned on his shoulder. "I wish you didn't have to go back to the damn place. It's hateful."

He stroked her cheek and tilted her chin up, looking into her eyes. "You don't have to come back ever."

There was a shriek from the children as Paul lost his balance and toppled over. Frances stood up, propped him with the pillows again, and kissed them both.

As Mueller watched them, he felt a surge of love. He tutted, smiled at them, and said, "You stay here, Froggy. I'll come home whenever I can. It will all be fine, I promise."

"And when will that be?" Frances asked.

"I have no idea. There's nothing planned."

"I need to know when I will see you," she said, "so I will visit at the end of February and stay a few days." She plonked herself back down on the sofa.

"Well, that's going to put pay to my philandering," he said, frowning and scratching his head. Frances picked up a cushion and whacked him with it, and she was surprised at how quickly he could move with all his injuries. He grabbed her around the waist and dragged her onto his lap. "I suppose the positive is that if you are there, I won't have to pay anyone."

Frances shrieked and grabbed the cushion again, but he held her tight and smothered her face with kisses, making her scream with laughter. The twins joined in with the laughter as well. Anna's voice made them all sit up straight.

"So, I guess you two won't be wanting dinner, as you're now eating each other." She shook her head, scowled at them, and as she left, said, "And in front of these children, too."

* * *

The defence's opening statements began on January 29th with that of Karl Brandt. His defence lawyer, Rober Servatius, read: "One can condemn the defendant Karl Brandt only by imposing on him the duty of revolution and having a different ideology to his environment." A little later, he also asked the question that resonated with Mueller all through that night, that being, "What did the airman think who dropped the first atomic bomb on Hiroshima? Did he consider himself a criminal? What did the state think who ordered the atomic bomb to be used?"

Mueller recalled his time on UBA when he ordered Allied vessels to be sunk. The first few kills had excited him. Each sinking was reported, and the crew would celebrate afterwards, usually with a beer. But then, as the war had progressed, didn't he get tired of it, sick of it, even? Particularly when he looked on as men threw themselves into an ocean already ablaze with leaked oil or heard the bows of a ship crack as it sank with all men onboard. *But it was them or us*, he thought. The poor bastards that Brandt and his cronies carried out their so-called operations or experiments on were sitting ducks. *There was no us, just them.*

There was the difference, Mueller thought with relief. These men on trial appeared to derive pleasure from inflicting suffering on others through their mock experiments. There was no battle to win apart from that of prolonging the suffering of another human being or thinking up the cruellest way to maim or kill.

He was shocked by the number of witnesses who came forward in Brandt's defence, not just for Brandt. Also, during February, Siegfried Handloser and Oscar Schroeder, two other men, had their defence heard. Like Brandt, they had multiple witnesses defending them. Hosler had an affidavit signed by twenty doctors extolling his virtues and praising his dedication to caring for the sick and wounded without taking leave. He swore he knew nothing of the medical research discussed during the trial. So maybe, thought Mueller, there is at least one decent man amongst those in the courtroom.

The other man defending himself in February was Oskar Schroeder, Chief of Staff of the German Air Force medical officers. He had high-altitude and freezing experiments carried out on people. As before, he received a strong defence.

Mueller couldn't tear his eyes from the men. He wanted to see a show of human emotion from them during their defence, but there was none. Were they being stoic or just utterly inhuman, he wondered.

He wanted to discuss everything he'd seen and heard that month, but who with? He looked around the courtroom. There were a few men he knew by sight and to whom he nodded good morning, but after his encounter with near death, he wouldn't trust anyone he didn't know.

It was a huge relief when, at the end of the month, Frances arrived in Nuremberg. She went straight to their hotel suite and watched for his arrival from the upstairs window, which looked onto the street below. When she saw him coming, she flew from the room to meet him, relieved that he appeared to be now walking without the help of crutches or a stick. He opened his arms wide when he saw her, giving her an even wider smile, and once she was in his arms, he buried his face in her hair, breathing in her scent to shift the stink of the courtroom from his nostrils.

They went upstairs to their rooms, and once inside, he said, "My God, I've missed you, Froggy. How was the journey, and more importantly, how is everyone? How are Pa and the children?"

"Everyone is fine. The children are fine, and I am fine now that I have seen you." She helped him off with his overcoat and threw his hat over the room onto the table, casting her eyes over him. "You have lost weight, and I want to know why, but not yet. There's something even more important." She stretched her arms around his neck, pulling his head down until their lips met, kissing him passionately. "First things first," she said.

* * *

It was early the following day. Frances had ordered coffee and toast to be sent to their room. While she waited, she studied Mueller, who was sleeping the sleep of exhaustion after only managing to drop off a couple of hours before.

After making love the previous evening, they walked to a restaurant about a twenty-minute walk away, and Frances could feel Mueller's uneasiness. It was unlike him; he had always been at ease with himself. He scarcely ate and was distant, even when she talked of the children. They returned to the hotel, downed a brandy, and turned in. She soon drifted off as he held her in his warmth but was woken a short time later by him tossing around and moaning in his sleep. Gently waking him, she questioned him about what was wrong, but he had merely apologised for waking her up and told her he was fine, and for her to go back to sleep.

She closed her eyes but slept no more that night. She kept vigil as he tossed and turned until it was almost light. Then, he lay exhausted beside her, with only a couple of hours left before he must go to court.

And now there was a gentle knock on the door. She donned a dressing gown and opened it to the girl who had brought them their breakfast. She thanked her, closed the door, carried the tray to the table, and briefly looked out onto a dark, damp morning in Nuremberg.

Placing a cup of coffee on the bedside cabinet, she climbed back into bed with a plate of toast, deciding to let Mueller sleep for another hour and then order a fresh breakfast for when he woke. She chose not to question him that morning but instead said that he had a sleepless night. She would wait until that evening to talk things through.

Mueller was in a mood and a rush when Frances woke him an hour later. He declared he had no time for breakfast and would grab just a coffee, but Frances insisted that he sit for ten minutes and have two cups of coffee, toast, and honey.

"What time do you think you'll be back?" she asked as he donned his overcoat and grabbed his hat off the table.

"I don't think I'll be late. We have just one more witness in the Schroeder case, so I could be back early afternoon, but don't worry if I'm not. It will just be taking longer than I expected. What will you do with your day?"

"I thought I would go for a walk and see if there is anything at all that Nuremberg has to offer. But first, I will have a long bath and wash my hair."

"Good." He kissed her on the cheek and left. She wandered over to the window and watched him walk away until he was out of view, lost in the remains of the old historic city. She was worried about him and hoped he would be in the mood to talk when he came home.

After bathing, she walked into the old town of Nuremberg, although finding its boundaries amidst the debris was challenging. Mueller had told her that ninety percent of the old city was gone, and she had to admit that seeing an entire building was like looking for a needle in a haystack. The local people amazed her as they had in Berlin. They were making the most of what was left and going about their business as best they could.

The children grouped, searching for American GIs who might have chocolate in their pockets or a coin or two to give away. Frances's heart went out to them; they had the same hollow cheeks and starved look as those she had seen when they visited Inga. She silently prayed that her children would never know war.

She continued walking into the ruins of the old town, along what was left of its narrow, cobbled streets. Making towards the centre and the remnants of the castle built on its colossal sandstone plinth. She could only imagine what it must have looked like before its destruction; it was old, that was clear, and she wondered if Kristian would know anything of its history.

Continuing her walk, she found herself in the marketplace, which was still busy despite its near destruction. Catching the smell of something delicious, she went in search of it. Someone had set up an oven in the marketplace and was cooking what turned out to be gingerbread. She bought more than she should have, hoping to enjoy it later with Kristian. Wishing to find a bottle of something alcoholic to go with it, she began a conversation with the woman selling the gingerbread.

The woman told Frances that her gingerbread was from an old family recipe. "Of course, Nuremberg is famous for its gingerbread."

"It must have been a very lovely city," Frances said, making conversation.

The woman looked sad. "The bombs managed to destroy six hundred years of history in less than an hour. The number of residents here has halved."

"I'm sorry," Frances said.

"They are trying our countrymen as criminals at the courts. No one mentions what happened here and in our other bombed-out cities. Wasn't that criminal too, don't you think?"

Frances struggled to think of a suitable answer without upsetting the woman further. So as not to appear rude by just walking away, she scanned the marketplace, hoping something would catch her eye. "What is the name of that lovely old church over there?" she pointed to the remains of a church building.

"That's St. Sebaldus," the woman said. "Our glorious composer Johann Pachelbel played the organ there, though I don't suppose you have even heard of him."

"I most certainly have heard of Johann Pachelbel," said Frances, bringing a broad smile from the woman.

"He was born here, you know, and he's buried in the St Rochas cemetery," the woman informed her.

"Then that is where I will go next," said Frances. "I will visit dear Johann."

"The cemetery is a good walk away," the woman told her. "It's outside the city walls. The plague victims were buried there."

Well, it's something to do, thought Frances as she walked off toward St Rochas with a piece of gingerbread in her hand. With Pachelbel's canon playing in her head, she forgot to ask the woman where she might find something alcoholic.

Chapter 26

When Frances pushed open the hotel's doors, she found Mueller leaning on the reception desk, chatting with two young women.

"Oh," he said loud enough for her benefit. "I'd better go, or I will get a beating from my wife." When Frances reached him, she gave him a shove. "See," said Mueller, "she's started already." The women giggled together.

Frances looked the two women straight in the face. "Don't think he's cute," she said, "because he's not." She grabbed his arm and walked towards the stairs.

"You are awful," she said as they reached the door of their suite. "You're almost old enough to be their father."

"My God, do I look that bad?" Mueller asked, following her into the room.

"To be honest, you don't look good."

"Truthful as always, Froggy, huh?" He noticed the bags that she'd put on the table. "What have you got?" he asked, picking up one of the bags and peering inside. She watched as a smile creased his face, which grew wider when he opened the second bag. "Where on earth did you find this feast?" He picked up the gingerbread bag a second time and was about to take a piece when Frances snatched it from his hands.

"This is for later, Kristian. After you've eaten a good meal."

"You sound just like Anna," he teased. "You have done well, though, Froggy. Firstly, you've found some fine brandy, and secondly, it's German."

"All the good French stuff had gone," she said with a toss of her head. She took off her coat and hung it in the wardrobe.

"So, where have you been all day?" he asked her.

She told him of her walk around the old town and her visit to the castle's ruins. How sad she found that what must have been a beautiful old medieval town was now a pile of dust. "The people, though," she sat on the couch and patted the seat beside her until he joined her. "The people are just as they were in Berlin. Not complaining or feeling sorry for themselves but getting on with whatever they need to do to survive. The ruins of the marketplace were buzzing. That's where I got the gingerbread," she said. "I spoke to the woman who made it, and it was quite odd; I asked about the ruins of a church, and she told me that Pachelbel had been an organist there." He was smiling at her enthusiasm. "What?" she asked.

"Who the buggery was Patchy Bells?" he asked.

She threw up her hands. "Just one of the most significant early composers. I played his music at Sara's wedding, Kristian."

He shrugged. "I've heard of Bach. Is he any good?"

"Who, Bach?"

He laughed at the horror on her face that his comment had made. "No, even I know Bach was a great musician. I meant your mate, Patchy Bells?"

She tried not to laugh but couldn't help herself. "Trying to give you a musical education is a waste of time. After visiting the marketplace, I searched for old 'Patchy Bell's' gravestone. He isn't even buried inside the city walls. Isn't that sad when he was born here?"

Mueller had left the couch and walked back to the table. Picking up the bottle, he asked, "So, how on earth did you come across a bottle of Asbach?"

"There was a wine shop on the far side of the city that had escaped the bombing."

He nodded. "So, are you ready to sample good German brandy?"

"No, and neither are you. We are going to eat in the restaurant here tonight, and then we are coming back to the room and—"

"Are you going to make a pass at me again, Froggy, because I have to tell you I'm knackered?" He laughed, and she could tell it was all forced. He was trying too hard to be himself; it was a giveaway.

She stood and crossed the room to him. Reaching her hands, she cradled his face and looked deep into his eyes. "After our meal, we are coming back to this room, and you are going to sit down with me, have a very large brandy, and tell me everything."

"Nothing to tell," he replied, trying to shift his gaze from hers.

"You are going to tell me how you are feeling, or I will leave tomorrow and not come back until this damn trial is all over."

"Might be for the best," he muttered.

"Best for who?"

He shrugged, moved her hands from his face, and walked away. "I'm going to bathe before dinner," he said. "Have you booked us a table?"

"Yes," she said as the door to the bathroom closed behind him.

* * *

244

The meal had been quietly tricky. Neither said much, except Frances insisted Mueller eat his dinner. It had taken him an age to pick his way through it, even though the steaks had been surprisingly good. As he placed down his knife and fork, Frances stood up.

"Come on then," she said.

"What, no pud for you?" he remarked.

"We have the gingerbread. Come on."

She left the dining room and climbed the stairs back to their suite. Mueller was unusually quiet. She had to wait for him to open the door, but once inside, she grabbed the two brandy glasses from the night before and ordered Mueller to sit. She opened the Asbach and poured two large ones.

"Does it matter where I sit?" he asked with more than a touch of sarcasm.

"Just sit, Kristian, please," she replied, "anywhere but the couch." He sniffed and took a hard chair at the table. "So, you are going to be awkward, are you?" she asked with some irritation.

He sighed. "This is all unnecessary, you see."

She drew up a second chair and sat close to him, placing the brandy on the table. He took one of them, and she grabbed his hand and looked deep into the blue of his eyes.

"Let me in, Kristian. You're hurting. I know you almost as well as I know myself. Talk to me. Please. Let me help you with your demons."

Mueller downed the brandy and, taking Frances's hand, squeezed it. "I'm fine," he said. A whisper of a smile crossed his face. "I'll sort my demons; don't you worry, Froggy."

She poured him another drink, and, taking a sip of her own, she was pleasantly surprised that anything other than French brandy could taste so good. He downed the second brandy in one gulp.

"Kristian, I've been close to death, too. Look how long it's taken me to understand what happened and its effects on me," she said.

He shook his head. "It's not the attack. That's just something random that happened. I was in the wrong place at the wrong time. I can cope with that."

She felt a smile rise from deep within her. He was going to talk, and she'd been afraid he wouldn't. She poured him another drink and pushed the gingerbread towards him. "What then?" she asked.

He blew out his cheeks and exhaled with a sigh. "It's this damn trial, Froggy. You're going to think I'm mad." He took a bite of the gingerbread. "It's since the witness statements. I have this dream, you see. It repeats itself, and I'm one of them in it."

"In court being tried, you mean?"

"No, no," he shook his head. "It's still the war, and I'm with them. The men standing trial."

"Taking part in the atrocities, you mean."

"I haven't seen me taking part, but I've witnessed it and felt —" He stopped talking. He bit on his lip as he fought to find the right words. "Enjoyment," he eventually said. "I'm feeling enjoyment seeing the suffering of others. It's not me, Froggy. I hate myself for feeling that way."

She took both hands and held his gaze steady. "Tell me. Tell me your dream," she said.

He looked away from her and muttered, "They're freezing them. They're freezing men and women." Taking a deep breath, he raised his eyes to hers. "Sometimes they hold them down in the water, and it's freezing. They're freezing them alive, and men are laughing. I am laughing. There are people left outside in the cold. Their clothes are removed, and they are left outside and timed until they lose consciousness." He drew his hand through his hair and exhaled before continuing. "And then they look for ways of warming them. Some are plunged into boiling water, and we laugh as they scream in agony. And we laugh when women are brought in to warm those submerged in tubs of ice for hours. They warm them with their nakedness, and —I laugh. I laugh when limbs are taken without anaesthetic from one person and transplanted onto another. I laugh at their pain. I fucking well laugh, Froggy."

She raised her hand and caressed his cheek. "It's a dream, Kristian, that's all, and I believe we are all capable of feeling pleasure in the misery of others. What I am going to say cropped up with your father when we were discussing Karl Donitz, and I believe I said the same thing to you in a hotel room in Munich." He gave her a questioning look, and she reminded him. "You asked me, don't you believe in good and evil—"

"And you answered, 'No, there's just men," Mueller said, taking her hand. "That really saddened me."

"I still believe it. I think we are all capable of both. Whether you listen and act upon that evil side makes you the man or woman you are. And I happen to know you would only ever act on one side, and that's the good side."

"You forget I'm responsible for killing more than just a few men, Froggy."

"That was war. That's different. You were part of the machinery."

"Did you say that to the women you shared the block with at Auschwitz?"

"And that was different, too. And it's absolutely what we are talking about. These people standing before you in court chose to listen to the dark side of their nature and were rewarded for it."

"By an evil madman," Mueller said.

"Yes," she replied. He gave her a questioning look.

"What?" she asked.

"I thought you didn't believe in good and evil."

"Even your Adolf was just a man, Kristian," she said.

"Some might question that," he replied.

They sat silently for a few moments, contemplating each

other's words. It was Mueller who eventually broke the silence. "Let's have another drink, more gingerbread, and sit on the couch where we can relax."

She stretched out her hand and pushed his hair back from his face. "Come on," she said, "you take the gingerbread, and I'll pour one more drink."

"What do you think is going on at home?" he asked as she joined him.

"Mayhem," she suggested, and he smiled—not the forced smile of earlier, but the smile that crinkled his eyes and lit his entire face. "We're lucky to have help, aren't we? I don't know how I'd cope without Mutti and Anna," she said. She saw that he was studying her. "What?"

He rubbed his chin thoughtfully. "Tell me your secret. How have you rid yourself of your demons? You scarcely have those moments anymore."

"I've replaced them with your children," she said, and he laughed. "No, really," she said. "I have no time for them, Kristian. My mind is fully occupied with other things. Better things. I've sent my demons to hell where they belong so that I can concentrate on the things that matter—my family. I refuse to let my demons ruin my life. You can do the same, you know. I could drink a coffee. Shall I go downstairs and get one?"

He nodded. A little later, she returned with a pot of real coffee and, after pouring two cups, returned to the couch and sat beside him.

"It's really odd, you know," she said, turning to him.

"What's odd?" he asked.

"I feel different. I think by talking to you about letting go of your demons, I've realised I have let go of my own. They're not important, are they? We are important, and our future together with our family. They are just vestiges of our past. Vestiges of what we've seen and been through. I don't want to hang onto that."

Mueller wrapped his arm around her, and she shuffled her body close to him and laid her head on his shoulder. "Those men who are standing trial, I feel sorry for them," she said.

"You do?" questioned Mueller with some surprise. "Why's that, then?"

"Because they're stuck with their demons, aren't they? They will carry them to the grave."

* * *

Frances returned to Schonen Felder two days later, and Mueller felt lost and lonely. He'd had a good night following their talk, and there were no demons to encroach upon his sleep. The second night, the one before she left, he'd slept deeply following their lovemaking, and it was a wrench for both of them to say their goodbyes.

They sat at the table the morning she left and ate breakfast, knowing it would be some weeks before they'd be together. Frances's eyes landed on Mueller's briefcase. "I don't know why you cart that thing backwards and forwards," she told him. "What have you got stashed away in there?"

"All my notes."

"What on earth do you write about?" she asked.

"Everything. Who says what? How I feel the defence is going. The questions the prosecution asks."

She questioned him again, "But do you need to do all that? I thought Konrad just wanted you to sit in the courtroom and ensure fair play."

"He does," Mueller replied whilst chewing round bread and sausage.

"Do you think he will bother questioning you on individual cases?" she asked.

"Doubtful," came the reply, along with a shrug. "It's the lawyer in me, I guess."

"Can I make a suggestion?"

"Can I stop you?" She was relieved to see the smile tugging at his mouth. "Go on," he said.

"Just sit in that courtroom and only bother writing down notes if you think something is unfair or unjust. After all, that's all you've been asked to do."

"Hmmm," he said, rising from the table. "I have to get ready to leave, or I'll be late. Are you sure you'll be okay getting yourself to the station?"

She nodded and sat on the couch for several minutes until he returned from the bathroom.

"I've been thinking about what you just said, Froggy, and you're probably right regarding the note-taking, but what the fuck else can I do while I'm sitting there all day?"

"Come here," she said and undid the robe she was wearing, revealing her nakedness beneath it.

He walked to the couch, eyes wide, a smile playing on his mouth. "Froggy, I haven't got time for this," he said.

"I know, but sit, anyway. I won't make you late. I promise." Unable to resist, he obeyed and sat beside her, his eyes glued to her body. She climbed onto his lap, legs straddled across him, and he watched the fire kindle and burn deep within her eyes and felt his hardness, demanding release from his clothing.

"Froggy?" he questioned with a groan as she ran her fingers through his hair and met his lips with her own, delivering the most sensual of kisses. And then she was off his lap and standing before him, with her robe pulled tight around her, grinning like the Cheshire Cat. "And that was for what?" he asked her with some confusion.

"That was to give you something to think about when you're sitting in that damn courtroom," she said.

He nodded, smiling back at her, and checked his watch. "I will be late if I don't leave now," he told her. "And by the way, you've given me a pain in my balls."

"Sorry," she apologised, standing on tiptoe and kissing his forehead. Then, grabbing his overcoat, she helped him with it and buttoned it up as he stood with his arms around her, breathing her in until he knew he had to leave.

"Think about me and your children and home," she said, passing his hat. "Fill your mind with us, and there will be no room for your damn demons."

"That's not going to be hard. That vision of you will be stuck in my head for some time. I wish you didn't have to go back," he said.

"But I do. To our children, who are probably driving your household up the wall by now. Call me every evening, won't you? And remember, Kristian Mueller, you are nothing like those men standing trial. I wouldn't love you if you were."

CHAPTER 27

MARCH 1947

There was a change in Mueller the next time he took his place in the Nuremberg courtroom. He decided that Frances was quite correct. Konrad wasn't looking for a journal. All he wanted to know was that there had been fair play. He'd have known that if he had taken the time to think things through and listen to his feelings, which he had to admit were totally dishevelled.

All the time he'd been scratching down copious notes; he'd been doing it for himself. It was to lock it all in his mind so that he could sift through the day's happenings later when he returned to the hotel and search for some sense in it. Frances was right again. There was none, and he now sat back in his chair, scarcely taking any notes and feeling much more relaxed.

That air of relaxation quickly abandoned him when he answered the knock on his hotel room door on the evening of the last day of March. He sighed as he put down his copy of Shakespeare's Sonnets and, opening the door, was surprised and a little shocked to see his visitor.

"Miriam? Victor? Which one are you today?" he asked with some sharpness and a great deal of sarcasm.

"Mueller. There's no need to be like that. I thought we were friends," Miriam drawled.

"Friends? You think?" Mueller shook his head and scowled. "No, we just shared a moment," he said dryly. "Didn't Frances tell you to sod off?" he questioned.

"Manners," Miriam returned, holding his gaze with her own. "You're speaking to a lady."

"Oh, I doubt that," Mueller retaliated.

He attempted to close the door, but Miriam quickly placed her foot in it to prevent him from doing so. He raised his fist without thinking, then, remembering that he was talking to a woman, he let his hand drop to his side.

"I need to speak to Frances. It's urgent," Miriam said. "Is she here?"

"Don't you think she'd have joined us by now if she were?" he suggested.

"Mueller, it's really urgent." She looked over her shoulder and around the hotel corridor. "I can't speak out here. Let me in. You need to know."

Mueller sighed, opened the door and bowed her in.

"Can I sit?" she asked.

"You won't be staying that long," Mueller replied. "Say what you need to say and go."

"We have Mengele."

She watched as surprise crossed Mueller's face.

"Mengele, are you sure?"

Miriam nodded madly.

"Why do you need Frances?" he asked.

"We need a positive ID from someone who spent time with him," she replied. "The bastard is denying he's who he is. But it's him, all right. Enough of us have seen the bastard during selections or at the gate to recognise him. We may not be enough, though. Frances knows him, some say intimately," she said with a smirk which Mueller chose not to react to. "They couldn't ignore her if she identified him."

"It would destroy her if she saw him. I won't let you do that to her," Mueller told her.

"She's tougher than you think, Mueller, and I wouldn't do anything to harm her. I love that girl; you should know that."

"Hah! You love nothing more than your greed for revenge, Miriam. You'll happily overlook the aftermath to get the result you want." Mueller shook his head. "I won't let you put her anywhere near Mengele."

"Surely, Frances should have a say in this, huh? How will she feel when she finds out she could have brought him to justice, but you stood in the way?" Miriam asked. "And I will make sure she finds out."

"Of course, you fucking will," he spat.

He walked over to the window and looked out, watching the headlights of the cars lighting up the road as people went about their business. Miriam had backed him into a corner. Frances would never forgive him if Miriam told her they had Mengele in their grasp but couldn't get a positive ID. She'd accuse him of protecting Mengele when he only wanted to protect her. His head was thumping, and he rubbed it before facing Miriam.

"I'll tell her. I'll also tell her she's a fool if she goes anywhere near the courthouse and Mengele. Now leave."

Miriam looked him full in the face and nodded. "I'll go, and I know she'll come. Nothing you say will stop her."

She left, and Mueller knew she was right. Frances returned to Nuremberg two days later.

* * *

"Are you okay?" Mueller asked Frances. She nodded. "You know what you will have to do when you get inside the courtroom?" he continued, and she nodded again. He squeezed her hand. "I wish I could come in there with you."

"I'll be fine. Will you wait here or with Miriam and Simeon in the foyer?" she asked him.

"No, I'll wait here," Mueller replied. "I'm not that happy with Miriam and Simeon, you see."

They were waiting in an area near the courtroom. Outside the courtroom, in the foyer, a small crowd had gathered: newsmen, witnesses from the main trial, members of various organisations with an interest, members of the public, and a few troublemakers. Word had spread that Mengele had been found and was about to face justice.

Mueller wished they would get a move on; he could feel Frances's mounting agitation as she was kept waiting. It was playing on her nerves. After a wait of fifteen minutes or so, the door to the courtroom opened, and Frances was asked to take the stand. She grabbed Mueller's hand tightly, and for a moment, he thought she would pull out. She looked into his face, and he nodded. Following a deep breath, she followed the clerk, and the door closed behind her.

Frances was unsure what she felt as she came back out. She immediately sought Mueller's eyes and shook her head. She could see the worry on his face as he walked to her side and took her arm.

"Are you okay?" he asked.

"Yes, yes. I'm fine, but, Kristian, it wasn't him," she told him.

"Are you sure?"

"Oh, he resembled him. He was small with an Italian look. She shook her head and continued, "But it most definitely was not Mengele."

"So, what happened in the courtroom?" Mueller asked her.

"They told me to point to the man in the courtroom known as

Josef Mengele. The poor man fell to the floor, weeping, when I told the clerk I couldn't. I think they thought I was joking. They asked me if I was certain, and I assured them that I was. I know Miriam, Sim, and the rest of their friends are going to be disappointed."

"Hey, don't worry about that," said Mueller. "You went in there and told the truth. I'm proud of you. How did you feel when you saw him?"

She shrugged. "I knew straight away it wasn't him, so I didn't feel anything apart from pity for the poor chap. He must have been terrified. We should go and let Miriam and Sim know the bad news."

There was a buzz when they walked back into the foyer, and Mueller gave Frances's hand a squeeze. Miriam sped to Frances's side when she saw her, closely followed by Sim.

"Have you done it? Miriam asked.

"I have," Frances said, and Miriam crowed. "But Miriam," Frances continued, "it isn't Mengele. The man in the courtroom isn't Josef Mengele."

"You're joking, you sod," Miriam half-smiled, and Frances shook her head as Miriam's eyes widened. "Fuck! Are you certain?" she asked.

"I am certain. I know you wanted me to come out of that room and tell you that you had the bastard, but the man in there is innocent. At least, he is as far as Mengele's crimes are concerned. I'm sorry. I feel as though I've let you down."

"You haven't let us down," Sim interceded. "You've saved an innocent man from being killed. Others were going to just shoot him instead of bothering the courts. Thank goodness they didn't."

"Because that would have been another damn mistake," Mueller shot.

Several more people joined Miriam and Sim; clearly, they were other Nazi hunters. Two men drew Sim and Miriam to one side; they were beyond disappointed. Mueller saw the anger bubbling up within them.

"The woman was his whore, they say," one of them uttered.

Mueller felt his hackles rise and made a move towards him, but Frances pulled him back.

They listened as Miriam told the men, "She wouldn't lie. If she said the man isn't Mengele, then he isn't Mengele. We got it wrong. Next time, we'll get it right."

The men returned to the others, muttering, and they heard and felt a ripple of condemnation that took a pathway through the lookers-on.

"Come on, time to go," Mueller said, picking up on the growing unrest.

"Us too, I think," Simeon agreed. "We'll leave together."

"Come back to the hotel with us for a while," Frances suggested. She turned to Mueller. "That's all right, isn't it?" she asked him.

"If that's what you want." He gave them all a nod.

Miriam threaded her arms through Frances's. "Are we friends again?" she asked.

"No, not friends," Frances replied, "but I do love you, you know." Miriam rewarded her with a smile as the four crossed the foyer of the courtroom together.

More people were gathered outside. As the four left the court building, the American guards parted to let them through. They were only several yards away when a shout came from behind them, "Mueller, I've got that bullet you were so desperate for!"

They all turned as Lisha fired a shot. Mueller felt the impact of the bullet. As a second shot was fired, he watched as Lisha fell to the ground and became aware of Miriam clinging to him. He looked down at the blood on his hands, realising now that it wasn't his. Grabbing hold of Miriam, he held her close to prevent her from falling as mayhem broke loose. There was a scream nearby, and Mueller watched as Frances dropped to her knees, sobbing uncontrollably.

Still holding Miriam, he turned to Simeon and ordered him to leave, and quickly. "They'll arrest you for having a gun. I'll sort things here." Simeon hesitated as he realised the enormity of Miriam's injury and saw how Mueller was holding tight to the woman who clung to him—the woman who had taken the bullet meant for him.

Those around the court building shouted and ran from the scene as guards appeared. Some wanted to help, and others, out of pure nosiness, made their way to where a woman had been shot.

Mueller, Frances, and Miriam had no awareness of anyone. There were just the three of them. As Mueller gently laid Miriam on the ground, she was already gasping for breath. She reached up and laid her hand on his cheek. He bent over her and lifted her head, folding his coat beneath her to give her some comfort, though he knew any comfort he gave would be short-lived.

She forced a smile onto her face, looked him in the eyes and groaned as she uttered, "Are we having another moment, Mueller?"

"I do believe we are," he said, smiling back at her, holding her gaze and gently pushing back the hair from her face.

"Sir," said one of the guards stepping forward. Mueller turned and scowled, holding up his hand to silence him. Understanding the situation, the man took a step back as Miriam continued to speak to Mueller.

He bent over, closer, to hear her. "I saved you for her. Do you think she'll ever be my friend again?" Miriam searched Mueller's face for an answer.

"Why don't you ask me?" Frances said, dropping down on her knees beside her and taking Miriam's hand. As she heard Frances's voice, Miriam struggled to pull herself into sitting and fell back into Mueller's arms with a sigh.

"You bloody idiot, "Frances spoke through a deluge of tears.

"Well, it was me or him, girl." Miriam forced the shadow of a crude laugh from her lips. "I thought your preference would be Mueller," she continued. Then she turned her eyes to him, her breaths now shallow.

"I can't say," her face twisted from the effort of speaking. She nodded at Frances and gasped an inhalation. "I can't say I blame you for that." She forced a smile to her lips. "He's a good one." She lifted her brows, "Never thought I'd say that about a Kraut. Hold on to him, eh?"

She coughed, blood ran from her mouth, and she licked her lips. "Fuck," she whispered and held out her hand to Frances, who took it as Miriam forced herself to say more. "We are friends now, aren't we?" she asked, taking her last breath and smiling into the molten ocean of Frances's eyes.

"Yes, we're friends now," murmured Frances. Bending over Miriam's body, she kissed her brow and spoke through tears. "Aleha ha-shalom. Peace be upon you, my dearest friend."

* * *

It was hours later before Mueller and Frances could return to the hotel. They were both questioned regarding Miriam's death by the American military police. Frances had little to say except that she had been called to the court to identify a man and had left with her husband and a friend. That friend had saved her husband's life.

Mueller almost came clean. He told them of his near death at the hands of Lisha, who believed he was in the court to support the men on trial and that the man clearly wanted to finish the job he had started. He followed on by saying that his wife's friend, Miriam, had saved his life. Then he was questioned as to why his wife's friend had sacrificed her life on his behalf and found that, in truth, he was unable to answer that.

Neither of them mentioned Simeon and prayed that in the mayhem that followed the shooting, he was able to disappear.

* * *

A little less than thirty-six hours later, there was a knock on their hotel room door. Mueller answered it and invited Simeon in.

"How are you?" Mueller asked, placing a hand on the man's shoulder sympathetically. Simeon broke down before them both, and Frances poured him a brandy and ushered him to a seat. She drew up a chair and sat near him, taking his hand.

"I'm responsible for her death," Simeon announced. He punched his forehead with his fist. "How can I live with myself?" he asked them.

"I thought you had sorted fucking Lisha," Mueller snapped. Frances cast him a look. He'd been odd since they'd returned from being questioned the day before. He was quieter than usual, and there was a latent anger in him. She wondered if he was carrying some guilt over Miriam's death, too.

Simeon shook his head; he struggled to speak. Fighting back his tears again, he said, "I should have done it. I intended to. Lisha told Miriam he had a couple of kids, and she talked me out of it." He turned to Frances. "She told me about you losing your child. She felt so much guilt over that. I'm so sorry."

Frances squeezed his hand as he continued, "I told Lisha we didn't need him in the organisation as he was untrustworthy. I thought that was the end of it. I'm sorry, Mueller, I put your life at risk again, and because of my stupidity, I've lost my Miriam. I don't even know where her body is," he sobbed.

"With the undertaker," Frances told him.

Simeon wept more. "I can't leave her in this God-forsaken place."

"Can I make a suggestion?" asked Frances. Both men shot their eyes at her. "I think she should be returned to Paris," she said. "There are Jewish cemeteries there. That's where she belongs."

"There's no way I can do that," Simeon said. It would cost more than I have."

Frances glanced at Mueller; he was watching her intently. He nodded his agreement.

"I can sort it. I want to do that for her," she told Simeon.

After Simeon left, Frances phoned for a pot of coffee to be sent to their room. When it arrived, she poured them a cup and put one on the cabinet by Mueller, who was lying back on the bed.

"Kristian, have I done something wrong?" she asked.

"I wouldn't blame you if you had," he replied, "but I would like to know."

She placed her cup on the cabinet on her side of the bed and lay back. She expected him to turn towards her, but he didn't.

"What?" she asked, and he sighed. He turned to her then and took her hand.

"Mengele," he said. "I'd just like to know, that's all."

"You think I should have told you if, as people so nicely put it yesterday, I was his whore? Kristian, I haven't told you because nothing happened. The last time I saw him was at his house at Auschwitz. He placed his hands on my shoulders and said, 'I wonder what you would do if I made love to you'."

"And how did you reply to that?" Mueller asked, holding onto her gaze.

"I told him I couldn't stop him." She heard Mueller's intake of breath and took his hand. "I suppose I took his threat away when I said that." She pushed herself up on her elbow and turned to him. "Look, what you don't understand about Mengele is that he was into terrifying people, not having sex with them. He thrived on their fear. I was petrified every time he sent for me. I never knew if I would leave alive."

"And he never touched you?"

"No, he never did." She was thoughtful for a while, then gave a little laugh. "I knew he could: of course, he knew I knew that too. That must have been enough for him. And he had a real love of music. Thankfully."

Mueller exhaled and rubbed the back of his neck.

"Come here," he said. She rolled over on the bed to him, and he took her in his arms.

Chapter 28

October 1947, Boston U.S.A.

Mueller was in a reflective mood. Seated in the bar across the road from the Boston Symphony Hall, he had left Frances getting on for an hour ago. She was nervous, he thought. He had annoyed her with his banter, so she eventually banned him from her dressing room.

The last concert on this first trip to the States was important to her, as Charles Munch was conducting. Over the last couple of years, he had shown himself to be a loyal friend. He had arranged a couple of concerts in Europe, and this was her first visit to the States with promises of more tours to come. They were alone for this tour, and the children were home with Anna and his parents.

The thought of the children made him wonder what they were up to. He was carrying a smile on his face just by thinking of them. Karin and Paul were fourteen months old now. His daughter was a handful. She was a wild child and enjoyed being outside, especially around the horses. A Mueller through and through. No fear, he thought. The child showed no fear, and he wasn't always sure that it was a good thing.

And then there was Paul, who had inherited his mother's

colouring and wolf's eyes. He was more delicately put together than his sister, but what he lacked in physical size and strength was more than made up for with his strength of character—a little too outspoken already and argumentative, just like his mother. His favourite word was 'no.'

Mueller sipped his brandy and turned his thoughts to his wife. It was over eighteen months since he had declared his feelings for her on that night in Paris, and he hadn't regretted a second of the time they'd spent together. They still had spats; he hoped they always would, as making up was so delicious.

He was glad that he'd never looked for a larger property for them in Bonn. He frowned. Two attempts on his life. He was lucky to be alive. Lucky to be sitting in this bar now. He sighed loudly, drawing attention from one or two others in the bar, and he nodded an apology to them.

Konrad had been very apologetic when he learnt of the first attempt on his life and the torture he'd been put through at the hands of Lisha. Frances had been angry that he'd wanted to stay and continue with the job he'd been given. She ensured that Herr Adenauer was informed of every last detail.

Konrad had sent him a telegram giving him the chance to leave Nuremberg, but he hated the thought of leaving the job unfinished. Frances had said Konrad knew that before the telegram was even sent. "He's a wily old sod," she told him. That wily old sod he thought was now in a good position when the time came to take charge of the government. In a small way, he had helped Adenauer achieve that goal, and for that, he was proud. And of the trust Adenauer put in him for the work he'd been doing.

Following Miriam's death, he and Frances had left Nuremberg and spent a few days at Schonen Felder before leaving for Paris for her funeral. He was one of just three people who attended the burial of a young Parisian woman who, after surviving Auschwitz and Bergen Belsen extermination camps, had been shot in Nuremberg, Germany, almost two years after World War Two had ended. He found that devastating.

Frances had sorted everything so that Miriam was laid to rest in the Jewish part of the Parisian cemetery of Bagneux following her body being flown home for burial.

He'd been told to take time off to deal with the funeral and its aftermath. They had been away from the children for so long that they had taken them to Paris with them, along with Anna, who was in a state of both apprehension and excitement as she left Germany for the first time.

Once the funeral was over, they let her loose on the Parisian populace, giving her as much free time as she wanted. He'd looked after the children a couple of times, too, so that Frances could take Anna on the tour of Paris that most women would wish for, the fashion houses. Anna, of course, was not like most women, and that particular tour was cut short and they ended up in the Louvre Museum.

They now tried to visit Paris every month, more often when Konrad had needed him there, which became quite regular. Frances had teased him mercilessly over his becoming a pen pusher, and she was correct. It wasn't him; he disliked being couped up; he was an outdoor man. However, having played such an integral part in Germany's change of fortune had made up for sitting behind a desk for hours and, more recently, in the Nuremberg Court.

He had returned there following Miriam's funeral and taken up his seat again in mid-April. The defence had progressed to Gerhard Rose, another physician involved in experiments with new vaccines. Witnesses said Rose spoke out against testing on human guinea pigs. Mueller had rightly thought at the time that would save his life.

The defence continued. There were another nine doctors. Mueller took a different approach and noted witness statements that he thought might save their lives, as with Rose. The last doctor to stand was Adolf Pokorny, his application to join the Nazi Party in 1939 had been turned down as he had married a Jew, even though they were divorced four years earlier.

Following the last witness statement for Porkorny on June 27th, the defence and prosecution made a series of statements, which concluded with the defendant's own statements, and began on July 19th.

The Tribunal rendered its judgment on August 19, 1947, and the defendants were sentenced on August 20, 1947. That evening, Mueller phoned Konrad Adenauer. He told him that seven of the defendants had been sentenced to death, nine defendants were convicted and would serve prison terms, and seven defendants had been acquitted. He also told Konrad of his decision to return to the farm to help his father, who wasn't getting any younger. That's where he belonged, Schonen Felder, and by working the farm, he would help Germany's recovery in his own other, but no less critical, small way.

He looked at his watch. After another few minutes, he would have to return to the Symphony Hall. As usual, he had promised Frances that he would stand in the wings for her performance, where if she wanted to, she could see him. She told him that just knowing he was there would keep her calm. He hadn't understood how or why that should be the case but knew it was something left over from when Steven had been there. That night, she was playing some piece by some chap Bartok and was worked up about it.

"Charles has given me this on purpose," she told him when she had received the program. "It's a test to see if I'm as good as he is. He's renowned for playing it. It belongs to him, and it's bloody difficult."

"You're as good as him, aren't you?" he replied.

"Don't know, we'll have to see," she said. He'd grabbed her and kissed her then and told her it didn't matter if she wasn't as

good a player as Charles Munch because she was much prettier, for which he had received a kick in the shins.

He wondered if she had got into her new dress yet and smiled to himself in recollection of their last visit to Paris. She had dragged him along to some new designer, Dior, and his 'New Look.' He told them both that the look wasn't new and that pinched waists and frippery were a flash from the past. He could remember his grandmother wearing a corset. Dior had assured him that no corsets were necessary beneath his clothing as the cut of the garments achieved the pinched-in waist. He wasn't sure his comment had gone down too well with Dior, and neither had his other one when he said that Frances looked like a Christmas tree when she tried on one of his gowns, but Dior assured him that in the correct size, Frances would look stunning. He thought she didn't need a dress for that. She would be wearing it for the first time tonight, and Dior listened to him when he suggested that the dress should be made of bottle, green, silk.

He returned to the symphony hall with ten minutes to spare and knocked on her dressing room door. He was knocked off his feet when she opened it.

"Wow," he said. "That's some dress, Froggy."

"You like?" she answered with a huge smile.

"I like it very much. I'll enjoy getting you out of it later."

"You will keep your mittens off it, Kristian Mueller. This is now my new favourite and will bring me luck."

"You don't need luck, do you? Come here." He kissed her cheek and whispered, "Knock 'em dead, sweetheart." He then left her and took up his position in the wings. He was overwhelmed with pride as she took her bow following the concert to monstrous applause and a huge basket of red roses, which Munch delivered to her on stage.

Following the concert, Frances went to the hall's foyer to sign programmes, where he and Munch joined her. As an adoring public surrounded her, Mueller and Munch watched her from a few yards back. They got on well, which was no surprise, as Charles Munch was German, too.

* * *

The programme signing had just about finished, and Frances thought it was time to join Mueller. Suddenly, she was overwhelmed by the scent of lavender. A hand on the back of her shoulder froze her to the spot.

"Frances, my dear. Well played. How are you?"

Her hands flew protectively to her stomach, and she forced away the lump in her throat to answer the man who had positioned himself in front of her.

"Herr Doctor?" she muttered, and as her eyes widened, she looked into Josef Mengele's smiling face. Adrenalin pumped into her body, and she felt the urge to run, but he still had a hold on her shoulder, and she felt he was digging his fingers into it a little too hard.

"I always hoped you would make it," he continued, "and as you see, I have too. You have such talent, my dear, and it could have all been wasted."

"Frances, Frances?" She heard Mueller call. It was distant. Her eyes were stuck on Mengele, who was still speaking, and she fought the feeling of nausea that washed over her. Mengele looked towards Mueller and watched as he approached.

"And I see you found your Kapitan, too. Well done. I do like a happy ending."

And with that, he was gone, and she found herself wrapped in the safety of Mueller's arms.

"Who was that man?" he asked her. She couldn't answer for a while and stared wide-eyed into his face. "Froggy?" he questioned and gently shook her.

She swallowed and took a deep breath before muttering, "That man is Josef Mengele."

Mueller shouted to Munch. "Charles, look after Frances, will you?" He turned to Frances, and spat, "Stay here. I'll find the bastard."

She grabbed hold of his arm. "No. Let him go. Let him spend the rest of his life looking over his shoulder and wondering if that day would be his last. We've suffered enough. Let's not get involved, Kristian. We have children to think of. It's time for us now," she said.

He stood a while, digesting her words. She had laid his hand on her womb. "Are you telling me?" he asked. She nodded, smiling into his eyes.

"How many this time?" he gasped.

"Just the one," she answered.

"Thank Jesus for that," he said, wiping his brow and making her laugh. "Is it time to go home, do you think?"

She placed her arms around his neck and kissed him. "Yes, most definitely, Kapitan Mueller. It's time to go home."

Afterword

Who were some of the real characters mentioned in the War Torn Novels?

Grand Admiral Karl Doenitz

Following the suicide of Adolph Hitler, Karl Doenitz succeeded him as head of state of Nazi Germany. Doenitz was an odd choice for Hitler to make as his successor. Doenitz was a gifted naval officer who had risen through the military ranks, not the Nazi party like other prominent leaders of the Third Reich.

In 1918, he became a U-boat commander, and after scuttling his boat to prevent it from being taken, he spent time in a British POW camp.

In 1935, he was chosen to reconstitute Germany's submarine force, and under his command, the U-boats sank more than 3,500 Allied vessels. The German Navy lost 784 U-boats in the process, and Donitz lost both of his sons who had served in the German Navy. He was known for being kind and thoughtful to his men, who received many awards from him.

In 1943, Doenitz took over all command of the German

Navy. Until then, he had little to do with the Fuhrer, but his new post meant twice monthly meetings, and Doenitz developed a strong attachment to Hitler. He joined the Nazi party in 1944 and remained loyal to the end.

Hitler named Doenitz his successor in his will, and Doenitz was elevated to sole leadership of the crumbling Reich, surprising him and many others who hadn't even heard of him. Doenitz claimed that Hitler chose him "because he doubtlessly felt that only a reasonable man with an honest reputation as a sailor could make a decent peace."

As Germany's military situation deteriorated, Doenitz attempted to negotiate a favourable surrender with the Western allies to save as many German soldiers as possible from falling into Soviet hands. He was eventually forced to surrender all German forces unconditionally.

Doenitz was sentenced to just 10 years in prison following the Nuremberg war crimes trials. He remained unrepentant for his Nazi beliefs for the remainder of his life and died at the age of 89.

Charles Munch

Munch was born in 1891 in Strasbourg, Alsace, into a family of musicians. He wanted to be a locomotive engineer but ended up studying the violin at the Strasbourg Conservatory. He was conscripted into the German army in 1914 as a sergeant gunner and was gassed and later wounded. Munch considered himself purely and profoundly German, but that he was a friend of many countries and, first and foremost, a musician and conductor.

Munch remained in France during the German occupation, believing he could help maintain the French people's morale. He refused to conduct in Germany and also refused to perform contemporary German works. He protected members of his orchestra from the Gestapo and contributed from his income to the French Resistance. For this, he was awarded the Legion d'honneur with the red ribbon in 1945.

Munch is probably best remembered as conductor of the Boston Symphony Orchestra, which he joined in 1946.

Konrad Adenauer

Konrad Adenauer: a pragmatic democrat and tireless unifier

Konrad Adenauer was born in Cologne on 5 January 1876. He studied at Freiburg, Munich and Bonn universities before becoming a lawyer. He became a member of the Cologne City Council and, in 1917, lord mayor of the city. In 1920 he became president of the Prussian State Council, making him one of the most influential politicians in Germany.

Adenauer was replaced as mayor of Cologne after the Nazis came to power for refusing to decorate the city with swastikas for a visit by Hitler and was briefly imprisoned. He was also arrested by the Gestapo in September 1944 and accused of involvement in the failed July bomb plot against Hitler.

The United States, which liberated Cologne, appointed Adenauer mayor again, but the British military government dismissed him soon after. Adenauer formed a new political party, the Christian Democratic Union (CDU). In 1948, he was made president of the parliamentary council that drew up a constitution for the three western zones of Germany, which the French, British, and Americans occupied. The Soviets occupied the eastern zone of Germany and installed a Communist government.

Adenauer was elected chancellor of the Federal Republic of Germany on 15 September 1949. His main aim was to ensure West Germany's transition to a sovereign, democratic state. The military occupation of West Germany ended in 1952, and in 1955, under Adenauer's leadership, West Germany was recognised internationally as an independent nation. It joined

NATO in 1955 and the European Economic Community in 1957.

JOSEF MENGELE

Mengele was considered a promising young geneticist with academic aspirations before the war. He came from a wealthy, respectable background and decided to study medicine, human genetics, and physical anthropology in the 1930s. He became a member of the Nazi Party in 1938, and at the same time, he joined the SS.

Mengele studied at the Frankfurt Institute for Hereditary Biology and Racial Hygiene, a research body closely aligned with official Nazi Ideology. He served as a medical officer in the Waffen SS Viking Division and was posted to Auschwitz in 1943.

He was one of the core doctors, medical staff, orderlies, and nurses posted in the camp. He is remembered for the selections that took place at the gates to Auschwitz, where those arriving were separated left to right with a raise or drop of the thumb to work or to die in the gas chambers. All officers took part in these selections, though as Mengele began his research on twins and dwarfs, he spent more time there looking for those who could aid him in his study.

He performed experiments such as unnecessary amputations and would inject a twin with a disease and then transfuse blood into the other. If one twin died, the other would be of no importance and would be killed. Similar experiments were carried out on dwarfs, people with physical abnormalities and pregnant women. He was fascinated with eye colour, and it's said that he had a massive collection of every eye colour.

Mengele firmly endorsed Nazi racial theory, and many of his experiments aimed to illustrate those beliefs. He never wavered from these beliefs, nor did he ever show remorse for what he'd done.

He was a strange dichotomy of a well-educated character and a music lover. He would take to a person on a whim and show kindness to the people working for him; however, that could change on the spin of a coin.

On the night of January 17, 1945, as the Soviet army approached Poland, Mengele fled westward from Auschwitz. He joined a retreating Wehrmacht unit and swapped his SS uniform for a Wehrmacht officer's uniform. He was arrested 400 miles west of Auschwitz by the Americans and was held in a camp for two months. He was eventually released as they couldn't prove he was the same Josef Mengele on the wanted circular for mass murder and other crimes. Known for his vanity, Mengele had refused to have his blood type tattooed onto his chest or arm when he joined the SS. The fact that it wasn't there clinched his freedom.

With help from his well-to-do family and a network of friends, he escaped to South America. He eventually settled in Brazil and died in 1979 from a stroke whilst swimming in the sea. He was buried under a false name.

About the Author

Jan Lloyd is an author living in Mid Wales with her husband and 2 Cavalier King, Charles Spaniels.

Before retiring, Jan taught maths and science at the secondary level before becoming a junior schoolteacher. In the last few years of her teaching career, she taught English as an additional language.

Jan enjoys walking, gardening, and spending time with her children and grandchildren.

She would like to thank you for reading her books and hopes you enjoyed them. She would love you to leave a review and thanks you in advance.

Find Jan

Website: Janlloyd.uk If you're interested, you can sign up for Jan's newsletters here or send an email.

Facebook: www.facebook.com/profile.php?id=100090941768112

Instagram: janlloydauthor

X: @jan_oghanlloyd

Books by Jan Lloyd

War Torn Series: - WW2 story of betrayal, love, and survival

Book 1 The Mermen and the Doctor

Book 2 The French Girl

Book 3 The Aftermath

Fragments of Time: - A historical time-slip story.

Presently working on a Tudor/Stuart story.